DATE			

Bad Thoughts

Bad Thoughts

Dave Zeltserman

FIVE STAR
An imprint of Thomson Gale, a part of The Thomson Corporation

THOMSON
GALE

Detroit • New York • San Francisco • New Haven, Conn. • Waterville, Maine • London

THOMSON
GALE

Set in 11 pt. Plantin.

LIBRARY OF CONGRESS CATALOGING-IN-PUBLICATION DATA

Zeltserman, Dave, 1959–
Bad thoughts / Dave Zeltserman. — 1st ed.
p. cm.
ISBN-13: 978-1-59414-540-7 (alk. paper)
ISBN-10: 1-59414-540-7 (alk. paper)
1. Police—Fiction. 2. Serial murderers—Fiction. 3. Cambridge (Mass.)—Fiction. I. Title.
PS3626.E396B33 2007
813'.6—dc22
2007008158

First Edition. First Printing: July 2007.

Published in 2007 in conjunction with Tekno Books and Ed Gorman.

Printed in the United States of America on permanent paper
10 9 8 7 6 5 4 3 2 1

Bad Thoughts

Chapter 1

November 9, 1997. Morning.

The fingers on his right hand—the ones that had been broken and mangled when he was thirteen—were being squeezed hard, forcing him to move through the cold and darkness. He tried to fight it, tried to see who it was behind him, but the grip on his fingers tightened, heightening the pain. He gave up and let himself be pushed forward.

He had no idea where he was. It was too dark to see anything. There was no sense of anything around him except that presence forcing his arm behind his back and squeezing his two fingers. He could smell a faint but oddly familiar odor, like formaldehyde and rotting garbage.

Up ahead was something white and small. As he got closer he could see it was a woman. He was about thirty yards from her, but he could tell she was beautiful, thin and slender with yellowish blond hair. But there was something wrong. Her mouth looked funny, bigger than it should've. As he was forced closer he could see she was naked and her hands and feet were bound. He could see pure terror shining in her eyes. A red piece of cloth had been stuffed in her mouth. Thin red lines crisscrossed her body.

Panic overtook him. He tried to fight whatever it was that was squeezing his fingers. He tried, but the pressure tightened and the pain became unbearable. And that smell . . . it was stronger now, gagging him, making his head reel. Whatever strength he had bled out of him.

A knife was lying on her naked belly. He was forced forward until his free hand was inches from it. The pain made him pick it up, made him place the point of the knife against her throat. The pain was trying to force him to stab her in the throat. There was an unspoken promise—push the knife a little further, just break the skin—only draw a drop of blood, and the pain will stop. He tried to fight it. He looked in her eyes. A muffled sound escaped from her as she tried to scream. He dropped the knife to the ground. A loud obscenity was barked out from behind him. The voice was vaguely familiar. Where did he know it from . . .

Then his fingers were twisted with a hard jerk, twisted to the point where they were about to break. The pain exploded inside him.

And then somehow he was free. Falling . . .

Bill Shannon awoke in bed. He was doubled over in pain, his two fingers throbbing, a cold sweat soaking his body. He grabbed his fingers and tried to massage them, tried to ebb the pain flowing from them. They were thicker than his other fingers and were a slightly bluish-purple color. It had been almost twenty years since they had been broken. They had been so badly damaged the doctors at first didn't believe they could be saved. They were never quite right, though. Always stiff, always slightly purple in color, and at times, especially when it got cold and damp, they would throb like all hell.

The pain faded. He pulled himself up and leaned forward until his forehead rested in his hands. His skin felt cold, clammy. At least he didn't wake up screaming, god, at least he could be thankful for that. 'Cause if he had . . .

It was still a few minutes before the alarm was set to go off. Susie stirred next to him. He looked down and studied her. She was an exceptionally beautiful woman. Although the only blood in her was Irish, she had a dark, exotic Mediterranean look about her. Small and petite with long black hair that now lay across her oval face. As she slept, Shannon almost didn't recognize her. She looked so calm and at peace, so much younger than her twenty-nine years. Even though they had been married for ten years, at that moment it seemed incredible to him that they knew each other.

Susie opened her eyes. As she recognized Shannon, and then as she focused on the perspiration dampening his skin, the color left her face.

"You're having nightmares again," she said hoarsely.

Shannon didn't say anything.

"What was it about, Bill?"

"I don't know," he lied. "I really don't. But I don't think it's anything to worry about."

She rolled over and turned her back to him. "It's early for you to be having nightmares. About three months early. You told me you were making progress with your therapist, that this year was going to be different."

"I really don't think this is anything to worry about," Shannon repeated weakly.

Susie lay quietly for a few moments. Then she got up and headed towards the bathroom. Before closing the door she turned to him and told him she hoped he was right. "I don't think I can take it again this year," she said.

She closed the door behind her. A minute later the shower was turned on. Shannon fell back onto the bed and listened to the soft drone of the water. Susie was right, it was too early for him to be having nightmares. February tenth was still three months away.

He closed his eyes and thought about his dream. Usually he couldn't remember them. They'd be right at the edge of his subconscious, right where he could just about get a finger or two on them, and then they'd slip away. God, if this is what he dreamed about he could be thankful for that. This one, though . . .

He never saw that woman before. He knew that. She seemed so real, though. Shannon shivered thinking about her eyes, the pure, raw terror that flooded her blue eyes. And that smell. It was so damn familiar . . .

Neither of them had any appetite for breakfast. Shannon drank some instant coffee and then he drove Susie to the law office in South Boston where she worked as a legal secretary. During the ride she sat frozen, her small hands pressed together, her eyes rigid as they stared straight ahead. As she got out of the car she gave her husband an uneasy look.

"Bill," she said, her face softening, "please tell your therapist about your nightmare. Promise?"

"Sure." He tried to smile at her. "But I don't think it's anything to worry about. People have nightmares sometimes, right? It's normal."

As she stared at him the softness from around her eyes faded, leaving her face both drawn and tired. Without a word she turned from him and walked away, her movement as frigid as the November morning air. Shannon watched as she headed towards the building's entrance. He struggled to keep his smile intact. For some reason he hoped she'd turn around, that she'd relent and give him a reassuring look, let him know there was nothing to worry about. He watched as she disappeared into the building, not once looking back at him. He couldn't blame her. He knew in the pit of his stomach his nightmare was anything but normal.

But, as he told himself, February was still three months away. He could still beat it. Just block the damn thing out of his mind because nothing happened. Nothing but a crazy nightmare. His lips pressed into a tight smile as he pulled away from the curb. Twenty minutes later his jaw muscles ached as he drove into the back lot behind the Cambridge Central Square police station.

Captain Martin Brady was hanging by Shannon's desk talking with a couple of the other detectives. As Shannon approached, Brady's pale blue eyes took him in. "You're looking a bit gaunt this morning," Brady said, a thin smile on his lips.

"I had some trouble sleeping last night."

"Not ill or anything, I hope?"

"No. I just had a little insomnia."

Brady's pale eyes held steady on Shannon for a good twenty seconds before blinking. "Sometimes alcohol can interfere with your sleep. You haven't been drinking, now, have you?"

"Not a drop."

"That's good." Brady inhaled, obviously trying to detect booze on his detective's breath. Satisfied, he backed away. "Joe's waiting for you in interrogation room B. He's with a Kyle Rowley. Rowley's wife, Janice, never made it home last night. Her car was found this morning in an industrial park off First Street. No sign of her."

"That doesn't sound good. Any reason to suspect him?"

"There is." Brady showed his thin smile again, a smile that never made it anywhere near his eyes. "He came down to the station last night around seven to report his wife missing. Mind you, she was only an hour late at that point. Sounds like he might've been a bit too anxious to set up an alibi."

Shannon nodded. "Yeah, it does sound that way."

"I'd like to see this wrapped up quickly." Brady hesitated as a queasy look pushed the smile from his lips. "An abduction is going to scare people here. If it's the husband let's get this finished with this morning before the media gets a whiff of it."

"What about the car?"

"Forensics is going over it. Talk to the husband, okay, Bill?"

"Sure."

"And, Bill, get it finished with this morning."

Shannon gave his captain a nod and then headed off in the direction of the interrogation rooms. He stopped off at the lunch room to pour himself some coffee, and then stepped outside so he could smoke a cigarette. Cambridge had a smoking ban in the work place, and even though over half the cops in the precinct smoked, it was strictly enforced. Getting caught cost you a thirty-dollar fine, and he had already racked up a hundred and fifty in fines over the past three months. If Susie knew she'd be pissed, he thought with a slight smile. When he was done, when his nerves had for the most part settled, Shannon went to interrogation room B and stuck his head in.

Joe DiGrazia was leaning back in a chair, his eyes half closed, his hands folded on top of his thick belly. Sitting across from him was a man in his early thirties, tall, lean, with a sallow complexion and a day's growth of stubble covering his face. The man, Kyle Rowley, looked like he hadn't gotten much sleep the night before.

DiGrazia caught Shannon's eye and gave him a signal that they needed to talk alone. He then turned to Rowley and told him he'd be right back. Rowley nodded dully in response.

Outside the interrogation room DiGrazia took a deep breath, expanding his chest half a foot. He was built like a bull, about five feet eight inches tall and practically the same width. A short, thick neck, not much hair, and a face like a granite block. He exhaled a lung full of air and made a face.

"I don't know about this, partner," he said. "I think the man's genuine."

"Why'd he report it so early?"

DiGrazia shrugged. "He was worried."

"Tell me about him."

"There's not much. He's a white-collar type, a software engineer, married four years. They have an apartment near Porter Square. And his wife's missing. That's about it . . ."

DiGrazia stopped, his eyes narrowing as he studied his partner. "Are you feeling okay?" he asked.

"I didn't sleep well last night," Shannon said.

"You don't look too good. Kind of nervous," DiGrazia observed.

"I'm fine. Let's go talk to the husband."

They went back into the interrogation room and Shannon introduced himself to Rowley. Rowley seemed only partly aware of it, his eyes searching off into the distance.

"What time was your wife supposed to be home last night?"

"Six o'clock," Rowley said, his eyes drifting towards Shannon but not quite making it. "Janice called me at five and told me she'd pick something up for dinner. She asked what I wanted and I told her to pick up whatever she was in the mood for. She told me she'd be home by six."

"And after being only an hour late you thought something had happened to her?"

"I knew something had happened to her." Rowley's eyes met Shannon's. They had a sickish, jaundiced look about them. "I don't know how I knew, but I did. I came down here last night, but the officer at the front desk told me Janice had probably just stopped off someplace for a couple of drinks."

"Wasn't that possible?"

"No."

"She's never been late before?"

"Of course she has. There have been times when she's been stuck at work, or she has a hair appointment that's running late, but not like this. She called before leaving work that she was going to pick something up for dinner and be right home."

"Where does she work?"

"In Watertown. She's an accountant. Here's her business card." Kyle Rowley took a card from his wallet and handed it to Shannon.

The card had Janice Rowley's work address and phone number. Shannon put it down in front of him and considered Kyle Rowley for a long moment.

"How have you and your wife been getting along?" Shannon asked at last.

Rowley tilted his head to the side, shaking it slightly. His lips pulled into a thin smile.

"I need to ask you this."

"This isn't anything like that," Kyle Rowley said, his voice tired. "My wife and I love each other very much."

"There haven't been any problems, no fights or anything?"

"No." Rowley's eyes shifted upwards to lock in on Shannon's.

"If we were to ask around we'd hear—"

"You'd hear the same thing. That me and my wife love each other. That's all you'd hear about us."

Shannon took a pack of cigarettes from his jacket pocket, shook one loose, and looked at it for a long moment before pushing it back into place. He noticed DiGrazia staring at him from the corners of his thin, narrowed eyes.

"Could your wife be seeing someone else?" Shannon asked.

"No."

"Is there the possibility—"

"No. Janice is not seeing anyone. There's not even the possibility of it."

"What about someone she works with?"

"I told you she's not seeing anyone—"

"But you have suspicions, though."

"What do you mean?"

"You had her business card ready for me. You obviously have suspicions about somebody there."

Rowley thought it over. "I don't think so," he said. "You asked me where she worked. Anyway, I thought it could help to give it to you. Maybe somebody saw someone suspicious in the parking lot. Maybe somebody heard something. I don't know. But that's why I gave you her card. Janice is not seeing anyone."

"How can you be so sure?"

"Because I know my wife," Kyle Rowley said. "I know how we feel about each other."

Something about Rowley being so cocksure of his wife bothered Shannon. Shit, half the cops he knew sooner or later found their wives in affairs. Stubbornly he kept at it. "If your wife is seeing someone I need to know about it—"

"She's not seeing anyone. This is not anything like that."

"What is this then?"

Pain pushed through the dullness in Kyle Rowley's eyes. His entire face momentarily was flushed with it. "Janice was abducted," he said. "Somebody took her. You realize that, don't you?"

"Okay," Shannon said, "let me be straight with you. What I realize is your wife is missing, either because she wants to be, because somebody did something to her, or because you did something to her. If we can rule you out then we can focus on the other two possibilities. Which means if your wife really was abducted, the quicker we can cross you off, the better the chance we'd have of finding her. Will you give us permission to search your apartment?"

"It's not going to help at all—"

"I could get a warrant, but it would take time. I don't think we want to waste time right now."

Anger turned Rowley's skin a soft purple. "This is ridiculous," he started to argue, his jaw muscles hardening, "there's nothing in my apartment that's going to help you find my wife—"

"If you're involved, you're doing the right thing by stonewalling us," Shannon said.

"I'm not trying to stonewall you," Rowley said. "Goddamn it." He shook his head. The color drained out of his face, leaving it the same unhealthy yellow it was before. "Do whatever you want as long as it gets you looking for Janice."

"Are you willing to take a polygraph test?"

"I'll take whatever you want me to take. Just find my wife."

Shannon stood up. "I'm going to get you a pad of paper. I want you to write down any place your wife might have stopped off last night to pick up dinner. Any place you can think of. I want you to also write down anything unusual that might have happened over the last couple months, anything your wife might've said that seemed out of place—"

"Like what?"

"Like somebody coming on to her at work, or threatening her, anything like that. I also want you to write down everything you did from the time you left work yesterday to coming here this morning." Shannon hesitated. "Do you have pictures of your wife?"

"I didn't bring any. I can go home and get some."

"That's okay. Just give me your keys. While you're writing down what I asked, Detective DiGrazia and I will search your apartment. I need to get a photo of your wife out on the wire. Do you give me permission to remove photos of her from your apartment?"

Kyle Rowley told Shannon to do whatever he needed to do and told him where they kept their photo albums. He took a pair of keys off a chain and handed them to Shannon. "Janice's still alive," he said. "I know it. Goddamn it, I don't know how I know it, but I do. Don't let her die. She's my life. I don't think I can make it without her."

"I'll do everything I can. I promise. I'll be right back with that pad."

DiGrazia, before leaving, put a hand on Rowley's shoulder and told him to hang in there.

Out in the hallway DiGrazia remarked how he let Shannon do all the talking.

"Yeah, I noticed."

"I wanted to give you every opportunity to form an unbiased opinion."

"Thanks."

"You thought there was something funny about him pointing us towards her coworkers?"

"No. I just wanted to ask him about it."

"So what do you think," DiGrazia asked, "is he genuine?"

Shannon thought about it. "What I think is we've got a woman in pretty bad trouble."

Before leaving the precinct they stopped to talk with Brady. Forensics took a couple of partial prints off the steering wheel, nothing else.

"Of course," Brady went on, "they're most likely the victim's, but we'll check them. Bill, tell me about the husband."

"He's given us permission to search his apartment and he's also willing to take a polygraph. I've set it up for one this afternoon. Do you want to be there?"

"I don't think that's necessary. Is he responsible?"

"I don't know."

"What do you mean you don't know?"

Shannon shook his head. "I don't have a feel yet, Martin. I really don't know."

Brady gave DiGrazia a questioning look, but DiGrazia cut him off. "I don't know what the fuck's going on," he said.

"You're disappointing me," Brady said to the two cops as

they walked away from him.

Brady stood watching them, shaking his head, a dour look forming over his soft features. "And I'm not at all happy about it," he said to no one in particular.

Chapter 2

Shannon only half heard his partner puffing as they made it up the three flights to Kyle Rowley's apartment. He couldn't help thinking about Rowley, about how certain Rowley was of his wife's feelings. If it was Susie, could he say for sure she wouldn't spend the night with another man? When they first got married he probably could've, but now he'd only give even money on what she'd do. At best, they were the same odds for whether he'd care . . .

As Shannon opened the door to Rowley's apartment a smell stopped him; a rotting, sour smell that had assaulted him in his dream. It was fleeting, though, disappearing almost as soon as he breathed it in. Still, it unnerved him.

"Did you smell anything?" Shannon asked.

"What am I supposed to have smelled?"

"I don't know. Something like bad body odor. Except worse."

"Sorry, pal, I didn't smell it. I'll take the kitchen."

The apartment was neat, orderly, no evidence of a recent struggle. Shannon found a picture of Janice Rowley in the living room. He picked it up and studied it. She was attractive, blond and petite with a nice, easygoing smile. There was something appealing about her smile, something warm and genuine about it. A cold numbness pressed against Shannon's forehead as he stared at that smile. The woman in the picture was the same one from his dream.

He put down the picture and found a chair. He sat down

until the coldness went away. Then he thought, what the hell. He couldn't help what he dreamed about. He got up, found the clothes hamper in the hallway, dumped its contents onto the floor and started sifting through it, searching for any torn or bloody clothing. He was at the bottom of the pile when DiGrazia yelled out to him to meet him in the kitchen.

DiGrazia had a hard grin etched on his face as Shannon met him. "Notice anything?" he asked.

A drawer was opened showing a set of steak knifes. One of the knives was missing.

"Did you check the rest of the kitchen for it?"

"Yeah," DiGrazia said, "it's not here. So what do you think?"

"What am I supposed to think?"

"That maybe our guy stabbed her in the heat of the moment, that he then dumped her and the car, and fed us that abduction story."

"They got wall-to-wall carpeting. I haven't seen any blood stains."

"He could've been lucky with the way she bled."

Shannon was shaking his head. "If she arrived home at six and he showed up at the precinct at seven it wouldn't have left him enough time to dump the body and the car and also clean up."

"The car wasn't discovered until this morning. He could've gotten rid of both her and the car after reporting her missing. He probably knew he'd be told to go home and wait."

Shannon was shaking his head.

"What about the knife, then?"

"Knives get lost. It happens."

"Come on."

"If she was abducted," Shannon said, "maybe the perp came back for it."

"What do you mean?"

"He'd have her keys and her address. Maybe it struck him as an amusing thing to do—use one of her own knives on her."

"You're kidding, right?"

Shannon stared straight at his partner. "I don't see any blood stains on the carpeting, I don't see anything to indicate she was stabbed here. I don't think we're being conned. And one of the steak knives is missing."

"Jesus Christ," DiGrazia swore softly. "You got a twisted way of thinking." He paused for a moment. "You see any point in getting the apartment dusted?"

"It's cold outside. I'm sure our guy was wearing gloves. Assuming the knife wasn't just lost."

DiGrazia was scowling, a deep, hard scowl that creased the bottom half of his face. "If it's working out that way, partner—"

"The knife could just be lost," Shannon suggested without any real conviction.

"Shit," DiGrazia swore. Then he stopped and gave Shannon a long, hard stare. "Is something wrong, partner? You don't look too good."

Shannon shook his head and muttered, "nothing" before heading towards the door. He wasn't about to tell DiGrazia that he had seen the missing steak knife in his dream.

The story they got at Janice Rowley's office was consistent; their missing coworker was happily married and was not looking for anything extracurricular. One of the accountants remembered her leaving shortly after five. Like the others interviewed, she seemed visibly shaken on hearing that Rowley was missing.

Shannon tried getting back to the extracurricular angle, asking whether there were any guys in the office who had a tough time taking no for an answer.

The woman just shook her head. "They're accountants," she

said as if that explained the matter.

When they got back to the station Kyle Rowley complained about how long he had been sitting there waiting for them.

"I'm sorry about that, but we've been busy," Shannon explained. "We've put a description of your wife out on the wire and we're faxing her photo to every department in New England. We've also released the story and photos to the local stations and newspapers. If anyone's seen Janice we'll know soon."

"Did you get anything from her car?" Rowley asked.

Shannon shook his head. "I'm sorry," he said. "We didn't find anything that's going to help us."

Rowley seemed lost for a moment, his eyes dazed before focusing on DiGrazia and then Shannon. He reached over and handed a pad of paper to Shannon. "Here's what you asked for," he said. His body seemed to crumple as he sat back in his chair.

There were about a dozen restaurants listed on the front sheet. Shannon quickly read through the rest of what Rowley had written and then handed the pad to DiGrazia.

"I can't believe this is happening," Rowley said to no one in particular. "Oh, Jesus, poor Janice."

"We'll do everything we can to find her."

"I should be home," Rowley said.

"I'd like you to stay a little while longer. We have a polygraph set up for one."

"I have to get home. Somebody could be trying to call."

"There were no messages on your answering machine. I don't think this is a kidnapping."

Rowley's long face screwed up as if he were trying to keep from crying.

"Do you know if any of your steak knives are missing?" Di-

Grazia asked.

"What?"

"One of them is missing. Do you know about it?"

"No. I don't know what you're talking about."

"Don't worry about it," Shannon said. "Another half hour and you'll take the polygraph test. Then you can go home."

"I don't like this," DiGrazia stated in a low, guttural voice to his partner when they were alone. His complexion had turned a dull gray, his eyes closed to thin slits.

Shannon didn't say anything.

"Why would some freak have to go back to her apartment to pick up a knife? I just don't like it."

"It may not be that way." Shannon felt tired. Maybe more beat than tired, as if he were dragging cement blocks from around his legs and arms. He poured himself a cup of coffee. "I want to see if I can pick up her trail. Would you mind hanging around for the polygraph? Maybe you could do a computer search, see if anyone's been released who could fit this."

DiGrazia nodded slowly. "Yeah, sure. Give me a call if you find anything."

The manager of the Bombay House recognized Janice Rowley's picture. "Yes, she was here."

"Do you remember what time?"

"She used a credit card. Wait, let me get the receipts." He bent down under the register and pulled out a tin box and brought it up to the counter. After sifting through it he pulled out a slip of paper.

"Here it is," he said as he handed the receipt to Shannon. "She was here at five forty-five. I had written the time in the left corner. It helps me keep track of when we're busiest."

Shannon noticed Janice Rowley's signature on the receipt.

He asked whether the manager remembered anything else that could help.

"No," he shook his head after thinking about it. "She paid for her food and left. She's a nice woman, though. She comes here often. I hope nothing has happened."

The restaurant was in Somerville, five minutes from Janice Rowley's apartment. Shannon thanked the manager for his help, then checked out the small parking lot in back. It would've been dark and the cars there would have been obscured from the street. As Shannon stood in the parking lot a chill ran through him. He lit a cigarette and breathed in deeply, trying to pull some warmth from it. Janice Rowley had parked there last night and someone had gotten in her car and had waited for her. Sometime later that person had dumped her car at the industrial park. Shannon closed his eyes and imagined what it had been like. Janice Rowley walking briskly, almost running towards her car to get out from the cold. Sitting in the front seat, putting the key in the ignition, and then a hand from the back covering her mouth, another grabbing her by the throat. Her slipping out of consciousness . . .

Shannon opened his eyes, cold sweat running down his back. For a brief heartbeat he had smelled that sickly pungent odor again. For that same brief heartbeat he had a vague image of the person who had been hiding in Janice Rowley's car. An image of someone large, of diseased flesh, and of evil. He couldn't hold on to it, though. It slipped away into the ether.

Shannon took another drag on his cigarette and then tossed it to the ground. The question was, What happened next? Did he drop Janice Rowley off someplace and then dump the car, or did he exchange cars at the industrial park, moving Janice Rowley to the trunk of his car? It would've been about six o'clock by the time he drove to the industrial park and there would be too many people around. It would've been too dangerous to move a body between cars. No, he left Janice Rowley someplace first, then got rid of her car and walked back to her. He got to the Bombay House parking lot the same way, by walking.

On his way back to the station Shannon made a detour to the industrial park to talk to security there. No one saw anything unusual the night before, nor did they have any video security cameras for the parking lot.

When Shannon arrived back at the station he told DiGrazia about finding where Janice Rowley had stopped to pick up dinner and his thoughts about what happened afterwards. DiGrazia listened patiently and then told him that Kyle Rowley's polygraph test had been inconclusive.

"That's too bad. Was there a feel one way or another?"

"Nah. You know Parker, if the results are fuzzy then the test is inconclusive. That's all he's willing to say. I didn't get any type of read from watching Rowley."

"Anything about the steak knife?"

"Inconclusive, just like the rest of the test."

"Where's Rowley now?"

"I sent him home."

Shannon was shaking his head. "It would've been nice to have that test back him up, but I don't think he's involved. I have a strong gut feeling Janice Rowley was abducted from that parking lot."

"She could've gotten home with the food. She could've been killed in the apartment and then dumped. That nasty odor you got a whiff of could've been spoiled Indian food. Hubby could turn out to be as inconclusive as his test results."

"I don't think so." Shannon paused as he tried to block out an image from his dream of Janice Rowley bound and gagged with red lines crisscrossing her naked body. "Not from the vibes I picked up from that parking lot," he added after a while.

DiGrazia gave his partner a hard look. He was going to make a crack about whether Shannon had called the psychic hotline, but he trusted his partner's intuition, maybe more than his own. "You think she was left somewhere within walking distance of where her car was dumped?"

"More specific than that, I think she was left somewhere between that restaurant and the industrial park. It's about four miles between the two. I think our guy walked a couple of miles to get to that restaurant. He probably didn't want to walk more than a couple of miles from where he left her car. My guess is his hole is closer to the industrial park. He'd be too anxious to get back to his victim to want to walk too far."

"And you think she's still alive?"

"What time did Kyle Rowley leave his apartment this morning?"

"Around five. He said he had to do something, so he drove around looking for his wife's car. He came to the station around seven."

"Sometime after five this morning our perp would've retrieved that steak knife. Yeah, she's still alive."

DiGrazia made a face as if he had stomach problems. "I don't know," he said. "If it was an abduction I don't see why he couldn't have moved her to another car. He could've parked somewhere and waited until the industrial park emptied out."

"He'd be too anxious to wait."

"Yeah, well, I'm still not convinced. Anyway, take a look at what the computer spat out."

DiGrazia handed Shannon a folder. Inside was a listing of sexual offenders who had been released over the last six months. Each of them had a prior history of either abducting their victims or using knives on them.

"Four of them are in the Boston area," DiGrazia said.

"This is going to keep us busy."

"I still have to check on their addresses—"

"Take your time. I want to talk to Brady. I want to see if I can plant a bug in his ear."

DiGrazia took the folder back and scanned through the listing, his eyes closing to the point where it looked as if he were going to start napping. As Shannon walked away he heard his partner pick up the phone and start dialing.

After Shannon entered his office, Brady told him to pull up a chair and then asked him whether he knew that Rowley's test results had been inconclusive. Brady showed a thin smile; his eyes, though, remained as dull as a mannequin's.

"I don't think he's involved," Shannon said. "I found where his wife stopped to pick up dinner last night. An Indian restaurant in Somerville. My gut feeling is she was abducted in the parking lot."

"Any witnesses?"

"No."

"No one heard or saw anything?"

"Not that I know."

"But your instincts tell you she was abducted there." Brady's smile faded, his expression becoming as dull as his eyes. "You have no evidence of any kind she was abducted. For all we know she picked up dinner, went home, and met an untimely end at the hands of her husband. Statistically, that's most likely what happened. The little evidence we have seems to suggest that; her husband's inconclusive test results, his behavior, the missing knife."

"About the knife—"

"Yes, I know. Joe told me your theory."

"I have a real strong feeling about this. And I think I have a solid read on the husband."

"You didn't have any read when I asked you earlier."

"I've got one now."

"Is that right?" Brady's eyes opened a bit wider but his soft, round face remained unperturbed. "That's just wonderful, Bill. By the way, since the twelve o'clock news ran I've gotten calls from both our local universities, wanting to know what we are going to do to protect their student population from being randomly abducted."

"You could tell them to keep their students out of Somerville."

"Very constructive, can I quote you on that?"

"Feel free."

"I wish you had cleared it with me before going to the media," Brady said, his round face deflating a bit. "If this turns out to be a domestic situation which we could have wrapped up—"

Brady stopped himself and took a deep breath. "Prove it's an abduction. Find me some evidence, any evidence. Talk to the individuals from Joe's computer search."

"Here's what I'd like to do." Shannon took a map from his inside jacket pocket and unfolded it on Brady's desk. Both the Indian restaurant and the industrial park were marked off and a circle drawn between the two. "I'd like us to do a door-to-door search of all properties within the circle."

"This is another attempt at humor, right?"

"She's being held somewhere within that area. She's still alive, Martin, she's got to be. If we move quickly we can save her."

Brady sat staring at his officer, his small eyes bland, his expression incredulous.

"Trust me on this, Martin—"

"Find me some evidence," Brady stated softly, impatience edging into his voice.

Shannon stood up, took the map from Brady's desk, and then shrugged and moved towards the door.

"By the way," Brady called out, "she had a hundred thousand dollar life insurance policy."

"Yeah, I know," Shannon answered without turning back. "It's a company benefit. Her husband wasn't involved with it."

"It's still motivation. Find out if he's having financial problems, or better yet, a girlfriend. Do your homework. Then talk door-to-door search to me."

Back at DiGrazia's desk, Shannon was asked if he was ready to visit some freaks.

John Roper was soft-looking, round, and mostly bald with a few wisps of blond hair scattered on his head. He had a pockmarked complexion, and a thin, affable smile. Nine years earlier he had drugged a young woman in a bar in Providence, got her to his car, and then held her captive for four days in the basement of a condemned building. During those four days he sexually assaulted her and terrorized her with a straight-edge razor. One night while sleeping he left the razor edge down against her throat. Somehow, even though both her hands and feet were bound, she was able to free herself with it. John Roper was arrested and later sentenced to a minimum of twenty years. In August, the State of Rhode Island paroled him and he relocated to Revere, Massachusetts.

He was the third sex offender Shannon and DiGrazia had tried to visit. The first one, a twenty-four-year-old who had raped a couple of teenage girls while a juvenile, was living with his mother in Arlington. The mother insisted her son was with her the previous night, got belligerent, and threw the officers out. They talked with a few of her neighbors, none of whom could confirm the mother's story. The general feeling they got from their talks was the son wouldn't have had the initiative to get to Somerville by himself.

The next person on their list turned out to be in police lockup in Boston, arrested two weeks earlier on a narcotics charge. Now they were with Roper at the auto garage where he worked, and Roper seemed nervous about it, rubbing his hands against his overalls and forcing an overly affable smile. He asked whether they could question him someplace else.

"What's wrong with right here?" Shannon asked. "Your boss must know you're an ex-convict?"

DiGrazia said, "He probably does, but I bet he doesn't know what you were in for, does he, John? If he's got a wife or daughter he might feel differently about having you around his garage."

"Come on, guys, there's a doughnut shop across the street. I'll buy you a couple—"

"Are you trying to be funny?"

"No—"

"I think he was trying to be funny," Shannon said.

"Come on," Roper pleaded, "I'm trying to start a new life here. I've been paroled—"

"By Rhode Island," Shannon observed. "I don't think Massachusetts had any say in it."

"I bet you're right," DiGrazia agreed. "So, John, why'd you pick our state to settle in?"

"My sister lives here. I'm staying with her—"

An older man with large, grease-stained hands and a cigar stub stuck in his mouth had walked over to them. He asked whether anything was wrong.

"We need to ask your employee some questions," Shannon said.

"What about?"

"About a crime that was committed last night."

"What type of crime?"

"A woman was abducted."

"And you think John's involved?"

"From his criminal record we need to talk to him."

Alarm showed in the older man's eyes. He looked quickly at Roper and then away from him, settling on a spot near his feet. "I had no idea," he murmured to no one in particular, his voice dropping to a hoarse whisper. "I better leave you officers alone," he croaked as he moved away.

Roper's smile disappeared. His skin had turned a blotchy white, his eyes becoming nothing more than small, gray holes. He trembled slightly as he watched the older man walk way. "I'm going to lose my job," he moaned. "Fucking Jesus Christ, I'm going to lose my job because of you assholes."

"Shut up," DiGrazia stepped forward and pushed a thick finger into Roper's chest.

"One of my conditions for parole is being employed," Roper said, his tone not quite human, "another is chemical castration. I get shots every week. I got nothing down there anymore. What the fuck would I want with a woman, you assholes?"

"Nice mouth on this guy," DiGrazia said.

"A real sweetheart," Shannon agreed.

"Maybe we should take him back to the station. If nothing else we can teach him some manners," DiGrazia said, moving closer to Roper.

Roper took a step back. "You don't have to take me anywhere—"

"Shut up," DiGrazia said.

"Are you going to be civil to us?" Shannon asked.

"I didn't do anything," Roper said. "I told you, with the shots I'm getting I don't have any use for a woman."

"We'll check that," DiGrazia said. "But even if you can't get it up anymore there's still the violence part of it. You're a violent man after all, John."

"You still like to cut them, don't you, John?" Shannon asked.

"No, it's not like that—"

"I read the report on that woman in Providence. You cut her over sixty times. It's a wonder she didn't bleed to death."

"Those cuts were superficial. I didn't really hurt her that bad. And it's not like that anymore, not with the treatment I've had and the shots I'm getting—"

"You don't have to explain, John. We understand. You like to cut women. The one you took last night, where is she now? Where'd you leave her?"

"I didn't do anything. I tell you, with the shots—"

"We're sick of hearing that crap," DiGrazia said. "Where is she?"

Roper closed his mouth. Something shut down within his small, gray eyes. "I'm not talking to you anymore," he said. "I want a lawyer."

"Your choice, John," DiGrazia said. He had Roper put his hands behind his back and then he cuffed him. DiGrazia and Shannon then led him out of the garage to their patrol car.

Back at the station, DiGrazia read Roper his rights and had him initial different paragraphs of it and sign at the bottom.

"We'll get you your lawyer now," DiGrazia said. "Then I'm going to get a search warrant for your room at your sister's. I'll find something that will break your parole."

Shannon said, "A couple of grams of coke in his sock drawer would do it."

"That's usually a good place to find it," DiGrazia said. "Then we'll send you back to Rhode Island. I'm sure your friends in lockup will be glad to see you again, especially now you've been turned into a fat, little eunuch."

"Should be loads of fun for them," Shannon agreed. "They'll have a ball."

Roper started to cry. "I didn't do anything."

Shannon said, "You don't have to talk to us. You've already asked for a lawyer."

"I swear to you I didn't do anything."

"Are you telling us you've changed your mind about wanting a lawyer?" Shannon asked. "You willing to talk to us, see if you can clear this up?"

"Sure," Roper said. He was still sobbing. He rubbed both his palms against his eyes. "We can clear this up 'cause I didn't do anything."

"A woman was abducted last night. It looks a lot like what you did in Providence."

Roper took both palms away from his eyes and looked at Shannon. His small eyes had a pinkish look to them, like rat's eyes. "I was home all last night," he said, sniffling.

"Home—you mean your sister's house?"

He nodded. "They have a small in-law apartment in the basement they're letting me use. I was tired yesterday. After work I went home with a bottle of vodka and a quart of orange juice."

"What time did you get off work?"

"Five. Kelley, the owner of the garage, can back me up on that. I bought the vodka and juice a block away from my sister's house and was home by quarter past."

"Your sister see you?"

"I don't think so. I have a separate entrance."

"She doesn't check up on you?"

Roper shook his head. "She might've heard me. I turned on my stereo when I got home."

"That's it?" Shannon asked. "You didn't talk to anyone or see anyone last night?"

Roper looked away from Shannon. "I don't have any friends here," he said. "And there's really no point to me trying to date."

DiGrazia moved his chair close to Roper's, and then leaned forward until his face was inches from the ex-convict's. At first Roper tried to ignore him, then he tried to push his own chair back. DiGrazia stopped him.

"You fucking with us?" he asked.

"No, I'm not fucking with you—"

"I think you are," he said. "I like you for this one, John. If you took this woman, I'm going to find out. Trust me, I will. And if you did, and if you've been sitting here lying to us, when we get you I'm going to make sure you don't go back to Rhode Island. I'll pull whatever strings I have to get you into the Federal system and into Danamora. It's a nasty place, John. A fat eunuch like you won't last a month there."

"I'm not lying."

"If you've been lying, right now is the last fucking chance you'll get to come clean. Have you been lying to us?"

Roper just shook his head. He bit down on his bottom lip, his small, pinkish-gray eyes bleary with tears.

"What time did you get to work this morning?" Shannon asked.

Roper hesitated. Shannon said, "If you've been telling the truth so far, don't start lying now. Your boss will be able to answer this one for us."

"I came in after ten," Roper said. "I was hung over from the vodka."

"Okay," Shannon stood up. "We're going to go talk with your sister now."

"Am I free to go?"

"No. If you want a lawyer we'll arrest you and process you on a kidnapping charge. Maybe you'll be able to get bail afterwards. If you're willing to sit until we talk to your sister, we'll let you go if she backs up your story. You want a lawyer?"

Roper shook his head.

As the two cops got to the door, Roper spoke to Shannon. "You two put me through a lot for no reason," he said.

Shannon considered the ex-convict. "I'm not sure I agree

with that. We questioned you, John, that's all. It's not like we held you hostage for four days, sexually assaulting you and cutting you with a straight-edge. Any scars came from you, not us."

Shannon closed the door on him. DiGrazia was waiting in the hallway. He gave his partner a hard look. "I think that sack of shit is lying to us," he said.

A weary sigh broke loose from Shannon. "Maybe. Let's go talk to his sister."

Chapter 3

John Roper's sister was married and had a triple-decker house a couple of blocks from Revere Beach. When Shannon knocked on her door, a large, barrel-chested man wearing a tee shirt and a pair of dirty khakis answered. He squinted at Shannon's badge and when Shannon told him what he was there for, the man's face turned a deep red.

"God damn it," he swore, "we never should have let him move in here." He turned away from the officers and bellowed, "Wendy, your pervert brother's been at it again!"

A large woman with a strong physical resemblance to John Roper came to the door and the barrel-chested man left. She stood silently, her eyes darting suspiciously at the two officers.

"Are you Wendy Soretti?" Shannon asked.

"What of it?" the woman answered, her lips barely moving. Shannon couldn't help noticing her skin color was way too pale. The stark whiteness of her skin made the black moles along her face grotesque.

"We'd like to ask you a few questions about your brother."

She said something that Shannon couldn't quite pick up and he asked her if she could repeat it. She said she wanted to see his badge, her lips again not visibly moving. Shannon showed her his badge. DiGrazia asked her if she ever worked as a ventriloquist. In response, she glared at him.

"We're hoping you could tell us where your brother was last night," Shannon said, pulling her glare away from DiGrazia.

"According to John, he worked late last night and came home around eight. Then you, him, and your husband went out together for Chinese food and didn't get home until eleven. Is that true?"

She stared bug-eyed at Shannon for a long moment and then told him that's exactly what happened.

"Your brother was having a tough time remembering the name of the place you went to. Could you help us with that?"

"May Ting's on Route One in Saugus."

"You're lying," DiGrazia said.

"No, I'm not."

"Your brother didn't tell us he went with you for Chinese food," Shannon said.

Wendy Soretti blinked at them stupidly.

"Anyway, you answered whether there's any point trying to talk to you," Shannon continued. "There's no point, is there? And you don't know where your brother was last night."

"I do, too."

Shannon gave DiGrazia a questioning look. DiGrazia said, "She don't know shit."

"He was wherever he said he was," she said in a low whisper.

"And where was that?" Shannon asked.

She blinked a few more times before repeating, "Wherever he said he was."

"You're not helping your brother any," DiGrazia said.

"It would help him if you'd let us look in his apartment," Shannon suggested.

She stared blankly at both officers. "Not without a warrant," she said after a long moment.

"That's not going to help John."

She shook her head stubbornly. "You're not coming in without a warrant."

"I'll get one then," Shannon said. "My partner will be outside the apartment entrance with a flashlight. If he sees you or anyone else tampering with anything inside he'll break down the door and arrest you for tampering with evidence. By the way, do you have any children?"

"I don't have to answer that," she said, her voice tinny, barely audible.

"I thought I heard a girl's voice from inside."

"That's my daughter—"

"How can you have him live here when you've got children?"

Her eyes shrunk as she stared at Shannon. "He's family," she said stubbornly. "And it's none of your business." Then she closed the door on him.

DiGrazia let out a low whistle. "What a piece of work. Were you serious about having me hang around here while you get a warrant? It's cold as hell, partner."

"You're going to have to," Shannon said. "She'll clean out the place if you don't. I'll bring you back some coffee and a couple of doughnuts."

"Son of a bitch," DiGrazia swore. "I'm going to freeze my ass out here." He walked over to the in-law apartment entrance and peered in. "Get me some chocolate glazed."

Judge Harold Coen was explained the urgency of the matter, and although he grumbled about the thinness of the evidence, he issued a search warrant for John Roper's apartment. When Shannon returned to the triple-decker, Joe DiGrazia was breathing into his cupped hands. He gave Shannon a long, pained look, and Shannon handed him a cup of coffee and a bag of chocolate glazed doughnuts.

"Anything happen?"

DiGrazia took a sip of the coffee. "She snuck down at one point, but when I flashed the light at her, she scurried back upstairs."

"They're still home then?"

"Yeah, no movement."

Shannon walked up to the main entrance and rung the bell. There was no answer. After waiting, he knocked on the door and yelled out that he had a warrant.

"Hell with it, we've got a warrant, right?" DiGrazia asked without waiting for an answer. He broke the glass pane on the basement door and unlocked it from the inside.

Roper's apartment was nothing more than a room with a bed, a worn-out sofa, a TV, a cheap stereo, and a table. In the corner was a small galley kitchen and next to that, a bathroom. A staircase led to the upstairs level. Dirty clothes and tissues littered the floor. Dishes were stacked up in the sink, a layer of grease covered the kitchen countertop. The apartment smelled faintly of urine. Shannon found a vodka bottle lying next to the bed. It was two thirds empty and rotgut quality.

The door to the upstairs level opened. Wendy Soretti bounced down the stairs wearing a large, ratty bathrobe. Her husband peered down the staircase after her, but stayed where he was.

"You broke into my house," she accused, her voice harsh but barely above a whisper.

"We have a search warrant," Shannon said. He handed her a document. "You failed to open the door for us."

She glared at the paper and then at Shannon. "I didn't hear you. Look at my door—you're destroying my property. I'm calling the police."

"Feel free to do what you want," DiGrazia said. "Just don't interfere with our police work."

The husband's face disappeared from the top of the staircase. Wendy Soretti walked over to the phone, picked it up, and then put it back down. She glared at both officers. "I'm going to watch you," she said. She took a small notebook and pen from her bathrobe pocket.

"Do whatever you want," DiGrazia grunted as he pushed the mattress off the bed.

Shannon had found a collection of porn magazines and metro bus schedules buried within a pile of newspapers. He called DiGrazia over and showed him what he found. Wendy Soretti peered angrily at them and jotted something down in her notebook.

Shannon noted that it was an interesting collection for a guy who had been chemically castrated. DiGrazia suggested that Roper probably had them for the articles.

"Yeah, I'm sure that's it." Shannon pointed out the bus schedule Roper had for Somerville. "You notice, partner, there's a five-twenty bus from Revere that gets to Somerville by five forty."

DiGrazia stared at the bus schedule, his eyes narrowing as he studied it. He turned towards Roper's sister. "Do you know how long he's had these?" he asked her.

"I'm not talking to you," she said.

Shannon placed the bus schedules in an evidence bag. He helped DiGrazia move the sofa. Underneath it they found more hardcore magazines, this collection even more sordid than the ones Shannon had already found.

In the back of the closet they found a shirt splattered with blood droplets. A sick, weary feeling hit Shannon as he looked at it. He could see DiGrazia's jaw muscles tightening. They put the shirt in a separate evidence bag.

Wendy Soretti protested. "You got no right taking my brother's possessions," she croaked as if her voice was squeezed out of her.

"Read the warrant." DiGrazia said.

When they were done, they left the apartment and stood by the curb. Shannon could see Roper's sister peering at them from the window. He lit a cigarette and offered his partner one. The cold air felt good against his face, the cigarette smoke helped erase the stale smell of urine that lingered from Roper's apartment.

"Any reason we shouldn't settle on this freak?" DiGrazia asked.

"I don't see any," Shannon said. He took a long drag on his cigarette and held it in for a good ten-count. He studied the smoke as he let it out. "Let's say he took the five-twenty bus to Somerville, he would've gotten to the Indian restaurant about the time Janice Rowley did. And if he'd been scouting for empty buildings in Cambridge he'd know where to dump her. Later, he takes a bus home. It seems to fit."

"What do we do now, sweat him some more?"

"Let's talk with Brady."

DiGrazia laughed sourly. "A lot of good that's going to do us. It's nine o'clock. Our boss has long been home with the wife and kiddies."

They ended up catching Brady in the police parking lot. Brady, his soft features bleary with fatigue, complained that the abduction story given to the press had forced him to work well into the night. Shannon and DiGrazia listened sympathetically and then filled him in on what they had found.

"You'll test the blood on the shirt."

Shannon nodded.

"He's an auto mechanic," Brady added. "He's going to cut himself on the job. The blood could easily be his."

"It's possible. What do you want us to do?"

Brady let loose a tired sigh. "Try and get him to talk. If the blood type matches the victim's, then arrest him."

"What about a door-to-door search?"

"It's nine-twenty. I'm not going to wake up half the city now.

Check the blood type, talk to Roper. If we still haven't located the victim by morning, we can talk more about a door-to-door search."

Brady gave his officers a curt nod and wished them luck.

John Roper looked uneasily at the porn mags that had been dumped on the table in front of him. "They're not mine," he said.

"What were they doing in your room?"

"I don't know."

"Your brother-in-law storing them down there, is that it, John?"

"I don't know. Maybe."

"What is it, John, yes or no?"

"I don't know. There's no law against having them, is there?"

DiGrazia smiled thinly. "No, there isn't. But I thought you were being chemically castrated. What the fuck use do you have for these magazines?"

"They're not mine."

"You're lying, John. You think we're fucking idiots?"

Roper didn't say anything.

"You still like hurting women, don't you, John?"

"No."

"You at least like looking at pictures of them being hurt."

"I told you those aren't mine—"

"John," Shannon asked, "tell us why you had this bus schedule."

Roper, distracted, looked over at what Shannon was holding. As he peered at the schedule and noticed the Revere to Somerville route, his small, gray eyes seemed to dull. "I never saw that before."

"You never saw it before, huh?" DiGrazia asked. "And we're fucking idiots, is that what you're trying to say?"

Roper's mouth opened and closed. He shook his head.

"John," Shannon explained, "we found a shirt of yours stained with blood hidden in your closet. We're having the blood analyzed right now. We know your blood type, we know the victim's, we're going to know pretty soon if you abducted her. Why don't you help us now while it can still do you some good?"

Roper's eyes glazed over as he listened to Shannon. The phone rang. DiGrazia picked it up and listened for a moment. When he put the receiver down his face was flushed with anger.

"Where is she, you little shit?" DiGrazia demanded.

Roper blinked several times at him, his small eyes seeming to grow more distant. DiGrazia moved quickly towards Roper, grabbing him by his shirt collar and swinging him out of his chair. He pushed the ex-convict hard into the wall.

"I asked you where she is," DiGrazia demanded, breathing hard, his face inches from Roper's.

"I want a lawyer," Roper said, his tone impassive, his expression calm.

DiGrazia reached back and swung a thick, ham-hocked fist into Roper's gut. There was a soft thud and Roper's skin turned a queasy gray, but other than that there was no reaction from him. DiGrazia reached back and delivered another blow, this one to the side of Roper's skull. Roper fell to the floor, but again there was no real reaction from him. DiGrazia backed away, his smile stretched tightly, his eyes sharp, black points. When Roper could, he asked again for a lawyer.

"John, we've got you for this one. You might as well help us," Shannon said.

Roper pushed himself to his feet. He looked through Shannon as he again repeated that he wanted a lawyer.

DiGrazia gave Shannon a questioning look but it was obvious Roper had shut down and no amount of beating him was going to get him to tell where he had left Janice Rowley. Shannon told

Roper that they were going to book him for kidnapping and he could see a lawyer in the morning.

Susan was sitting on the living room sofa watching TV when Shannon arrived home. It was past two in the morning and she was wearing a red flannel robe, her skin pale white in contrast to it. Dark lines ran under her eyes. She looked exhausted. Shannon explained why he was so late and why he had missed his appointment with his therapist. He knew Susan knew about him missing his appointment. Susan listened to his explanation and while she didn't like it, she accepted it.

That night he had a restless time of it. Every time he'd start to drift off he'd see images of Janice Rowley, her thin body dotted with blood, her hands and feet bound, her eyes wild with terror—and he'd be jolted awake. Eventually he fell asleep. A little after four he woke with his heart pounding. He jumped out of bed and dressed quickly. He felt a sense of urgency, one he didn't quite understand. Before leaving the bedroom he whispered to Susan that he had to go. She murmured something unintelligible and fell back asleep.

A light rain fell as Shannon drove towards the industrial park where Janice Rowley's car had been found. When he got to the park he turned left and headed in the direction of the Indian restaurant where she had stopped to pick up dinner. He drove a half dozen blocks and then turned down an alleyway. Lining the alleyway were a series of rundown warehouses. The one on the end had boards nailed over its windows.

Shannon got out of his car and checked the entranceway to this warehouse and found the door bolted shut. He then walked around the building and checked the windows. With just a little pressure from his hand, the boards covering one of the side windows slid off. Someone had pulled them off recently and had placed them back in position. Shannon shined a flashlight through the hole and saw a small body lying in the corner. Something glinted from it. Shannon ran back to his car and radioed for an ambulance. He then ran back to the window and climbed through the opening in the boards.

The body lying on the floor was Janice Rowley's. She was naked, her hands and feet both bound. A red rag had been stuffed in her mouth. There were cuts all over her body, small lines of blood everywhere and one big puddle under her neck. The glint came from the steak knife that had been pushed into her throat.

Shannon removed the rag from her mouth and then put his fingers against the side of her neck. He was able to detect a faint pulse. She was still breathing, barely, but still breathing. He covered her with his jacket and told her everything was going to be okay, that help was on the way. He squeezed her hand but got no reaction.

He checked the door to the building and saw he needed a key to unbolt it. Swearing to himself, he kicked it once and felt something crack in his shin. He clenched his teeth and kicked the door again and felt the wood frame give way. The third time the door kicked open. At least the EMV guys would be able to get in . . .

Whatever he did to his shin hurt like hell. He hobbled back to Janice Rowley. Her breathing was fainter. He knew she was slipping away. A heaviness welled up in his chest as he pleaded with her to hang in there. He didn't know what to do with the knife in her throat. The blade had been pushed in about an inch. He got on his knees and gave her mouth-to-mouth resuscitation. She was gone before the ambulance arrived.

Chapter 4

Later, he found that John Roper had committed suicide in his cell. Roper had wrapped his jail-issued blanket around his head and had asphyxiated himself. It would've been a painful way to kill yourself. A difficult way to kill yourself . . .

DiGrazia arrived at the station after six in the morning looking hung over, his eyes bloodshot, his skin pallor not quite right. He admitted with a sick grin that he had hit the scotch hard before going to bed. He asked Shannon how he knew where to find Janice Rowley. Shannon couldn't answer him because he really didn't know. When he woke he had a grim realization of what he was going to find, but it wasn't until he had gotten in his car and started driving that he had any idea of where he was heading. It was as if something had taken over, as if something had delivered him to that warehouse and to Janice Rowley.

He told DiGrazia that he woke up knowing he was going to find her.

"Just something you dreamed about?" DiGrazia asked with a bit of skepticism.

"I can't remember what I dreamed about," Shannon said.

DiGrazia gave his partner a long look. "I'm thinking of a number between one and a hundred."

"Yeah, so?"

"Come on, you're psychic, guess."

"Go fuck yourself."

"But you knew where to find Janice Rowley."

"Yeah, somehow I did."

"Too bad you didn't wake up a couple of hours earlier."

Shannon didn't say anything.

"It's also too bad I didn't try a little harder to beat the truth out of that piece of shit," DiGrazia said. "Damn it. It shouldn't have had to end this way. We had that piece of shit. He knew we had him. Why couldn't he have just told us where he had her? Especially if he was going to check out anyways?"

Shannon shrugged. "Hell if I know. I have to get to an emergency room. My leg hurts like hell."

"What happened to it?"

"I hurt it kicking a door down. Look, I've got to get going."

"You haven't notified the husband yet?"

"Not yet. It's too early. I thought I'd try to let him have a decent night's sleep."

"I doubt he's been sleeping too well."

Shannon grabbed a bottle of aspirin from his desk, shook out three pills and swallowed them. He then pushed himself to his feet, grimacing. "I've got to get to an emergency room. Could you talk to the husband?"

DiGrazia nodded. "Sure, what the fuck. You need a ride?"

Shannon shook his head. "Just talk to the husband."

Chapter 5

January 5. Evening.

The cast had been taken off his leg a few days earlier. Even though his fractured shin had healed, it still felt stiff and Shannon showed a slight limp as he made his way across the street.

Throughout the day he had a tough time concentrating. DiGrazia had lost patience with him several times before finally telling Shannon he had enough of his bullshit. Red-faced, he informed Shannon he'd better get his act together and then stormed out, muttering how he wasn't going to waste any more time with a useless asshole. Susie called a little before five to see if he was coming home for dinner. He told her he would try. She told him not to bother on her expense and hung up on him. He knew from the iciness that had crept into her voice that she sensed something was wrong with him. Shannon couldn't help it, though. He couldn't help the pounding in his head. He couldn't help how damn dry his mouth felt.

He hung around the precinct until seven o'clock. It was cold out, both windy and sleeting. Central Square was mostly empty; partly because of the weather and partly because the students were still away on Christmas break. Shannon stood in front of O'Leary's, trying to find the strength to move on. The little resolve he had faded and he opened the door and walked in. Before he knew it he was sitting at the bar, staring at a bottle of bourbon.

The bartender looked at him, knew he was a cop from the

way he was dressed, and asked him what he wanted. Shannon had to clear his throat before he could say that he wanted a shot of bourbon. The bartender poured him a double and left it in front of him.

Shannon's hand felt unsteady as he picked it up. He tried to put it down, but he couldn't. His head was pounding too much to put it down. He drank it in one gulp. It didn't help any.

The bartender filled the glass again.

Shannon stared at the glass and found himself getting angry. It was too early for this. February tenth was still over a month away. He never started drinking this early. There was no reason for him to be starting this early.

Except he wasn't sleeping well at night. It was almost as if he were afraid of falling asleep, afraid of what he would dream about.

The first week after Janice Rowley's death, he would wake up with vague images of her haunting him. He would wake up wondering how he knew where to find her, wondering why he couldn't have woken up that night a few hours earlier so he could have saved her. Sometimes he found himself wondering about that dream he had.

After a week the images stopped. The last few days it was something else. Something much worse. He just wished he knew what it was.

Shannon pushed the glass away. He sat for a moment, his body trembling, and then forced himself onto his feet.

It was too damn early to start drinking.

Chapter 6

January 30. Twilight.

The pillow muffled his screams. Shannon almost fell out of bed as he jerked himself forward. After a minute he realized where he was.

He was so cold. He couldn't stop shaking, he couldn't keep his teeth from rattling. Slowly he put a hand to his forehead. His skin was soaked with sweat.

Goddammit, he swore to himself. He clenched down hard on his teeth to try to keep them from rattling. Goddammit. He looked over and saw with a small sense of relief that Susie was still sleeping. At least he didn't wake her, at least he could be thankful for that.

The last few weeks things had actually gotten better. He was starting to believe his therapist that this year was going to be different. But now it was starting just like it always did.

Shannon crawled out of bed, trying to keep from waking his wife. He made his way out of the bedroom and to the kitchen. There, he put on some hot water for coffee and lit the first of many cigarettes. He tried to pull some comfort from them.

He sat at the kitchen table, his head in his hands, a cigarette hanging from his mouth. He had no idea what he dreamed about. The whispers, though, were still buzzing in his head, but he couldn't make them out. Just like all the other years.

Chapter 7

February 6. Morning.

"Enough! Stop it!"

It was a pointless thing to say to himself. He knew he could yell it until he was blue in the face and it wouldn't help any, it wouldn't change that February tenth was only four days away. And as bad as it was now, Shannon knew it was going to get worse. A lot worse. Trying to psych himself out of it was about as useless as anything he'd ever tried in his life.

He'd been lying in bed since nine last night making it over sixteen hours flat on his back. Every time he'd try to move he'd feel his strength drain out of him like blood from an open vein. Susie had left hours ago, her face hard and cold. She was too pissed to say a word to him. Maybe more scared than pissed because she knew what was coming or at least had a good idea of it. She didn't know why, though. She had given up trying to find out why a long time ago, but as much as he'd promise her otherwise she knew it was going to be like all the other years.

Shannon started to think about February tenth, and as he did a dull ache radiated through his body and inched its way through his legs and to the heels of his feet. He took a deep breath and forced his mind blank. Then he pictured a mountain brook among golden aspen trees. He held that image in his mind. It was a technique his therapist had been urging him to use. He slowed his breathing, concentrating on keeping the scene intact. It was difficult, though, and the picture changed as other images danced in and out, scurrying every which way and perverting the pristine landscape he had built. Then they took over, pushing themselves to the front and playing themselves out in all their glory. There was so much blood in them. Shannon squeezed his eyes shut and shook his head until the images dissolved into a blur of redness. As he lay in bed listening to the uneven rhythm of his heart he realized his breathing had sped up dramatically. Not quite the effect his therapist had promised.

It was funny, but some days he actually thought he could beat it. That this year could be different. Then it would hit him how ridiculous the idea was and the realization of it would sap the strength out of him.

He became aware of the phone ringing. The answering machine clicked on and then his partner, DiGrazia, his voice muffled with frustration, left an address in East Cambridge that Bill had better meet him at. That they had a homicide to investigate.

Shannon thought about it for a long moment as he listened to a soft buzz running through the back of his head and then found the strength to push himself out of bed. He dressed without bothering to shower or shave.

The address DiGrazia left was typical of East Cambridge. A ratty, four-family house crammed between a street full of similarly ratty structures. Each front yard about the size of a large burial plot. Thin layers of sludge and dirty snow covered the ground. Neighbors and other passersby were standing in the street, gawking at the house. A few uniformed officers were keeping them at a distance.

There were a half dozen patrol cars and an ambulance at the scene, all left in the middle of the narrow street, blocking off traffic. Murders were unusual in Cambridge. Shannon dumped his car in line with the others and held the collar of his coat shut as he stepped outside. The wind had picked up, making the cold even more unbearable. Up ahead, Shannon spotted Gary Aukland's white minivan with the vanity plate, "GUTS." Aukland was the Boston coroner and was contracted out to Cambridge when needed. For some reason Aukland thought his license plate was funny.

Two ambulance attendants were standing by the doorway of the house enjoying a smoke. Shannon nodded as he walked by them. One of them warned him that it was a grisly one.

The murder had taken place in the second-floor apartment. DiGrazia was standing by its front door talking to one of the patrolmen. He eyed Shannon slowly and shook his head, not bothering to disguise his disgust. "Nice of you to show up," he said, his tone flat and without any feeling. His small, red eyes continued to stare at his partner, the disgust in his face deepening.

"You look like a goddamn disgrace," DiGrazia muttered softly, pulling his partner aside. "You couldn't even shave, huh? Why don't you at least go into the bathroom and comb your hair?"

"Nice to see you, too." Shannon forced a smile, glanced at DiGrazia's thick, ham-hock hands, and winked. "And if we want to talk about personal hygiene, those knuckles of yours could use a trimming. Want to go fifty-fifty on a razor?"

"Very funny." DiGrazia edged closer. "We'll talk later. Don't worry about that, buddy boy." He paused. "Let me show you what we got."

He led Shannon through the apartment and to a bedroom. Lying on the bed was a woman, fortyish, her eyes wide open and staring at the ceiling. She was dressed in jeans and a white turtleneck sweater. There were long, red gashes through the sweater that ran from her chest to her belly. There were other stab wounds along her torso and legs, and a deep one in the middle of her throat. She was long dead, her skin already turning a dull blue.

"A little like Janice Rowley," DiGrazia said.

"Except she's fully dressed. Janice Rowley was naked."

"Yeah, but look at how she was stabbed."

Shannon nodded. "She didn't seem to bleed much," he noted mechanically as he studied her.

"I wouldn't quite say that," Gary Aukland stated. He was sitting at a desk behind them, scribbling notes and sipping some coffee. He twisted his body around to face them. "She bled a lot internally. If we move her the wrong way, it will all come spilling out of her."

"We better not move her the wrong way then," DiGrazia said.

"Not unless we really want to piss off the apartment below."

Shannon's eyes hardened as he turned back to the dead woman. "Is it as it looks?" he asked.

"For the most part. She actually died of asphyxiation. Her lungs filled up with blood and she drowned. The autopsy will prove it, but you can push down along her sides and feel for yourself."

Shannon did just that, putting his hands under her sweater and pushing down.

Aukland smiled. "Kind of squishy, huh?"

Shannon nodded. "What else do you got?"

"Believe it or not, everything."

"Like what?"

"Murder weapon with prints—" Aukland held up an eight-inch knife wrapped in a clear plastic bag. "—hair and skin samples from under her fingernails. We've also got a couple of drops of blood next to her pillow that I don't think are hers."

"And," DiGrazia cut in, "we've got the murderer in the second bedroom."

"What's he doing there? Why haven't you brought him in?"

"Because he hasn't shut down yet. I thought you, with that silver tongue of yours, could coax the truth out of him. Save us all some aggravation. I know it's a lot to ask from you, since all the department is doing is paying your salary, but—"

"Shut up," Shannon ordered. Normally he could ignore DiGrazia, and more often than not get a good chuckle out of him. Now, though, the fat man was getting to him and he could feel a hotness flushing his cheeks. DiGrazia closed his mouth, a slow, satisfied smirk twisting his lips. Aukland bent over the desk, pretending to be oblivious to their spat.

"Anyway," DiGrazia said softly enough so Aukland wouldn't be able to hear, "I thought it would be good to get you out of bed. Susie called me earlier this morning. Later, you're going to tell me what's going on with you. No bullshit this time."

"Fine." Shannon found himself staring at the woman's dead eyes. He shifted his gaze to the rest of her face. A heavy weariness seemed to pull at her features. Even in death . . .

"So who do we have?" Shannon asked, looking away from the corpse.

"This is a real beauty," DiGrazia said, his eyes sparkling slightly. Aukland, sitting at the desk, shook his head, his lips pressed tight together.

"Her son's in the other bedroom," DiGrazia went on. "He did it, buddy boy. He hasn't talked yet, but there is no doubt about it. It's a done deal, right up to the fresh scratch marks running up both his arms. And guess what we also found in his room?"

"What?"

"A collection of articles about Janice Rowley." DiGrazia paused for a moment, and then his voice got lower, edgier. "This freak has probably been dreaming about this for months. If we take him in, Youth Services will shut him down. Let's crack him now while we got the chance. If we're lucky we might be able to get something to use to try him as an adult. Let's have him spend his formative years in Walpole bent over at the waist."

DiGrazia spat on the floor, his eyes now shining like red hot coals. "I would love to bring the piece of shit in here and do the questioning, but well—" he shrugged, his shoulders slumping helplessly "—I don't suppose the courts would be too happy about it."

"How old is the kid?"

"Thirteen."

Bill Shannon stood, blinking at his partner. He felt cold for a moment, very cold, especially around the forehead. "What do you mean, thirteen?" he heard himself asking.

"Just what I said," DiGrazia muttered, annoyed.

"A thirteen-year-old kid torturing and murdering his mother?"

"That's what it looks like," Aukland agreed.

"We've got to nail him, Bill," DiGrazia said. "It would kill me if he got through this as a juvenile. You agree?"

Bill Shannon found himself nodding. The coldness in his head was disorienting, like ice pressing hard against the inside of his skull. His eyes wandered around the room and focused on the gaping red hole carved out from the dead woman's throat.

"When I was a kid I used to spend my afternoons playing hockey. I guess times have changed, huh?" DiGrazia asked.

Shannon nodded again and let his partner lead him to a much smaller bedroom, maybe a third the size of the dead woman's. It was crammed solid with uniformed cops. A few nodded silently to him, their faces pinched, hostile.

"Someone open a doughnut shop in here?" Shannon asked.

"We're keeping the boy company," one of the uniformed cops grumbled.

DiGrazia winked, smiling broadly and showing off some denture work. "Okay," he announced. "Slumber party's over. Clear out."

As the cops squeezed past Shannon, one of them muttered he'd give a month's overtime to spend five minutes alone with the kid.

"There wouldn't be enough of that shit to put in a paper bag," he promised with deep conviction into Shannon's ear.

With the room emptied out, Shannon got a good look at Jamie Roberson, the dead woman's son. The kid was sitting on his bed, his head hung loosely as he stared at the floor. There was a puffy redness about his eyes, the rest of his face a sickly white. He had on the typical urban teenage uniform; army boots, a Beavis and Butthead tee shirt, and a pair of torn jeans. Long, red scratch marks could be made out plainly along his thin arms. The kid seemed so young, his face small, freckled, his eyes glazed and dull. As Shannon looked at him, he felt the coldness within himself intensifying, the ice pressing harder against his skull. For a split second he lost his balance and had to clutch on to an oak bureau next to him for support. He shifted his gaze past the boy to a South Park poster on the wall.

DiGrazia gave his partner a dig with his elbow, grinning, and then walked over to the boy, his face forcing a somber look.

DiGrazia to the boy: "Jamie, we appreciate your bravery in this. I guarantee you we want to catch the sicko who did this as bad as you do."

DiGrazia then turned to Shannon, his nasty smile back in place. "What Jamie tells us is when he arrived home his mom was already cut up, with the knife sticking out of her throat. When he tried to pull the knife out, like any good son would—now get this—his mom turns out to still be alive and starts scratching him like all hell, not recognizing her own son. Isn't that right, Jamie?"

The boy nodded, a tiny sob breaking out of him. As Shannon shifted his gaze downwards, he met the boy's eyes. The same dumb sort of look a deer gives when it turns towards oncoming headlights. It hit Shannon hard, harder than if he'd been cold-cocked. The room started reeling. A thick shadow fell over his eyes, thick enough that he could taste it in his throat. Then it darkened and his legs gave out from underneath him.

The world disappeared as he was swallowed up in an icy swirl of blackness. He could hear DiGrazia swearing and then the boy crying hysterically. Then the noise faded to nothing. There was a sense of movement. Shannon tried to step forward. He felt his body jerk spastically as if he had no control over it.

The sense of movement stopped. After a while the black faded into gray, and then into a mix of shadows. Finally shapes formed. Shannon realized he was sitting on something. Through the haze he could make out DiGrazia. His hand shook as he lifted it to his forehead. Touching his skin was like touching a wet corpse.

"What the hell was that?" DiGrazia demanded, his teeth clenched tight enough to crack them apart.

"I guess I fainted," Shannon said, laughing softly. He saw that he was in a bathroom propped up on a toilet. He caught a glimpse of himself in the mirror attached to the back of the door and laughed pitifully at what he saw. His eyes had a hollowed out look, his face flushed and shiny wet with perspiration. He leaned forward and dropped his head between his knees, rocking his body back and forth.

"That little puke's hysterical now," DiGrazia forced out.

"That boy was in shock. You had no right trying to question him."

"Is that so? The poor kid, all shook up because he butchered his mom like a piece of meat. Maybe pushing that knife into her throat afterwards traumatized the young lad. Excuse me for not showing enough sensitivity to the matter." DiGrazia's face quickly went from red to white. "Fuck you."

"You should've brought him to the station."

"Fuck you!"

"Yeah, sorry. I'm not in the mood. I'm sick."

Even with the buzzing in his ears, Shannon could hear the harsh rasping sounds of his partner's breathing. He could hear it speeding up, like a crazed bull blinded by blood and rage. Then with a dizzying whirl he was pulled from the toilet and slammed hard into the wall. DiGrazia's face was inches from his, his breath sour in Shannon's face.

"Get your hands off me," Shannon demanded weakly.

DiGrazia didn't say a word. He had his hands wrapped around Shannon's collar. He tightened his grip.

"I'll tell you what, you let go of me and I'll find some Girl Scouts for you to rough up. Or maybe some invalids. How's that sound?"

DiGrazia blinked twice, the rage passing slowly from his eyes. "What the hell's going on with you?"

"I got sick, that's all. I think it's some sort of virus. Get your hands off me."

DiGrazia let go and Shannon slid down the wall, ending with his knees tucked close to his chin.

DiGrazia turned towards the door and then spun around, staring down at his partner. His eyes closed to thin slits. He demanded that Shannon tell him what was going on.

"There's nothing to tell."

"Uh uh. Don't give me that crap. Every year around this time it's the same thing. You start coming in late or missing work altogether. You become unreliable. I can't count on you for a damn thing. Then . . . Are you hitting the booze already? Susie told me you hadn't started yet, but I'm not so sure. You kind of look it, pal. And it would sure explain why you collapsed in there."

"Come on. You know better than that."

"I do?"

"I'm not drunk. Okay? I haven't touched any alcohol since—"

"Since last year this time. So what the hell is it then?"

"Nothing." Shannon shook his head. "At least nothing I can't handle. I just need a little space right now."

"Bullshit. You've been telling me that for five years and it's always the same thing. I always end up getting fucked, just like today. You realize that?"

"That's not really true. You had no right questioning that kid without Youth Services present. You know that as well as I do."

DiGrazia regarded his partner slowly, dispassionately. His face relaxed. "Why don't you take a departmental leave until you're back to normal?"

"I can't do that. I've got to beat this thing now or I-I'll—" The thought died in his throat.

"Beat what?"

"Nothing." Shannon shook his head, cradling it in both hands. "You've got a suspect out there to interrogate, okay?"

DiGrazia turned so he wasn't facing Shannon. "I need a partner I can trust," he said. "Not one who goes wacko a couple weeks every year. You take a leave now and return when you're normal or I'll ask Brady for a switch. I don't have any other choice."

With that, DiGrazia left the room, closing the door quietly behind him. Shannon leaned his head back and banged it against the tile wall. The spinning had stopped and the coldness in his head had cleared somewhat. He wondered briefly why he had the reaction he did with that thirteen-year-old kid. He had seen far worse during his eight years on the force. Like the young mother who'd become paranoid schizophrenic and believed a devil cult was after her ten-month-old baby. To protect her child from being taken by the devil she split the kid open like a ripe watermelon. That one even had DiGrazia woozy, but not him, not with his stainless steel gut. So why would a stabbing—yeah, it was a gruesome multiple stabbing, but still only a stabbing—have this kind of effect on him? Causing him to pass out at the sight of a thirteen-year-old suspect? Of course, he knew he was only kidding himself. Deep inside he knew the reason for it. Whether he'd admit it to himself was another question.

Like clockwork, things were progressing as usual. First the nightmares, followed by bouts of listlessness, depression, and then simply the struggle to get his ass out of bed. He hadn't realized he had reached the next level until DiGrazia had pointed it out; that he had stopped taking care of himself.

But there was still a chance he could beat it—if he could keep away from the booze. Except February tenth was a long four days away. As it was, he felt now like he was barely holding on by his fingertips and whatever he was holding on to was slippery as all hell.

Bill Shannon sat for a long while. Sat until the whispers had quieted in his mind. Then he stood up slowly and studied himself in the mirror. His skin had a pasty sheen to it, his eyes a wild combination of yellow and red. If he didn't know better himself, he'd say he'd been tying one on—and a hell of a one at that. What was the point of staying sober if he was going to look like a stinking drunk? He blotted the thought out of his head. He knew better than that.

He turned the faucet on and ran his comb under it and slicked his hair back. It helped a little.

The corpse had been removed, and DiGrazia, Jamie Roberson, and most of the crew were already gone. As Shannon left the apartment he nodded to a couple of members of the forensic team that were tidying up loose ends. They both only gave him a blank stare in return.

Chapter 8

When Detective Ed Poulett spotted Shannon entering the squad room, he raised his hand to his forehead and swooned to the floor in the same overly melodramatic way Bette Davis made famous. Then he started moaning in a high-pitched voice as he let his feet twitch spastically. That brought out some hoots and catcalls from their fellow officers. Shannon watched for awhile, then applauded politely and sidestepped past him. Poulett, with a big, smart-alecky grin, jumped to his feet, and along with Jacoby and Mason followed Shannon to his desk.

"What the hell happened to you?" Poulett asked. "Sight of blood get to you?"

"Come on, level with us," Mason smirked, showing off yellowed teeth. "The suspect just scared the shit out of you, right? A real mean-looking muthafucka."

"Give me a break," Shannon said. "I got sick. I think I have some sort of virus."

"Virus, huh?" Poulett said. "Let me guess where you caught it." He put his head back and stuck his thumb near his mouth and made with the drinking noises. Then he broke out laughing.

"That's not funny," Shannon said.

"Maybe not," Poulett agreed. He was grinning, but his eyes had a coldness about them. "Neither is embarrassing us. How do you think the punks on the street are going to react to hearing about a pussy cop passing out at the sight of a thirteen-year-old? You better get a grip on yourself, pal."

Shannon pushed himself to his feet and leaned forward. "You better shut up," he said very softly.

Poulett stood his ground for a moment and then cracked a smile and stepped back. "You better get a grip, pal." He pointed a thick finger at Shannon as he walked away. "You need it bad."

"You know, it really doesn't look good—" Jacoby started.

"Shut up," Shannon ordered under his breath as he turned to face him.

"A little touchy, aren't we?"

Shannon turned and saw Captain Martin Brady standing over him. Brady's pudgy face was set in an unhappy frown.

"Yeah, maybe a bit," Shannon admitted.

"Bill, let's talk," he said and then turned and headed to his office in the back of the squad room. Shannon, not having any choice, followed him. DiGrazia was waiting for them, sitting impassively, barely looking up as his partner entered the office.

Brady went behind his desk and sat with his hands clasped in front, his eyes staring, unblinking. "You're having a rough time, are you?"

"Just got sick for a moment, some type of virus, I think."

"Is that so? Maybe you could use some time off?"

"I'm okay now. Nothing to worry about."

"Well, now, I think there is something." Brady showed a troubled smile. "Joe has been suggesting that two weeks of rest would do you a world of good. I agree with him, Bill. I'm going to put you on two week's short-term disability, effective now."

"You have no right."

Captain Brady didn't bother to say a word. He just continued staring at his detective, his smile showing some strain.

"I'm going to the union with this," Shannon threatened. "You have no cause to force me on leave."

"I'm not talking about a leave of absence. Only short-term disability."

"You've got no cause!"

"Absenteeism would be a damn good cause," Brady said, nodding slightly. "Unprofessional demeanor. Intoxication—"

"I haven't been drinking a damn thing!"

"Looks drunk to you?" Brady asked DiGrazia.

"Stinking drunk," DiGrazia answered.

"And that's from your own partner." Brady sighed. "Bill, I'm trying to do you a favor. Don't make this harder than it needs to be. At best, all you'd accomplish with a union protest would be to embarrass yourself."

"I'll be fine, you don't have to do a thing—"

"Yes, I do. There's a pattern with you, Bill. A weird pattern, but a pattern nonetheless. It's become pretty damn obvious." Brady lowered his voice into a conspiratorial tone. "I'll be honest, if you weren't such a damn good cop I'd've bumped you from the force years ago. It's kind of unsettling the way you fall apart a few weeks every year. But you are a damn good cop. Smart, determined, you keep your caseload moving. It would be a damn shame to have to lose you. So take the next two weeks off, relax, maybe go to Florida with the wife. Enjoy yourself."

Shannon had his eyes closed tight. He shook his head slowly. "You don't understand—"

"It might help if I did, but I don't suppose you'd tell me?"

Shannon opened his eyes and stared helplessly at his commanding officer. After a long silence he shook his head. "There's nothing to tell."

"I suppose not. Joe, why don't you take Bill home, see that he gets there okay. Give his wife a call also."

"Sure." DiGrazia stood up, continuing to avoid eye contact with his partner.

Shannon took a deep breath and then stood up and forced a

smile. "Well, Marty," he said. "I guess I'll be seeing you in two weeks."

"I certainly hope so. Send us a postcard."

The two men left the office in silence. As Shannon passed through the squad room he could feel his fellow officers staring at him with a mix of curiosity and amusement. He had an urge to grab Poulett and kick his smirking face in, but he swallowed it down and kept walking. At the door, he turned and addressed the room, announcing that due to his remarkable service he was being given two weeks paid leave and the rest of them could just go screw themselves. Someone threw a half-eaten doughnut at him. He barely got out in time to avoid the barrage that followed. DiGrazia hadn't been as lucky. His eyes burned as he picked part of a tuna fish sandwich out from under his jacket, but he kept his mouth shut.

Outside, they got into Shannon's Grand Prix, with DiGrazia behind the wheel. Shannon broke the silence, calling his partner an asshole.

"I don't know what you're bitching about," DiGrazia mumbled, stone-faced. "Two week paid leave sounds pretty good to me."

"You're an asshole."

"You're repeating yourself."

"Yeah, well, in this case it's well deserved."

"You didn't give me any choice," DiGrazia said. "It was either get you on leave or get another partner. And I don't want another partner."

Shannon sat quietly, his face forming a peevish look. Finally, he thanked DiGrazia for spreading the word about his fainting.

DiGrazia started laughing. "You're really losing touch with reality, aren't you, buddy boy? There were half a dozen fellow officers in that apartment watching me drag you out of the kid's bedroom. Think about it."

The ride turned silent again. Finally, Bill Shannon asked to be dropped off at an address in Brookline.

"I need to see my therapist real bad," he explained.

Chapter 9

Susan Shannon had been out of it all day, making mistakes, losing her concentration. As the afternoon wore on, her frustration built, severely creasing her brow and tensing her small face. When she lost an hour's typing by hitting the wrong mouse button, the color dropped right out of her. She sat frozen, struggling against the impulse to smash her computer against the wall. Then she stood up, her body rigid, and held her breath before heading towards the ladies' room. Sid Lischten, one of the law firm's partners, spotted her and was about to start bitching about how long it was taking to get his contract typed up. He opened his mouth and then closed it. Even though Susan Shannon stood only five-foot-one and weighed at most ninety-five pounds, at that moment she didn't look like anyone you wanted to tangle with.

When Susan saw herself in the ladies' room mirror she let out a disgusted giggle. Her face looked like a ridiculous parody of itself—frozen into a hard, anxious mask.

She leaned over the sink and splashed cold water over her face. After a while she could feel the hardness softening. She glanced in the mirror and saw her face was almost back to normal, only a little tightness stiffening her mouth.

There were obvious reasons for her anxiety. The workplace was stressful as all hell. The associates for the most part were bastards, the partners petty little tyrants. They were adapting well for the nineties, cutting three secretaries and dividing their work among the remaining four. The official message given to the office staff was just be thankful you have a job. The unofficial message was a little more blunt; if you complain about having to work lunches or coming in an hour early or leaving an hour late, then your ass—even if it's as pretty as Susan Shannon's—will be out on the street.

But that was only a small part of it. She could live with all that. What she couldn't live with was what was happening to her husband. As much as he promised her this year would be different—that he was making progress with his therapist—she knew it was going to turn out the same as it always had.

It was all starting up again. A week ago he jolted up in bed at four in the morning, moaning, his body soaked in sweat. It took her almost a half hour to get him out of it. Since then, the nightmares had come nightly. After the nightmares came the moodiness, the depression, his just staring into space. She didn't have a clue if he'd gone to work today. She had tried calling home a half dozen times and no one answered, but that didn't mean a thing. If he was home, he'd just let the phone ring. Probably wouldn't even be aware of its ringing.

Once he got out of bed he was better, almost functional, but getting him out of bed was becoming harder and harder.

She knew the signs as well as she knew anything. She'd been living with them for over ten years. Two days ago he had stopped showering or shaving or even brushing his teeth. That was bad. That meant the drinking was only a few days away, at best.

And once the drinking started . . .

Her stomach tensed thinking about it. Absentmindedly she put a hand to the pain and massaged it. Once the drinking started was when the real fun began.

The drinking would be heavy and intense, but it wasn't even like he'd get drunk. More like he'd just fade away from her. Sometimes he'd become catatonic, other times he'd move around their apartment like a zombie, looking through her as if she didn't exist, as if he didn't have any idea where he was. The more alcohol he'd pour into himself the more frequent his trances would come. Sometimes they would last ten minutes, sometimes an hour, and then he'd be back, staring at her blankly, not even aware that anything had happened. Not even able to remember that anything had happened.

Then one day he'd be gone. Just plain disappear. He'd usually come back a week later looking emaciated, like he'd just gotten out of a P.O.W. camp. One year, he was almost dead with pneumonia when he staggered back to their apartment. Another year, he had rat bites up and down both his legs. Then last year, he was so dehydrated he had to be hospitalized. The doctor told her another day and she would've been out shopping for a casket.

He would never be able to tell her what went on during his disappearances. The way he would explain it was that one moment he would be drinking in a bar or restaurant or out of a bottle in some alley and the next moment he would be someplace else, realizing he'd better get home. He could never remember what happened between those two moments even though they could've been more than a week apart.

They never found out what happened during his disappearances. Except for one year . . .

Three years ago, he had ended up in a crack house in Chelsea living with a prostitute. A few weeks after he came back home, the girl showed up at their apartment to give Susan back Bill's driver's license. She also wanted to tell Susan about it. She was no more than eighteen, haggard looking, thin, her skull just about shining through her flesh, her arms nothing but a mess of scars. It broke Susan's heart to look at her. The girl was pretty much doped up but she was able to describe in detail her week with Bill. She thought Susan had a right to know about it. She was also hoping that maybe Susan could give her some money.

Susan almost left him then. She came within a heartbeat of packing her clothes and getting the hell out, but she knew he didn't have any idea of what he'd done. That it was a completely blank screen to him. So he begged and pleaded with her, his eyes as tortured as anything she'd ever seen, and in the end what choice did she have? Besides, at the time she probably still loved him. She wasn't sure, though, whether she could forgive him.

As it was she wouldn't have sex with him for six months, and after that only with condoms for another year. And there were his periodic HIV tests. And time fixed things, at least it dulled the hurt.

That was three years ago. The year after that was when he came home with the rat bites up and down both legs. And then last year . . .

It was all starting up again . . .

Of course, he would never tell her what triggered his yearly breakdowns. Whenever she pressed him, he'd become silent and distant. He knew what was behind it, but he wouldn't trust her with the knowledge. That was the one thing she couldn't forgive him for. Maybe more than anything that was why she thought constantly about leaving him.

Susan dried her face with a paper towel and then gave a quick glance in the mirror before leaving. She didn't like the look in her eyes, but under the circumstances she looked as normal as she could expect. On her way back to her desk, Sid Lischten, having been laying in wait, sprung out at her.

"You were in there twenty minutes!" he accused. He was an old man without much flesh around his face or body. As he stood staring at Susan, his mouth twisted unpleasantly.

"Excuse me?"

"What the hell were you doing in there, your laundry?" he

demanded, his voice booming throughout the office. It didn't seem possible for so much noise to come out of such a withered body. Susan could feel heads turning towards them.

"No, I wasn't doing my laundry," she stated slowly, her own voice trembling.

"What else could you've been doing in there for twenty minutes?" Lischten asked sarcastically. The unpleasantness around his mouth had spread throughout his face, leaving his small eyes bulging. "Unless you just needed to get away from it all. Is that it, a little vacation, huh? You've had over an hour and a half to get me the Haines contract. I could've typed it myself in half that time."

"I'll have it for you as soon as I can."

Susan turned and started towards her desk. Lischten yelled out to her back that if she thought she was too pretty to lose her job then she'd better think again.

By the time she sat down she was shaking. Donna leaned over and whispered to her that it would do the old bastard right if someone slipped Ex-Lax into his coffee. "Maybe it would loosen him up," she added. "He looks constipated, doesn't he? Anyway, we all know he's full of shit."

"I hope he chokes on it," Susan muttered.

"Yeah, you're not the only one. What do you call a hundred dead lawyers on the bottom of the ocean?"

"A good start."

It was a lame joke, one that they told each other whenever things got unbearable. Donna gave Susan's arm a little squeeze before turning back to her work. Susan was still shaking. She hugged herself tightly trying to stop. She couldn't afford to lose her job now, not if she was going to leave Bill.

The thought stopped her. Had she already made the decision?

The phone rang. It was Joe DiGrazia calling to tell her what had happened to her husband. She listened quietly and then thanked him. After getting off the phone, she sat for a minute and then forced herself to type up the Haines contract.

Chapter 10

As Bill Shannon lay on Dr. Elaine Horwitz's couch, he turned his head and caught her fidgeting with her pants, trying to smooth out a crease that had formed. The sight of her brought a genuine smile to his lips. She was pretty, maybe not as much as his wife, Susie, but in her own way very attractive. Frizzy red hair, dazzling green eyes, and the softest, most alluring smile he had ever seen. Maybe her complexion was a bit too pale, and her lips too full, and maybe there was a slight awkwardness to her body, but it all seemed to add to her sensuality.

He knew he made her nervous; he also knew she dressed up for him. On the days of his scheduled appointments she'd usually be wearing short skirts, sheer stockings, a soft rose–colored lipstick, and always her contacts and faint traces of Giorgio perfume. Whenever he would show up unscheduled she would almost always be in pants and wearing wire-framed glasses, barely any makeup and never any perfume.

She caught him smiling at her and she smiled back. "You seem to be feeling better," she said.

He nodded and kept smiling at her.

"I wish you hadn't missed your last appointment."

"Sorry, I wasn't feeling up to it."

"Those are the times you have to come here," she reprimanded, her smile weakening. "Tell me why you were so angry at being put on short-term disability?"

"I felt betrayed," Shannon said. "Sonofabitch should've cut

me some slack."

"Why is that?"

"Because of the job I've done for him over the years." His lips curled into an angry smile. "He owes me that."

"You don't see the danger—"

"That's bullshit. If I'm able to go in, I'm able to do the job."

"But not today."

Shannon didn't answer her.

"It might be a good idea for you to rest the next two weeks."

Shannon was shaking his head. "I need the work," he said. "It helps get me out of bed in the morning. It gives me something to focus on. To keep my mind off things. I think it's my only shot to beat this thing."

"That's not necessarily true," Elaine Horwitz said. "There may be better ways for you to heal yourself. Maybe keeping your mind off of murder investigations might be one of them." She reached over and started the tape recorder on her desk. "Tell me about the dreams you've been having. How much of them do you remember?"

Shannon thought for a while, his face rigid. "Not much at all. I really only have a vague impression of them."

Horwitz waited for him to continue. When he didn't, she asked about his impressions.

Shannon shifted uncomfortably on the couch. "That I was somehow responsible for my mother's death."

"How?"

"I don't know."

"And that boy today, the one who murdered his mother, he's thirteen?"

"Yeah."

"The same age you were when your mother was murdered?"

"That's right."

"And in your mother's death the body was found with a knife

stuck in her mouth. In this case the woman had a knife left in her throat."

Shannon didn't say anything.

"Do you think that's why seeing that boy had the effect it did on you? That it reinforced your feelings of guilt towards your mother?"

"Maybe," Shannon shook his head. "I don't know. But I didn't kill my mother. This kid did."

"No, you didn't. But you could still be feeling guilty about it. Maybe feeling if you'd come home earlier, instead of hanging out with your friends, you could've saved her. Do you think that's possible?"

"That I could've saved her?"

"No, that you *think* you could've saved her."

"Maybe I could've," Shannon admitted.

"Except the man who murdered your mother was twenty years old. You were only thirteen. What chance would you have had against him?"

A slow anger started in him, and he could feel the heat rise up his neck. "Maybe I could've done something—"

Elaine Horwitz had gotten up from her chair and moved over to him so she was kneeling by his side. She took hold of his hand with both of hers.

"Bill, you wouldn't have been able to do anything. He would've overpowered and murdered you, also. That's all that would've changed if you had come home earlier. I guarantee you, your mother wouldn't have wanted that."

Shannon looked into Elaine Horwitz's eyes and felt his heart skip a beat. Her hands felt nice holding his, nicer than anything he could remember. There was a warmth, a softness to them that he didn't want to let go of. He found himself momentarily lost in her green eyes.

"I think we're making a real breakthrough here." She gave his hand one final tight squeeze before letting go. Then she stood up and went back to her chair.

"I really feel positive about today," Horwitz said, a soft smiling breaking over her face. "I really believe you're going to be fine."

Shannon waited a ten-count before clearing his throat, waited until the effect of her smile passed through him. Then he forced a shrug. "I was feeling that way also until I started to fall apart. Just like all the other years."

"But this year it's different. You're more committed to healing yourself."

"I've seen other therapists before."

"But you've never opened up like this before. You've told me so yourself. And this breakthrough today is real. These feelings of guilt have been lurking within your subconscious for a long time. They're baseless, of course, but they've still been doing a number on you. Now that they've been brought to the surface, let's squash them completely. Admit to yourself there's nothing to be guilty about, that you couldn't have done anything to have saved your mother. Please, Bill, admit it out loud."

He obliged her, more for her benefit that his. Usually he had a strong intuitive sense when he was on the right track. That was what allowed him to close more cases over the past six years than any other detective in the precinct. The only thing he was feeling in his gut now was queasy. He mentioned to Horwitz about not being sure if she was right.

"Guilt can be a very destructive force. It can manifest into physical as well as mental illness. You've been suppressing your feelings of guilt concerning your mother's murder for twenty years. They're the root cause of your depression and blackouts."

"And I only feel this guilt for a couple of weeks a year?"

"No. I'm sure you feel it all year long. It probably becomes unbearable around the anniversary of your mother's death. The depression allows you to numb out these feelings, the blackouts allow you to hide from them."

Shannon thought about this. It made sense in a way. Maybe he needed to hit the booze when the depression no longer did the trick, and when the booze stopped working the blackouts did, offering the necessary escape. It was possible. He swung his legs around so he was sitting on the couch facing her.

"So that's it?" he asked doubtfully. "I'm cured?"

"You're well on your way." She paused while she rubbed a finger along the length of her cheek. "I would like to see you tomorrow. How is three o'clock? We've talked about hypnotism before, and I know you have strong feelings against it, but I believe at this point it's crucial. I'm going to invite a hypnotherapist to tomorrow's session."

"I'd really rather you didn't—"

"Bill," she stopped him, her green malachite eyes determined. "We're at a crossroad right now. If we can tap into your subconscious, we can allow you to fully come to terms with your guilt. Your recovery requires it. You don't have to have a breakdown this year." She paused and gave him a reassuring smile. "The hypnotherapist is very good," she added. "I've been working with him for years."

The idea of opening himself up to hypnotism troubled him. He had told Elaine only part of what happened with his mother. Only a small part of it. Still, it was more than he had ever told anyone, even his father. All Susie knew about it was his mom was dead.

He wasn't sure if he could bear Elaine finding out the other part. And there were other reasons. Like Dr. Eli Woodcock. Years ago, he was seeing him in Cambridge and after six months of pressing he submitted to Woodcock's requests and allowed himself to be hypnotized. Afterwards Woodcock dropped him without explanation. He refused to say a single word about it.

He didn't need to, though; the look on his face told the story.

But still, if she was right and this was the answer, how could he turn it down? Resistance fizzled out within him. Like a dying ember buried in snow. He told Horwitz to go ahead and make the arrangements, that three o'clock would be fine. As he started to get up, he stopped himself and gave the therapist a sheepish smile.

"You know, I haven't eaten anything all day," he said. "Want to get something?"

She seemed taken aback by his offer. She noticed her tape recorder still running and reached over and turned it off. "I don't know if it would be a good idea," she started, her peaches and cream complexion quickly turning a warm pink. "And you're married—"

"I'm not asking you on a date," Shannon said.

"I don't know." She hesitated, the warm pink now brightening into a deeper red.

"I feel good around you," Shannon explained. "I guess right now I don't know if I can handle being away from you. At least for the next few hours."

She sat studying her patient, the little resolve in her eyes weakening. After a long silence she nodded. "I am hungry," she admitted.

"Then let's go."

"How about I meet you in a half hour?" she asked. She suggested a restaurant on Harvard Street in Brookline and Shannon agreed. He didn't know the place, but it didn't matter. She could've suggested a soup kitchen and it would've been fine with him. As long as she was going to be with him. He left her office feeling a little funny inside, but also feeling hopeful, maybe even upbeat.

Shannon had the restaurant sized up as soon as he stepped

inside it. A yuppie hangout with overpriced drinks and mediocre food. The type of place that put sun-dried tomatoes in everything and offered more types of pasta than anyone would ever care about. He sat down at the bar and studied the liquor bottles lining the back wall. He was surprised to find he didn't want to sample any of them. The bartender, a beefy, football player–type with a crewcut and a thick, red neck, asked him what he wanted.

Shannon thought about it.

"What can I get you?" the bartender repeated, annoyance straining his smile.

"A beer," Shannon found himself saying. "A Bud."

When Elaine Horwitz showed up twenty minutes later, Shannon was still drinking from the same bottle. He almost didn't recognize her. She'd gone home and changed and had put on a tight-fitting green dress and black stiletto high heels. Shannon had seen her dressed up before but not to this extent. And she looked different out of the office. More curvy, more sexual.

He called out to her. She turned, caught sight of him and started to grin. Then she spotted the beer bottle in his hand.

As she approached him, Shannon noticed she had on a richer shade of lipstick than usual. As she got closer, he could smell the Giorgio perfume from her skin.

"Do you think that's wise?" she asked, her voice subdued, her eyes focused on the beer bottle.

Shannon held the bottle up to the light and studied it casually. "It's the only one I've had," he said, smiling. "And it's the only one I'm going to have."

He left the unfinished bottle on the bar and led her back to the front of the restaurant. There, a young girl wearing way too much gold costume jewelry showed them to a table. Shannon sat to the side of his therapist. She still seemed subdued.

"Why did you do that?" she asked.

"To see if I could," he told her matter-of-factly. "You know, I'm not an alcoholic. During most of the year I can walk away just as easily after one drink as I can from half a dozen."

"But you told me you don't drink except before your breakdowns?"

"I stopped a few years ago." Shannon looked away from her and started to pick at a fingernail. "It made my wife nervous and after everything I've put her through . . ." He let the sentence die as a soft growl in his throat.

"You've put her through a lot?"

"Yeah, I'd say so."

"How do you feel about her?"

He glanced up and caught the tension in her face. There was more to the question than a therapist trying to treat a patient. He started laughing.

"I really don't know," he admitted after a while.

He leaned back in his chair and thought about it. It was a good question. He used to love his wife, he knew that, and he was also pretty sure she used to love him. Now, sometimes he'd look at her and know she was only a coin flip away from leaving him. The sad part was he'd just as soon give her the damn coin. Even though Susie never blamed him outright for what happened, even though she'd make a point of insisting it wasn't his fault, he knew deep inside she blamed him for everything. And she had every right in the world to. The problem is, over the years all the blame and apologies tend to wear thin, eroding little pieces of you. Shannon had a good idea what was dead inside and what was quickly dying. He didn't know, though, what, if anything, was still kicking and breathing. He told Horwitz about it, he even told her how the sex between him and Susie had the last few years become both infrequent and joyless.

As Elaine Horwitz listened her face took on a soft glow.

"You've opened up more tonight than the nine months you've been seeing me," she said after Shannon had finished. As she talked she leaned forward and her knee momentarily pressed against his. She let the contact linger for a long heartbeat before pulling back, all the while smiling a sly Cheshire cat smile. Shannon felt a rush of excitement. Simply caused by her knee touching his. The thought of it made him dizzy. Then he thought about Susie and felt ashamed.

He got to his feet and mumbled something about having to make a phone call and that he'd be right back. He then headed to the front door, stopping to ask the girl with the fake jewelry to leave a message with his date that something had come up and he had to leave.

Even if he didn't know what was still between him and Susie, he knew she hadn't deserted him yet. That as bad as things had gotten she'd stuck with him.

Shannon walked almost blindly towards his car and was halfway there before he felt the cold air biting through his shirt and realized he'd left his coat in the restaurant. He slowed for a second and then kept walking. Then he sped up his pace.

He could always buy another coat.

Susie was waiting for him at home, watching TV. She observed him quietly until he sat next to her. Then she told him Joe had called and that she had been worried sick about him. He explained how he'd spent the afternoon with his therapist, that she'd thought he had a breakthrough and wasn't going to black out this year or any year. When he was done he could tell she didn't believe a word of it. He couldn't blame her since he didn't, either.

She sat trying to smile at him, exhaustion sagging her face. For a moment she looked like an old woman. She asked what happened to his coat.

Chapter 11

February 7. Twilight.

Shannon squinted at the alarm clock. It was three in the morning. Susie was fast asleep, her small body clinging as tightly to her edge of the bed as it could. This had become routine. He knew she didn't intentionally do it; it was more her subconscious wanting as little contact with him as possible.

He lay on his back and stared at the ceiling, making sure to keep his eyes wide open. Because when he'd close them his mind would start racing and images would start snaking in and out. He didn't want to see those images anymore.

It was too quiet in the room. So quiet he could hear Susie's soft, shallow breathing. If he strained he was pretty sure he could also hear the quiet thumping of her heart. Too damn quiet. No matter how hard he tried he couldn't keep from hearing his own blood pulsing through his head.

When he would let his eyes close it would start to play out again in his mind.

What Elaine had been told about his mother's death was only partly true. He did come home and find her body and for the most part it was the way he had explained it. But she wasn't alone, and the killer wasn't caught weeks later, and he didn't die in prison. And the rest of it . . .

When he did get home that day he knew something was wrong as soon as he got to the front door and found it unlocked and all the lights out. He'd spent the afternoon playing street hockey with his buddies, and instead of leaving his hockey stick by the front door like he usually did, he kept it with him. And he moved as quietly as he could through the house.

He found them in the kitchen. His mother lying on the table, her legs hanging loosely over the edge, and him bent over her, looking as if he were caressing her cheek, his own head casually moving from side to side as a long, dirty ponytail swayed back and forth with it. At first all Shannon felt was embarrassed and confused, then he noticed the knife, the way it was coming out of his mother's mouth, the angle it was tilting at, and after an agonizing moment he realized why. His blood chilled ice cold with the realization. The room started to sway. Then all he could see through a blur of tears was that ponytail swinging back and forth. And then he moved.

His hockey stick caught the killer on the side of the face. The blow cut a jagged gash running the full length of his cheek and the shock of it knocked him over. The killer rolled with the blow, spun to his feet in a fluid cat-like motion, and twisted his body so he faced Shannon. As he stood up, he towered over him.

More than anything it was his face that stuck in Shannon's mind, permanently scarring his consciousness. Twenty years later and he could still vividly see that face leering at him. It was almost like a hatchet had been taken to it, leaving it with only a tiny slit of a mouth and even less of a jaw. The gash had left him bleeding like a stuck pig. The killer put a hand to it, noticed the blood and showed a slight twisted smile.

"That was pretty stupid," the killer said.

Shannon swung the stick again but he was only thirteen and a good foot shorter than the killer and eighty pounds lighter. The killer let it bounce off his forearm and pushed forward, grabbing Shannon by the throat. Without much effort he lifted the boy and turned him on his stomach with Shannon's right arm twisted behind his back. He pushed back two fingers and broke them the way you'd break a pencil. When Shannon screamed, he gave the fingers a hard jerk. The pain was unlike anything Shannon had ever felt.

"What's the matter, boy, you jealous? Wanted your mommy all to yourself?" the killer whispered lightly, his breath hot against Shannon's ear. When he didn't answer, the killer applied more pressure to the broken fingers until Shannon repeated what the killer ordered him to.

"That's better," the killer whispered, his tiny, slit mouth close against Shannon's ear. "Let me ask you something, boy. You think you have the right to make a god bleed?" After working more on his broken fingers, Shannon screamed out that he didn't.

The killer jerked Shannon to his feet, one hand pushing the boy's head, the other twisting the broken fingers. Then he forced him forward, until Shannon's face was inches from his mother's.

"Go ahead," he whispered. "Take a good look. See what happens when you anger the gods." Shannon had his eyes squeezed shut, but the killer kept whispering to the boy, modulating the pressure on his bent fingers, using them the way a puppeteer controls a marionette by its strings. When Shannon couldn't stand the pain anymore he opened his eyes and looked into his mother's dead face.

"Now breath deeply," the killer ordered, "smell that beautiful smell of death." And Shannon did what he was forced to do.

"That wasn't so hard, was it, boy?" the killer asked softly. Then he jerked Shannon away from the table and applied pressure on his bent fingers until Shannon was kneeling on the floor.

"I was fifteen before I had my first chance to smell that beautiful smell," he whispered. "How old are you, boy?" A little twist made Shannon answer. "Aren't you lucky," he whispered, his breath obscenely hot. "Starting off so young. But this will be your only chance, boy. 'Cause you know what I'm going to do to you after this?" He described it in great detail, his breath flicking in and out of Shannon's ear, tickling it like a snake's tongue.

At times Shannon would black out from the pain. When he'd fade back in the killer would be whispering to him about how little time Shannon had left.

"Time to get up and kiss mommy good-bye," the killer breathed lightly as he escalated the pain. He forced Shannon to his feet and back to the table. The killer pushed harder on his fingers, trying to force him forward. The pain screamed through Shannon's head like a siren, exploding into a fiery burst. Then it went black. With the next twist, the pain reached a new level, a level beyond any conscious awareness.

The pain was no longer a part of him. It had gone beyond that. It was as if Shannon was outside of himself, observing the scene from a distance.

Something distracted the killer. Without being aware of it, Shannon swung his free elbow and caught the killer in the groin. There was a dull moan as he released his grip of the boy's broken fingers. Shannon scrambled forward and pulled the knife from his mother's mouth. Then he turned on the man.

The rest was only a dizzying whirl of images, with him slashing and stabbing at the killer, knocking the killer to the ground, then pulling at his dirty ponytail and yanking his head back and . . . and trying to sever that malformed ugly head from his body. Hacking away, again and again.

Someone pulled him off and twisted the knife from his hand. Shannon stared blankly at the man until he recognized him as his next-door neighbor.

"I heard you screaming," the man said, his face white as a

sheet. "Jesus Christ," he whispered as his face grew even whiter, his eyes scanning the room, "let's get you the hell out of here."

The police came. They put Shannon in a cruiser and took him to the hospital where he underwent surgery to save his badly mangled fingers. The doctor performing the surgery was more shocked than anyone that he was able to. Afterwards, Shannon was put on pain killers and sedatives, and put in a private room. Both the police and the reporters wanted to get to him, but only the police did and that was after a week of fighting with the hospital staff. Shannon stared into space as they questioned him, telling them only his mother was already dead when he got home. He wouldn't tell them anything else, not what the killer later did to him or any of it.

His mother . . .

The autopsy report showed bruises along her neck, but only the one wound inside her mouth. The knife had shredded her tongue and severed both her larynx and windpipe, and had cut through to the back of her neck. She actually had died of asphyxiation, unable to breath in air after the damage to her larynx. The police reasoned that she had been strangled until reflex forced her to open her mouth and then was stabbed. Most likely, the killer took a great deal of pleasure in letting her know what was going to happen as soon as she gasped for air. They were somewhat concerned about the lack of marks along the killer's wrists and arms. They were also bothered by the fact the only fingerprints on the knife were the boy's, but they were willing to accept that the killer must've wiped his off after the murder.

The killer . . .

He was identified as one Herbert Winters. His family was from Mornsville, North Carolina. Upper middle-class, his father a doctor, his mother a high school English teacher. They had no idea what he was doing in Sacramento. They further claimed they'd had no contact with him since he'd left home three years earlier. The police sent his picture and prints to the FBI hoping to tie other murders to him. Herbert Winters's death was ruled justifiable.

Bill Shannon ended up hospitalized for five months, most of it in the psychiatric ward for severe depression. His father visited him only a few times during those five months, and when he did, neither of them talked much or made eye contact. When he drove his son home from the hospital it was in silence.

Shannon's father was only thirty-four when his wife was killed. Before the murder he looked enough like Robert Conrad to have people stop him in the street. He and his wife used to joke about whether he should try and get a stand-in job for the *Wild Wild West.* Five months after the murder no one bothered to stop him. He no longer looked like Robert Conrad. He had aged, become an old man almost overnight. His hair more gray than black, the flesh around his face loose and sagging, his jowls hanging from his jawbone. It was his eyes, though, that had changed the most. They had become hollow and bitter.

Days would pass without Shannon or his father saying a word to each other. Sometimes Shannon would catch his father looking at him a certain way, the way you'd look at something you detested. Shannon would stare back and his father would end up averting his eyes.

One day Shannon felt his father staring at him. When he turned to face him, his father didn't look away. Instead, he kept staring at the boy, his lips twisting into something hateful. Then into something insane.

"Was your mom alive when you got home?" he asked.

"What?"

"You heard me, was she alive?"

Shannon stood with his mouth hung open, too confused at

first to answer, and then it hit him what was really being asked. A cold fury took him over. As he turned away, his father grabbed him by the shoulders and shook him until his teeth rattled.

"I asked you a question, was she alive?"

Shannon struck out, catching his father along the cheek. Then he watched as his father's eyes went blind. The older Shannon threw his son against the wall and then stepped forward, punching him in the ear and knocking him to the floor.

"Answer me, goddamn you!" he screamed, his face twisted like a wounded animal's. "You were there for over an hour. Was she dead when you got there? *And what the hell were you doing to her?*"

For awhile it was like it was with Herbert Winters, near the end anyway, with Shannon seeming to observe the scene from a safe distance, detached, only vaguely interested in what was happening. As if he were floating in a corner of the room, watching as his father slapped and punched at him. It seemed to last a long time. Then it was as if he were sucked back into his body. At that instant he could feel a mix of hot tears and humiliation and pain surge within him. As it took him over he told his father every hurtful thing he could think of.

The words hit his father hard, his body wincing with each one. He stood up, backing slowly away from Shannon, his body shaking like a drug addict's. Shannon didn't let up as the words poured out of him, as the words chased the older man out of the room and finally out of the house.

That was the last time they spoke to each other or even looked at each other. At seventeen, Shannon left both the house and California.

Shannon jerked his eyes open, a cold sweat breaking out along his upper lip. He sat up and reached over towards Susie, his hand finding her small hip. Still asleep, she pushed his hand off her. He stared slowly at her before squinting at the alarm clock. It was only three-thirty.

He got out of bed and went to the kitchen and found a pack of cigarettes. He sat and lit one after the other, inhaling the smoke deeply into his lungs. A half hour later the pack was nothing but ashes and burnt-out stubs. Shannon sat for a little longer and then went back to bed.

Come on, close those eyes. Let the Sandman come and put dust in those black holes of yours. I got a lot to tell you and I'm getting sick of waiting. More sick than you could ever imagine. And I don't know how much longer I can stay out. It's four-thirty already. The night's fading away.

Of course, waiting's not easy. It's damn hard. Everything moving at such an accelerated pace. It's a bitch to stay anchored in any one spot for too long. So close them, pal, there's so much I need to tell you and I need to tell you tonight. All about Phyllis Roberson, about how much fun I had with her. I don't know how much longer I got and the last thing I want to do is watch you lying there, too scared shitless to sleep. Well, that's not quite true. It's rewarding in a way, but it's not what I'm here for.

Goddamn it . . . losing my anchor . . . don't worry, pal, I'll be back . . . you can't keep a good man down for long. Bet on it.

It's always kind of weird when you lose your anchor. It's what happens, though, when you wait too long in any one spot. Oh, man, what a wasted night.

Early on I tried to find Phyllis, see if I could put the fear of God in her, so to speak. A lot of times if you catch them early enough, before they get a chance to get acclimated, you can really have a lot of fun. Get to them before they have their sense of bearing. Well, I didn't quite make it. She had a crowd around her, guiding her, explaining the ropes and all the rest. Oh well, you get your kicks when you can.

And now this. You're ruining my plans for the night, man. It's not good, but I guess it really doesn't matter. I'll be back. We'll talk. Only a matter of time . . .

See ya, Billy Boy.

Chapter 12

When the alarm went off Susie stirred slowly, eventually pushing herself out of bed and stumbling to the clock to shut it off. After killing the noise she stood for a moment rubbing her face before turning back towards the bed. Shannon was lying on his back, his eyes wide open, his face drawn in an grim expressionless stare.

"Sleep okay?" she asked.

He didn't answer, his eyes glazed and motionless, his body as still as a corpse's.

Susie began to lose patience. "What's so interesting up there?"

No answer. No movement, nothing. Was he even breathing? A quick panic overtook her as she ran to him and put her ear against his chest. The skin felt warm. She held her breath and could hear his heart beating. As she pulled away from him she could see his eyes focusing on her.

"Damn you," she swore at him as she choked back a rush of tears. "Damn you! I thought you were supposed to be getting better!"

He looked at her blankly before rolling his eyes back towards the ceiling.

She stood frozen, staring down at him. An angry, painful sob convulsed through her body. "Weren't you supposed to be all cured? Isn't that what your therapist has been telling you?" she asked, her face turning a hard white. When Shannon remained mute in response, she exploded, "Answer me! Are you even in there?"

"Where else would I be?" he said after a while.

She opened her mouth, closed it, and fled to the bathroom, slamming the door behind her. She stood frozen in front of the mirror and then started to sob uncontrollably. When she saw him lying like that, all she could think of was that he was dead. At least at first. After she realized he had just sunk deeper into his sickness, a hot anger had overwhelmed her, and if she were completely honest with herself she'd admit it wasn't just anger. When she first heard his heart beating there was something else. Something close to disappointment.

She stayed in the bathroom a long time. First, moving under the shower and turning the hot water on full until it was steaming. Standing there was therapeutic; the hot water calming her, dulling her senses, quieting her mind. After ending the shower, she slowly, methodically dried herself and then stood in front of the mirror and even more methodically applied makeup. By the time she was done it was almost impossible to detect the redness around her eyes.

"Still breathing?" she asked as she left the bathroom. Shannon didn't answer, but his head tilted towards her.

She dressed quickly, quietly. When she was done she asked if he wanted any breakfast. Shannon shook his head.

"Are you going to be okay?"

"I'll be okay," he murmured. "I just need some time."

"Well, you'll get that, won't you?"

No answer.

"What's going on? Can you tell me that?"

"I really don't know." He tried to smile at her.

"Can you at least guess?"

He shrugged, moving his shoulders up and down as much as an inch.

"So it's going to be like all those other years all over again," Susie said after a long pause, an angry harshness edging into her voice.

Shannon let his eyes close and placed a hand over them. "It's not going to be like that. This year's going to be different. I've already gone further than I ever have before."

As soon as Shannon said it, he felt the little strength he had left ebb away from him. Susie had become very quiet, very still, as she stared at him. After a long while she asked him what he meant by going further than in the past.

"I don't know," he said.

"Of course you do," she said, shrewdly, her voice as brittle as sandstone. "I want you to tell me what's behind all this."

"I don't know."

"That's a load of crap," she stated softly. "And I'm sick of it." Her bottom lip started to quiver. She bit down on it, turned and left the room. A minute later, Shannon could hear the door to their apartment open and close. Then he could hear the lock turn.

Around ten in the morning Joe DiGrazia called, leaving a message on the machine that he was just checking up on his asshole partner. Eleven o'clock DiGrazia called again and left another message.

A half hour later Shannon could hear a key turning in the front door, and then DiGrazia's low, guttural voice calling out. Then, his partner's heavy footsteps along the hallway floor.

There was a hard rap on the bedroom door and DiGrazia peered in, his granite-block face a bit exasperated.

"This is breaking and entering," Shannon muttered.

"Not really," DiGrazia explained as he walked into the room and pulled a chair up to the bed. "Susie called earlier and invited me over. She said you weren't doing too well. She's afraid you're about to slip over the edge."

"Especially with her pushing."

"That's a pretty shitty thing to say," DiGrazia said. "You're a lucky man to have a wife like that. Not only is she a sweetheart but she's as beautiful as all hell. Why the fuck she cares about you, God only knows." He gave Shannon a hard look. "Pal, you are more than lucky. I'll tell you, it would be a real shame if you lost something that good."

Shannon looked up but couldn't read anything in his partner's expression. "Am I about to lose something?"

"It could happen. Everyone's got their limit, buddy boy. I know I've already reached mine." DiGrazia let a sympathetic smile crack his face. "You really do look like hell," he said. "It's getting close to lunchtime. Why don't you get up and take a shower and shave. We'll go get something to eat."

Shannon declined, shaking his head slightly. He hadn't eaten anything yet that day or the day before, but he didn't want any food. What he wanted was a drink. Several of them. The impulse had been gnawing away at him all morning, working its way into his bones and into his blood. He wanted a bottle, bad. All he could think about was getting one, which was why he knew he had to stay in bed.

"That's what I get for trying to be a nice guy," DiGrazia snapped. "Fuck you anyways. I'm too busy to spend my time babysitting an ungrateful asshole like you. As you know, I'm kind of shorthanded at work with my partner flaking out. And our little mamma's boy hasn't confessed yet."

"You haven't beaten it out of him?"

"I wish I could. Youth Services has got our little mamma's boy wrapped up tight. They got a real asshole lawyer for him. The blood drops we found on the pillow weren't from the victim. This sonofabitch lawyer is fighting us every step of the way. The State Attorney has to go to court Monday so we can get blood samples from the kid. You sure you don't want to get something to eat?"

"Rather not."

DiGrazia pushed himself out of his chair and shook his head slowly. "Just trying to do Susie a favor," he said as he strolled out of the room.

A half hour later he returned sheepishly with a couple of subs. "I have to eat anyway," he explained as he wolfed down a sausage sub. He had laid out a meatball sub heavy with onions next to Shannon.

"You going to at least try it?" he asked.

Shannon didn't bother to answer him.

"You going to have to either eat it or get out of bed or lie there all day with it next to you," DiGrazia threatened, showing a bare-fanged smile and looking more like a bulldog than usual.

"Or toss it against the wall," Shannon observed.

DiGrazia wiped his hands on the paper bag the sandwiches came in and stood up. "I tried," he said. "You can't tell me I didn't. Have fun lying there and rotting."

Shannon closed his eyes. He didn't bother watching his partner leave. When he opened them the room was empty, just him and his meatball sub. He groaned as he looked at it. Smelling it made him nauseous. Since he didn't have any choice and really didn't want to look at it all day hanging from the wall, he twisted himself over the edge of the bed and stood up, his legs wobbly. He picked up the sandwich and moved slowly out of the bedroom and towards the kitchen. There, he tossed it into the trash. On the way back, he stopped in the living room and collapsed into his imitation-leather easy chair. It was amazing how bad he felt. Like he was hungover, his head pounding, a hard, tight pressure pushing against his eyes, his mouth feeling like he had gargled with sawdust. He leaned forward and held his head with both hands. It was over a year, forgetting about the double shot of bourbon he had a month earlier and the half a beer he had the night before, since he had any alcohol and it was like he was now suffering from the DTs. A year of being mostly sober and now this. Just like all the other years. Thinking about it made him laugh. The laughing hurt, though, especially in his stomach. He leaned further forward, rubbing his head slowly, trying not to think about how badly he wanted to sit with Jack Daniel's or Johnny Walker or any of his other old drinking buddies. After a while he stopped thinking altogether.

Of course, he had fallen asleep. Not really dreaming or conscious, just drifting along. Floating in a warm, peaceful blackness. Something was tugging at him, though, disturbing him, forcing an awareness within him.

And then there he was in front of him, grinning widely, ingratiatingly. Shannon knew him instantly. He was older than Shannon remembered—a good twenty years older—as if his memories had somehow aged equivalently with time. The man's skin now spotted and bloated and sagging slightly around the jaws. His body thicker around the middle. His hair thinner, almost nothing where the ponytail had been. But there was the same malformed chin. The same tiny, slit mouth. And the eyes, pale, almost translucent, like a rattlesnake's. Shannon felt a coldness as he looked into those eyes.

Standing in front of him was Herbert Winters. A forty-year-old version of him.

"Remember me, Billy?" Winters asked, his voice the same wispy singsong that had tortured Shannon all those years earlier.

"Yeah, I remember you. You're older. Why is that?"

"You got to ask yourself that."

"I don't have to ask myself a goddamn thing."

"Sure you do. Come on, boy, give it a try. Look deep inside yourself. The answer's there."

Shannon turned away, but Winters moved with him as if they were fastened together at the hips, hovering in front of him, his slit mouth grinning in an amused fashion.

"Just go away," Shannon pleaded. "I don't want you here."

"Sorry, Billy Boy. It don't work that way. You know why, don't you?"

Shannon had his eyes squeezed shut. He tried running, but he could feel Winters's warm, rancid breath against his face. There was no use running so he stopped. And besides, he felt too weak to run. His legs had quickly become rubbery and lifeless. When he opened his eyes Winters was still hovering in front of him, still grinning like only he knew the big joke.

"Too stupid to see the obvious, huh?" Winters asked, his grin shrinking to a thin, impish smile. "Let me spell it out to you. The reason I've aged twenty years since last we met is because we met twenty years ago.

"Still don't see it?" he asked, nodding at Shannon's blank stare. "Let me explain it to you. I'll talk slowly so you can follow. I'm inside you, dummy. I'm part of you. And I'm not too happy about it. But what the hell can you do, right?"

"That doesn't make any sense," Shannon started. "What do you mean you're part of—"

"Look," Winters interrupted, his smile taking on a malicious glint. "Think back twenty years ago, the day you murdered me. Let's try and remember what really happened, not the bullshit story you made up afterwards. Let's try and be honest with ourselves for a change.

"Your daddy knew what really happened," Winters continued, winking in a good-old-boy sort of way. "He knew just by looking at you. And you know, too. Come on, admit it, boy. Who really did kill your poor mother?"

"You did," Shannon said, dumbly. "She was dead when I got home. You were doing things to her. You were—"

"We were enjoying ourselves. That's all." Winters thin smile disappeared, leaving his mouth a tiny, dull slit. "Maybe it was a bit kinky making out on top of the kitchen table, but it was nothing serious. We even still had all our clothes on. And I guess we lost track of the time, huh? Didn't count on you sneaking in on us. Shit, were you quiet. A little mouse, weren't you?

"What's the matter, cat got your tongue?" Winters asked, chuckling to himself. "You remember what happened next, don't you? How, like the little pissant that you were, you snuck that butcher knife out of the drawer and then tippytoed over to your mother and plunged it into her mouth as she lay on that table minding her own business. And then you tried to use it on me."

"T-that's n-not true."

"Of course it is. Explains why only your fingerprints were on the knife. And why there were no other bruises on your mom, except a few along her neck when we were making out earlier and maybe got a little too rough. But nothing she didn't enjoy. I really had her purring, boy. Had her engine all revved up and ready to go until you killed the ignition.

"I had to break your fingers to get the knife out of your hand," Winters continued. "It looked like you were out cold. I went over to check your mom, see if I could save her. But I couldn't. She was as dead as dead can be. Her eyes bulging, almost popping out of their sockets like pale blue marbles. But you weren't out cold, were you, boy?"

Winters waited and then went on, smiling sadly. "You did a number on me, boy. Had the knife in and out of me a half dozen times before I realized what was happening. And then it was too late. Remember what you did to me afterwards—to my head? You had it hanging off my body by a thread. That was unnecessary, boy. Truly unnecessary."

"Y-you deserved it! A-and t-the rest . . . nothing but a lie!"

"Keep telling yourself that. Which brings us to why I'm here. You created me, you little shit. I'm the image that you needed me to be in. I'm part of you. Buried deep inside you. I'm the monster you had to conjure up so you could go along with your little fantasy of what happened. In all truth, I'm you. The essence of you. And it makes me sick to my stomach."

Shannon was overwhelmed with a sensation of vertigo. He squeezed his eyes tight as he felt himself spinning away. The invisible bond between him and Winters seemed to be weakening as he twisted upwards. He told himself that he was dreaming. That this was nothing but a bad dream. That he wanted to be far away.

"Not yet!" Winters ordered angrily, thick lines all of a sudden lining his stubby neck. "You don't leave me now! I've got too much to tell you, you little shit! All about Phyllis Roberson. You don't dare leave now—"

Shannon swung himself up in the easy chair, momentarily in free fall, his heart pounding, a cold sweat breaking over his face.

He was wide awake, Herbert Winters's image vivid in his mind.

He was alone in his living room, but he could feel Winters's presence. He could almost still smell the sourness of his breath. He could almost still feel it against his face. A draft from the window sill made him shiver.

Other than the one he had months ago with Janice Rowley, it was the first time he remembered any of his nightmares. In the past, there was nothing he could really hang on to except a vague sense of dread. If these were the type of dreams he was having, no wonder he'd been going nuts.

Shannon looked down at his right hand. He curled his fingers and felt the dull discomfort in his joints. In the cold weather the discomfort was closer to someone hammering nails into his bones.

There was no doubting they had been broken severely and worse. The torture he had undergone was real. The memories he had of that day were real.

So what about that dream?

Why was he conjuring up that murderer?

And what the hell did Winters mean about Phyllis Roberson? An image of the dead woman slid into his mind. In it he could picture the knife sticking out of the woman's throat. He could see her eyes staring into oblivion.

Shannon forced himself out of the easy chair. He was surprised to find himself as shaky as he was. He moved slowly to the bedroom and lay down on the bed. He couldn't keep from thinking about Phyllis Roberson. He couldn't keep the image of her out of his mind. Of that knife sticking out of her throat.

Chapter 13

Elaine Horwitz looked unnaturally pale, especially against the soft pink rim of her glasses. Part of the reason was her normally light complexion, partly that she had no makeup on; mostly, though, she was suffering from a wicked hangover. The type a cheap bottle of wine will cause. She sat staring at Shannon's folder, her fingers impatiently drumming along her desk.

Sonofabitch.

The night before she had waited nearly twenty minutes before getting the message that Shannon had run out on her. The sonofabitch had even left his coat at the table. Horwitz took the news with a polite smile and then ordered dinner and a bottle of wine. She was too humiliated to get up and leave, so she sat there with her high-gloss lipstick and her Giorgio perfume and her tight, sexy evening dress and tried not to look like as big an idiot as she felt. And she drank every last drop of the wine. She had even put black lace panties on for him . . .

On leaving, she took his coat with her and shoved it into a Dumpster behind the restaurant. It seemed the least she could do.

Sonofabitch coward.

She wanted to call him now and tell him to go fuck himself. That he could find himself another therapist. She caught herself in the middle of the thought and let a bitter smile pull up the corners of her mouth. A woman scorned, she chided herself angrily.

Of course, she got only what she deserved. She never thought about getting involved with a patient before, well, maybe thought about it, but not seriously, at least not to this degree. And this was not only a patient but a married one. So what did she expect? You play with matches, you get burned. You play with married men, you get dumped. And, what she had to keep telling herself, you play with patients, you lose your license. So she got off easy . . . But what the hell was it with him? Why couldn't she keep him out of her mind? Probably the pheromones he put out, making it completely physical and beyond her rational control. That had to be it.

He was already ten minutes late for his appointment.

Lousy, stinking sonofabitch . . .

Successful therapy requires both human interaction and caring, but she had let things go too far with him. Even going shopping to buy those black lace panties for the sonofabitch. From now on her relationship with Shannon was going to be completely clinical. Nothing else.

There was a knock on the door. She felt the butterflies in her stomach rise up as she stammered out for the person to come in. At that moment she felt more like a fraud than ever in her life.

The door opened and Mark Bennett, the hypnotherapist, shoved his face in.

"Sorry I'm late," he apologized, out of breath. "Parking out on Beacon Street now is murder. I ended up five blocks away."

"That's okay," Horwitz said. The butterflies settled back down like lead weights. "My patient hasn't shown up yet."

Bennett nodded, took his overcoat off and folded it over a chair and sat down, crossing his legs. With his fleshy face and receding curly hair and pear-shaped body he looked a little like Larry Fine from the Three Stooges. This is what's always interested in me, Horwitz thought, fucking stooges.

"Maybe you could tell me about the patient," Bennett asked, smiling pleasantly.

"He's a thirty-three-year-old police officer. As an adolescent he found his mother after she'd been brutally murdered. It seems that repressed guilt has manifested itself into both clinical depression and extended blackouts."

"What's he guilty about?"

"He feels if he'd come home earlier he could've saved her." Elaine Horwitz smiled joylessly. "He wouldn't have been able to."

Bennett settled back into his chair. "It sounds like you already figured it out. What do you need me for?"

"I don't have it all figured out," Horwitz said. "There's something else. I have no idea what it is." She sighed heavily and let her shoulders slump. "There's a yearly pattern to his breakdowns. I want to dig deep and see what we can find."

Bennett was frowning, making his long, rubbery face seem even more comical. "Yearly breakdowns? How consistent are they?"

"Very consistent. Every year around the anniversary of his mother's death. Same pattern of symptoms climaxing to a prolonged blackout, usually lasting a week, and without the patient having any memories of it."

Mark Bennett was frowning deeply and shaking his head, a perturbed look spreading over his features. "Lasting a week?" he muttered to himself.

Horwitz nodded. It sounded a lot worse when spoken out loud. Bad enough, actually, to make her regret not trying to have Shannon hospitalized. It made her wonder how much she'd let her personal feelings interfere with her treatment. A sick feeling crept into her stomach. She glanced at her watch. "He should be here by now," she said uneasily. "He's already fifteen minutes late. Let me try giving him a call."

She dialed his number and let it ring until the answering machine clicked on. When she put down the receiver she offered Bennett an apologetic smile.

"He could be on his way," she said. "I don't know. I hope so. He did have a setback yesterday."

"How so?"

Horwitz paused for a moment, and then explained about Shannon's latest homicide case and the similarities between it and his own mother's death. "All in all, a bizarre coincidence," she added.

Bennett shook his head. "One thing I've learned from years of hypnotherapy . . . there's no such thing as a coincidence."

"What do you mean?"

"Just that."

"Don't give me that crap. What exactly are you trying to say?"

"I'm not really sure," Bennett said, pausing, trying to smile. "I have to admit I've never heard of anything like this. This is pretty bizarre stuff. And now during the time when your patient suffers from his blackouts, a woman is murdered in the same freakish way as his mother—"

"You're way off track," Elaine Horwitz cut in, annoyance pushing some color into her cheeks. "First of all, my patient hasn't blacked out yet—"

"Excuse me, but how do you know?"

"Because—" Horwitz stumbled, trying to explain the obvious, partly because it was no longer so obvious. "Well, for one reason, his blackouts last a week."

"How do you know he doesn't have shorter duration ones, also? Does he remember them when they happen?"

"He knows when he has them," Horwitz argued. "Anyway, this wouldn't fit his pattern—"

"Again, how do you know?"

The thought left her stunned. "This is ridiculous," she said, her voice rising. "There's physical evidence tying a boy to the murder, and besides—"

"Elaine." The hypnotherapist had both hands up in an exaggerated sign of surrender. "I'm just talking. You know, just trying to kill some time."

"That's okay," Elaine Horwitz offered grudgingly. They sat in silence for the next several minutes with Bennett's attempts at small talk falling flat. Finally, he glanced at his watch and asked if it was safe to assume the patient wasn't showing. That got to Horwitz. Pretentious little prick. Couldn't just say that it looked like the patient wasn't showing up. Had to ask if it was a safe thing to assume. Horwitz told him it appeared to be a safe thing to assume.

Bennett stopped at the door before leaving. "When you hear from him again," he said, pausing as he stroked his chin, "give me a call. I'm curious."

February 7. Night.

It didn't surprise Susan Shannon to find an empty apartment when she arrived home from work. When ten o'clock rolled around and Shannon still hadn't come home it didn't faze her a bit. It was what she expected and all she felt about it was a heavy weariness. For the last few days she knew it was inevitable. So she called Joe DiGrazia, apologized for waking him, and told him that Shannon had disappeared. After that she had her first good night's sleep in weeks.

When she woke it was as if a hundred-pound weight had been rolled from her back. She pulled suitcases out of the closet and started packing her clothes. She had them filled when Joe DiGrazia called. He just wanted to tell her that he'd been out all night looking for Shannon, hadn't had any luck yet, but was going to take the day off and see what he could do. After she hung up the phone the weariness that had hit her the night before fell back on her like cement. All her resolve, her determination, crumbled away. She just sat on the edge of the bed and started weeping. It came out of her like a faucet.

It seemed a long time before she could slow it down, before she could breathe normally. Her lungs and chest ached from the crying. The thought struck her how a friend of Shannon's spent the night driving the streets for him while his own wife was all set to bail out, and as the thought stuck in her mind the sobbing started again. This time, though, it was silent and tearless. There wasn't anything left inside for tears.

When she was done, she stood up and unpacked the suitcases. After that she got the phone book and found a number she had circled months earlier.

Phil Dornich knocked on the door at eleven o'clock and Susan Shannon showed him in. A short, round man in his middle fifties wearing a cheap suit and a stained overcoat. As he smiled at her, she noticed he didn't have many teeth left in his mouth and what was there was in pretty bad shape.

"Nice to meet you, ma'am," he greeted her as he extended a hand. He had a handkerchief balled up in his other hand and was mopping his forehead with it. A cold winter's day and the guy was sweating like a pig. It nauseated her. Susan Shannon took the extended hand and let go on contact. She asked if he'd like a seat and maybe some coffee. He accepted both. First thing in the kitchen she washed her hands under the kitchen faucet.

When she brought the coffee in, Dornich was perched on the sofa in the living room, his overcoat opened and both a large paunch and a holstered revolver showing.

He grinned as Susan noticed the revolver. "I'm fully licensed to carry, ma'am," he said. "I hope this doesn't upset you."

Susan handed him his coffee and sat down across from him. "No, not at all," she said, smiling weakly. "I've been married to a police officer long enough that I'm used to it." She paused and looked down at her hands. "I'd like to thank you for coming. I don't think I was up to leaving the apartment."

"That's quite all right," Dornich took a sip of the coffee and then put it down so he could mop the back of his neck with his handkerchief. "Something about my metabolism," he smiled slightly. "I just can't keep from sweating.

"Now, just to explain," he continued as he shifted his body forward. "I'm fully licensed by the state of Massachusetts as a private investigator. My business, Dornich Investigations, has been around for eight years now. Before that I was a Boston police officer for twenty-five years and before my retirement I was head of detectives—"

"Very impressive," Susan said.

"Yes, thank you," Dornich wiped his handkerchief behind his ear and then along the side of his neck and under his chin. He leaned forward a little more so he had his elbows resting against his knees. "So there's no misunderstanding, let me go over my rates. One hundred and twenty dollars an hour plus any reasonable expenses. We won't charge you for gas or mileage or postage or stuff like that, but if we need to travel you will get charged for the airfare and hotel. By the way, how did you hear of us?"

"A friend recommended you," Susan lied. Actually, she had picked his ad out at random from the yellow pages. Dornich nodded, having the good sense not to push her for a name. Susan Shannon felt a sense of deflation. "I didn't know it would be this expensive," she murmured under her breath.

Dornich reached forward with his stubby arms and took hold of the coffee and sipped it slowly. "Well, it can be expensive," he agreed. "But we're the most experienced firm in Boston. All of my investigators are ex–police officers. My chief investigator worked on the Son of Sam cases in New York. Our forensics expert is often called on by municipalities all over the country."

Susan stared straight ahead as Dornich smiled sympathetically. With his mouth open all she could count were five teeth and a couple of them were nothing more than stumps. She found herself nodding slowly. For a long time she had convinced herself she was saving the money for them to buy a house, but she now knew she had only been kidding herself. The money had been her escape hatch and she had just nailed it shut. "Okay," she said. "I'd like to hire you."

"Well, now, that's good." He let his lips form a fragile smile. "And what would you like to hire me to do?"

"To find my husband."

He straightened up on the sofa, letting his head nod in a knowing way. "It happens all the time," he started.

"No, it doesn't. Not like this, anyway. My husband's sick. He's got some sort of amnesia."

"How long has he been missing?"

"Since last night."

"Last night, huh?" Dornich rubbed his face, his thick, stubby fingers kneading into the flesh. "What makes you think he's got amnesia?"

"Because he gets it every year," Susan said.

Dornich wiped his handkerchief across his face and then shifted his round body forward as he attempted to broach the delicate subject. "I had a client once," he began, "whose husband would sleepwalk every couple of months. He'd just get out of bed, hands held out in front of his face, and walk out of the house and then drive off." He demonstrated briefly, holding out his own two arms and looking ridiculous.

"A couple of days later," he continued, talking quickly, "he'd come back home completely disoriented, claiming he had no clue where he'd been. Well, one time the wife was worried so sick she hired me to find him.

"I found him shacked up," he said after taking time to wipe his face. "His girlfriend would come in from Atlanta every couple of months and he'd go through his sleepwalking act. Now, maybe your husband has some sort of yearly rendezvous—"

"He doesn't have anything of the kind," Susan insisted, rejecting the idea flatly.

"But—"

"There are no buts here. It's simple. My husband has amnesia and I'd like to hire you to find him. Do you want the job?"

Dornich sat with his mouth hung loosely open. He started to say something, obviously frustrated, then pushed his mouth closed, nodded and told Susan Shannon that he'd be happy to take her job.

"I'll need some photographs," he said. "Preferably a full shot and both sides. Also a list of all bank accounts and credit cards. And a list of his friends—"

"He's not with any friends."

Dornich stared straight ahead at Susie Shannon and smiled congenially. "Of course, he isn't," he explained. "But maybe he mentioned something to someone or—"

"He didn't mention anything to anyone."

"Of course, he didn't." Dornich forced a thin smile. He took a notepad from his overcoat pocket. "You said your husband's a police officer. Which department—here in Cambridge?"

"Yes. He's a detective out of the Central Square station. He's been working mostly violent crime cases."

"Who's his commanding officer?"

"I don't see how that could help you—"

"Well, it might. Maybe someone he works with knows something. It's possible."

"No one knows anything. If they did, Joe wouldn't have spent last night driving around looking for him."

"Joe?"

"Joe DiGrazia. His partner."

"His partner did that, huh? Hell of a nice thing to do. Could you spell his name?"

Susan hesitated, then spelled it out. Dornich wrote it down and got his home phone number.

"Well, now," he said, looking up, smiling. "Do you think you could find me those pictures?"

Susan got up. As she left the room the smile evaporated from his face, leaving it drawn, his eyes tired, glassy. He reached for the coffee and sipped it slowly. When Susan came back his smile flashed back on like a neon sign. He took the pictures from her and studied them quickly.

"Good-looking guy," he observed pleasantly. "How old, thirty, thirty-five?"

"Thirty-three."

"Thirty-three, huh? That's nice. I remember the way I was at that age. Boy, you can make real stupid mistakes when you're young, and probably even stupider mistakes when you're that good looking. I don't know about the last, but I do know about the first. You see, the problem is you start thinking with something other than your head . . ." He stopped himself. Actually, it was the look forming across Susan Shannon's face that stopped him.

"But then what do I know," he said, shrugging. "Except I'll need a five-thousand-dollar retainer."

She wrote the check out for him. As he took it from her, he hesitated and then asked if he should wait a couple of days before cashing it.

"The money's there to cover it."

"Of course it is." He folded the check and slid it gently into his inside overcoat pocket. "I'm planning on handling this job myself. I'll let you know as soon as I find anything."

As he started to get up to leave Susan Shannon stopped him. "There's something else," she said. "I'd like you to do something else."

Dornich looked up at her.

"There's a reason my husband's acting like this." She looked away from the detective. "I think it's something from his childhood. I'd like you to find out what it is."

She told him the little she knew about Shannon's childhood, that both his parents were dead and that he had grown up in California.

"You never met any of his family?"

"No. They had died before we met. And he won't talk about his family."

"So you think someone abused him as a kid? Maybe one of his parents? Or another family member?"

"Maybe. I don't know."

"And you don't know what part of California he's from? Or when he left?"

"No, I don't." A defensiveness edged into her voice. "He won't talk about it."

Dornich sighed heavily. "Okay," he said, "I'll see what I can find. Some of the stuff like where he went to high school should be on record at his department. We'll see where it leads."

He let her escort him to the front door. Once outside a gurgling noise seeped from his lips. He couldn't help it. He didn't want to laugh. He felt sorry for Susan Shannon, but it was just too damn funny.

Hell of a partner that woman's husband had. Hell of a guy, out the whole goddamn night for him.

Dornich didn't doubt it a bit, at least the part about being up all night for his partner's sake. The two of them probably spent it shacked up with a couple of hookers and a couple of grams of coke. As he wanted to tell the lady, he'd seen it a hundred times before.

As he walked to his car he gave the matter of how to approach DiGrazia some thought. There were a couple ways to play it out. He could wait until evening and then follow DiGrazia. Odds were their little party was going to last a few more days. The problem with that, though, was he didn't like the idea of tailing a cop. It's as good a way as any to get shot at. So it came down to either leveling with DiGrazia or playing innocent. Either way, word would get to the lady's husband to zip his pants back up and head home. Pretty soon he'd be recovering from his amnesia. Dornich had little doubt about that.

The other part, though, about digging into the guy's childhood sounded like a wild-goose chase. Well, first things first. He had a party to crash.

Chapter 14

"Oh God—"

Linda Cassen turned quickly behind her. She felt stupid as soon as she did. There was no one following her, no one lurking in the shadows. She was standing in broad daylight in the middle of Newbury Street which was probably the safest spot in the city. The only thing she had to worry about was being gouged in the pocketbook by one of the high-priced boutiques lining the street.

Still, she couldn't help feeling shaken. The fear was irrational but it was there and it was intense. A cold sweat started down her back. She turned and entered a gourmet coffee shop. Once inside she stood by the door and stared out at the street. People walked past, but no one paid any attention to her. No one looked in her direction. No one was following her. There was no bogeyman out there after her.

She felt even stupider. She ordered a large latte from the cashier and took it back to a table by the front window. As she sipped it she watched the pedestrians walk by. It had been a bitter cold winter so far, and February wasn't turning out to be any better. With the wind swirling off Boston Harbor it was below zero Fahrenheit outside. People were just about running past the store; men holding their overcoats shut tight around their necks, women moving in short, almost frantic strides.

Linda Cassen finished her drink and headed back into the cold. The air whipping across her face numbed her, making her feel as if her cheeks had been shot with Novocain. An uneasiness, though, swallowed her up quicker and more intensely than the cold did. It didn't make any sense. There was no reason for it. Stubbornly, she decided she wasn't going to let it affect her.

She came to the end of Newbury Street and cut across to the Public Gardens. The desolation there didn't help her mood. It looked like a wasteland. The pond for the swan boats had been emptied before winter and the trees scattered around the park were bare and lifeless. An old lady sitting alone threw bread crumbs to pigeons. She smiled blandly up at Linda. As she walked past the old woman she tried to smile back. Her heart skipped a beat as she noticed the street kids hanging by one of the benches along the other side of the park. All of them wearing hooded sweatshirts. They noticed her, also. Their sullen stares slowly drifted past her. She quickened her pace and got to the outside of the park and to Charles Street.

Once on Charles Street she darted into a convenience store. Winded, her heart racing, her legs shaky. A young clerk working behind the counter asked if she was okay. She mumbled something and grabbed a candy bar and bought it. Her hands shook as she peeled off the wrapper. She ate it greedily, as if it were the only thing she'd had in weeks. The sugar rush helped a little.

The clerk, a young kid, looked concerned. He asked if he should call her a cab. She thought about it but shook her head. Her apartment was only four blocks away. She'd feel more than stupid to have a cab take her four blocks. She thanked him anyway and walked to the door and peered outside. The street kids weren't in sight. They were probably still in the park. Probably beating the hell out of that old woman for her bread crumbs, she thought to herself as she slipped out the door.

The fear had quieted temporarily but was still in her. As she walked it seemed to take on a life all to itself. Making her panic about crazy things. That she'd forget how to breathe. That her heart would just stop on her. That she would collapse on the sidewalk. Then he would get her. She'd be defenseless against him. The thought stopped her. Who would she be defenseless against? Who was she so afraid of? There was nothing but a fuzzy image floating in her mind. Nothing she could really make out. Just a sour, rancid smell and the hint of a wispy, singsong voice breathing lightly into her ear. As crazy as it was, it became real. The panic became full-blown terror.

The terror wouldn't let her move her eyes. It kept them frozen straight ahead. It crept through her body, pressing hard against her chest. It made it difficult to breathe. She started to run. She couldn't help herself.

She ran two blocks up Beacon Hill before her legs gave out on her and she fell onto one knee. And then she started to cry. She didn't care anymore about feeling stupid. All she wanted was to get home. To be safe. She started making wild promises about what she'd do if she could only get safely locked behind her apartment door. About how she'd become a better person and start spending her weekends working at homeless shelters and her nights helping the impoverished. Anything, as long as she could be safe.

She got back to her feet. The terror was now crashing down over her, becoming something raw and primal. She could barely breathe against it. She could barely hear over it as it roared through her head and drowned out the noises around her. It made it impossible to tell if there were any footsteps behind her. But there couldn't be any footsteps behind her. Deep down inside she knew that, didn't she? She was simply losing her mind, going nuts, that was all. That's what she told herself. She was in the midst of a mental breakdown.

As she turned the corner, she saw her apartment building and started racing towards it, her legs rubbery as she pushed herself forward. And then she was at the front door.

She fumbled with her keys. They slipped back into her pocketbook. Then they disappeared among the clutter. A common nightmare of hers was where simple actions became impossible. Like running through molasses. Or trying to find her keys when her life depended on it. *Oh God,* she screamed internally as tears streamed her face, *please help me find my keys!* And then, miraculously, she had them and the main entrance door was open and she was racing up the three flights to her apartment. Her heart pounding within her, feeling as if it were going to explode out of her chest . . .

And then . . .

She had the door to her apartment open. The craziness of her fear and terror hit her hard and she started laughing and bawling at the same moment. All the emotion came pouring out of her.

And then something else hit her. Much harder than the emotion. Hard enough to send her sprawling face first across the hardwood floor of her hallway. She felt a dullness as her chin cracked against the floor and then heard a click behind her. Someone was locking her door. Then a knee digging into the small of her back. Her arms were pulled behind her, her hands tied together with some sort of cord, the material biting into her flesh.

It all happened so fast. Before she could utter a sound she was flipped over onto her back. A gloved hand was against her throat. Pressing hard and then releasing the tension. It made her think of the way a cat entertains itself with a mouse before the kill.

And then there was the knife—an eight-inch cutting knife. Her eyes grew wide as she stared at it. It was held inches from her face.

A soft, wispy, singsong voice breathed lightly into her ear. A vaguely familiar voice. "Go ahead," it said. "Scream. This knife has to go somewhere."

CHAPTER 15

Phil Dornich stood in the Central Square squad room shooting the bull with the desk sergeant. He recognized a few faces but didn't really know anyone there. It wasn't likely that he would. Boston and Cambridge police don't have much to do with one another. And after eight years off the force, the few cops he did know in Cambridge were long gone. Still, after twenty-five years as a cop he felt comfortable in any police squad room and he had no problem shooting the bull with anyone there.

"What about his personnel record?" Dornich asked with a thin smile.

A pained expression formed over the desk sergeant's face, like he had gas. Dornich pulled out Susan Shannon's retainer check and showed it to him.

"He just disappeared?" the desk sergeant asked. "Just like that?"

"That's right."

"And you think there's something in his folder that could help find him?"

"I think so." Dornich shifted his weight so he was leaning casually against the wall. "Maybe he went to his hometown or something. His wife doesn't even know where he grew up."

The sergeant said he was going to make some phone calls and he turned three quarters of the way around on Dornich. The first call was obviously to Susan. It was short and polite. The next call was longer. The way the sergeant joked around and by the language he used, it was to another cop. When he got off the phone he turned back to Dornich grinning widely.

"Shannon's wife said she hired you," he said, his shit-eating grin growing as he spoke. Dornich just smiled back.

"I also called a friend of mine who works out of narcotics in East Boston. Joe Wiley. He said you were a hell of a cop when you were on the force. That before you retired, you were head of detectives."

The name was only vaguely familiar. Dornich kept his smile intact. "Joe's a hell of a guy himself," he said.

"Yeah, sure. He wanted me to ask you how you got the nickname Pig?"

The fat detective's smile dulled a bit. "It's because of the way I sweat."

"You're sure that's the reason?"

"I'm sure."

"Nothing else?"

"No, nothing else. It's because I sweat like a pig."

The desk sergeant broke out laughing. "Quite a nickname," he said as he rubbed some wetness from his eyes. "Wait here. I'll see what I can get you."

Dornich waited patiently. He hated that nickname. Hated it more than anything. Even though he'd never admit it to himself, it was the reason he retired from the force. Head of detectives at fifty and retired at fifty-one. All because of a rotten nickname.

The desk sergeant wandered back. He stood very close to Dornich and pushed a wad of paper into his hand. "Slip this inside your jacket," he said, winking. The paper disappeared quickly into the fat man's jacket.

"What do you think about Bill Shannon?" Dornich asked after the sergeant got back behind his desk.

"A smart guy. Maybe too smart. But he's a good cop when he's not acting like a wacko."

"Does he have a girlfriend?"

The sergeant shrugged. "I wouldn't be the guy to ask."

"Any sort of reputation with hookers?"

A cautiousness darkened the sergeant's features. "Again, I wouldn't know," he said, his voice guarded.

"I can appreciate that." Dornich showed the few teeth he had left as he smiled broadly. "Of course, nothing I find out goes back to his wife. I just want to bring him home."

"I've never heard anything about Shannon playing with hookers," the sergeant said stubbornly.

Dornich took out his handkerchief and rubbed it quickly along the back of his neck. A grin crept along the sergeant's face as he watched. "Quite a nickname," he said.

"Sure was," Dornich agreed. "By the way, his partner . . . ?"

"Joe DiGrazia."

"Is he around? I'd like to ask him a few things."

"Sorry, he took the day off. Not feeling well."

Dornich couldn't keep from smiling. A real smile this time. Big surprise about DiGrazia. Obviously, the party was still going on.

"Let me leave my number in case he calls in," Dornich said.

"Sure, go ahead."

Dornich wrote it down and handed it to the sergeant. He hesitated. "I'll tell you," he started, a playful smile forming over his round face, "the world has changed since I left the force. Eight years ago murders meant something. Maybe a domestic situation that got out of hand or some scumbag trying to muscle in on some other scumbag's territory. But there was always something behind them. Nowadays they mean nothing. It can be simply because you look at a punk the wrong way. These days, words lead straight to gunplay."

"Yeah, these kids out there now are nuts."

"Not just the kids. You can just call someone the wrong name and have a Magnum .357 shoved up your ass. I'll tell you, though, it will clear away hemorrhoids better than anything I know. You might want to tell your asshole buddy Joe Wiley that."

The desk sergeant had the look of a man badly wronged. He reluctantly accepted Pig Dornich's sweaty extended hand.

It wasn't until after five o'clock that Dornich was able to reach Joe DiGrazia at home. He told DiGrazia what he wanted and DiGrazia gave him his home address and invited him to come over.

When DiGrazia answered his door, Pig Dornich knew he was on the right track. Eyes were bloodshot red, bags heavy enough to check in at the airport, and a hungover complexion that gave the cop's skin a feverish look. The general haggard appearance of a man who's been screwing and snorting hard all night.

DiGrazia gave the fat, smug detective a quick look up and down before stepping aside for him. "Susie hired you, huh?" he asked.

"She's worried about her husband. I was hoping you could help."

"Hey, anything I can do." DiGrazia seemed to lose his train of thought for a moment as his eyes wandered away. When they focused back he asked Dornich if he wanted a beer. Dornich said okay and DiGrazia asked him to follow him, that they could talk in the kitchen.

He tossed a beer can to the fat man and took one for himself, then sat down at the table and held the can firmly against the side of his face. "Got a real bad headache," he said, smiling. "I've been out all night and day looking for that sonofabitch. Just got home a half hour ago. I was going to take a quick nap and go out again tonight."

"Rough day," Pig Dornich agreed.

DiGrazia still had the beer can pressed against the side of his face. His eyes were half closed and dropping fast. He shrugged. "You find anything?"

DiGrazia slowly opened his eyes. He stared silently at the fat man for a few seconds, his face hardening. "What the hell do you think?" he said at last. "If I found anything, you think Susie would've wasted her money hiring you?"

"I was hoping maybe you found something."

"That's not what you meant," DiGrazia said. "Don't try and be a wise guy with me. You got something in your throat, spit it out. Otherwise, in the mood I'm in I'd be more than happy to do the fucking Heimlich on you."

"I was hoping you could tell me about his girlfriend," Pig Dornich said defensively.

"What do you mean girlfriend?"

"Just what I said. Who's he with now?"

DiGrazia stared long and hard at Dornich before shaking his head slowly. "Susie knows better than that," he said. "Where the hell you get that idea?"

"I don't have to tell the wife any of it. I just want to find him and bring him home. If his party ends a few days earlier than expected, that's too bad."

DiGrazia stared at the fat detective incredulously and then leaned back in his chair and closed his eyes. "There's no girlfriend," he said in a tired voice. "What did you think, that the two of us had a couple of hookers and some coke and were partying it up?"

"No." Pig Dornich hesitated. "I was just asking—"

"Yeah, sure. Let me tell you something. Bill does this every goddamn year. Completely flips out for a couple of weeks. Right now he's out there without a clue. You don't believe me, you can talk to his therapist. I'm sure Susie can get you her name and number."

Pig Dornich fidgeted uncomfortably. He knew he screwed

up, that he could've played his hand much better, but that wasn't what was bothering him. Doubt was beginning to work on him. "What have you been doing to find him?"

"Barhopped all over the goddamn place showing Bill's picture. Didn't get anywhere. I thought it might help if I knew where he'd been drinking last. That's the way it always works. He loses it while drinking. After last call I drove around places in Boston, Revere, and Charlestown where he's ended up in the past. Nothing there, either. But there probably wasn't any chance of there being anything. I don't think there's any pattern to what he does after he flips."

The phone rang. DiGrazia reached for it. "What is it? Ah, shit, I'm beat . . . No kidding? In the mouth? Yeah, does sound similar. Doesn't make sense, though. We got our guy locked away . . . Okay, sure, I better check it out . . . Thanks."

He put the receiver down and stared expressionlessly at Pig Dornich. "I have to go," he said, his voice dead tired. "Police work. Give me a call in a few hours. Maybe I'll drive around with you and fill you in some more. Maybe we can even find the sonofabitch."

Chapter 16

February 12. Midday.

The first thing he felt was the throbbing in his fingers; next he felt the cold. Shannon lifted his head and found himself squinting against the sunlight. As his eyes adjusted to the light he realized he was lying in a basement of what was probably an abandoned building. The sunlight he was squinting against was coming through a broken window.

The overall effect was disorienting. After all, one second Shannon had been in the Black Rose working on a bottle of bourbon the slow way, shot by shot, and the next he was lying on a hard, cold floor in some foreign basement.

He knew what had happened. That he had been gone since that second at the Black Rose. He pushed himself into a sitting position and looked over his hands, making sure there were no gashes or cuts. He quickly checked his fingers, feeling for frostbite and then felt over his body probing for any injuries or broken bones. It brought to mind a story he once read about a leper who was constantly checking himself for cuts, always worried about gangrene setting in. That was what it had come to for Shannon also, being unaware of what damage, if any, he had been doing to his body. For all he knew he could've been sitting there bleeding to death.

But he wasn't. His skin felt cold and raw but there were no cuts or broken bones. He ran a hand over his face and felt that his skin was intact; a few day's growth but no damage. His nose and ears felt numb but they didn't feel frostbitten.

He pulled himself to his feet. Other than the throbbing in the fingers of his right hand, he didn't feel that bad. Kind of dry in the mouth and his legs a little wobbly, but other than that, not that bad.

He was still wearing the same clothes as when he was drinking at the Black Rose. They were pretty much a mess. With some relief he found his wallet and badge were still in his pockets. He pulled out his wallet. There was still money in it.

The basement had a dank, musty smell. It was, for the most part, empty; a few broken bottles and some bags of garbage but not much else. He walked over to the broken window. There were pieces of glass lying along the floor underneath it.

Shannon walked up a small flight of stairs and found the door nailed shut. The wood, though, was rotting. He braced himself and then kicked it down. A couple of crack heads were sitting in the hallway smoking some stone. One of them was completely oblivious to him, the other one looked up from his pipe, kind of surprised.

"Hey, man," he asked, "what were you doing down there?"

"Hell if I know," Shannon said. He walked over them. The oblivious crack head never looked up. The other crack head started swearing.

"That's right," he sputtered out, indignant. "Just walk over us like we're trash."

Shannon ignored him. He heard some more crack heads upstairs arguing about who owed who for what they were smoking. The front entranceway had been boarded up but some of the boards had been pulled loose. As Shannon was squeezing through the opening, he heard the indignant crack head yelling at him.

"Just kick down other people's doors like they're your own," he was yelling. "No respect for other people's property. No goddamn respect."

It turned out he wasn't that far from home. The abandoned building was in Roxbury, a section of Boston located only a few miles from Cambridge. He bought a newspaper and was relieved to see that he'd only been gone five days. Five days was better than a week. Still, it was five days that were lost to him. Five days of doing God knows what. A chill ran through him. Like usual, whatever he was doing, he wasn't eating a hell of a lot. His clothes felt loose on him. At least this time, though, he wasn't sick. At least he made it past February tenth in one piece. He had to be thankful for little favors. When he tried hailing down a cab, the driver attempted to swerve past him, but Shannon stepped out in front of the cab and held out his police badge. The driver pulled over and Shannon climbed in and gave him his address.

As they approached the triple-decker that his apartment was in, Shannon saw the squad cars lining the street. DiGrazia was standing in front of the house next to his talking with a uniformed cop. Their eyes locked on each other. DiGrazia started moving in a trot towards the cab. He was at the door as Shannon stepped from it.

DiGrazia was breathing hard from his run. "Well, well," he grinned. "The prodigal son has returned. And looking kind of ripe at that."

Shannon couldn't help returning the grin. DiGrazia was looking worse than him. Along with the dark circles under his partner's eyes, the little hair DiGrazia had left was streaked with dirt and his clothes looked like they had been slept in.

"At least I have an excuse," Shannon said. "What's yours?"

"What's mine?" DiGrazia sputtered. "You sonofabitch. I've been out every goddamn night looking for you. I haven't slept in five days. That's my goddamn excuse." DiGrazia hesitated and then lowered his voice. "What have you been up to?"

"I don't know. I just woke up, so to speak."

"Yeah, well, it doesn't look like your rest did you much good." He paused, considering Shannon. "At least you're back in one piece."

"It looks that way. About spending your nights looking for me, I'd like to thank you."

"Yeah, sure you would. You really don't know what you've been doing?"

Shannon shook his head. "No idea. About an hour ago I came out of it in a crack house in Roxbury." He hesitated. "How's Susie been?"

"She hasn't left you yet. My ex sure would've." Exhaustion passed over DiGrazia's thick face, giving his flesh a wasted look. "I'm glad to see you, pal. I'll tell you, after the last week being run ragged both on the job and looking for you, I'm having a tough time thinking straight. Did you know Rose Hartwell?"

"Ah, shit. What happened to her?"

"You did know her?"

"Yeah, I know her. I know everyone on this street. What happened?"

DiGrazia started to say something and then stopped himself. For whatever reason he got cute. "You better look for yourself."

"All right. Let me wash up first—"

"Nah, don't worry about it. You're fine. Fresh as a goddamn daisy." DiGrazia had an arm around Shannon's shoulders and was veering him away from his building towards the triple-decker Rose Hartwell lived in. As they walked, DiGrazia asked whether Shannon knew if the Hartwells were having marital problems.

"Yeah," Shannon said, "I think things had kind of hit bottom for them."

"That's what I've been hearing," DiGrazia said.

There were about a half dozen plainclothes cops milling through Hartwell's apartment, all grim-faced, all wearing beige or maroon sports jackets. Shannon didn't recognize any of them. Rose Hartwell was waiting for them in the kitchen. She was lying on a small table, fully clothed, a knife sticking out of her mouth. She was dead. Gary Aukland was standing off to one side while a thin man with a short marine-style haircut examined the body. The man had an unnaturally pale complexion with lips that were way too red. His facial bones seemed to shine through colorless, translucent skin. Shannon didn't know him, either. DiGrazia murmured in his ear, "FBI."

There was no shock as Shannon looked at the body. He was surprised how calm he felt. Almost serene. It was as if he'd been expecting this for a long time. Maybe not Rose Hartwell, but someone. He asked the FBI examiner how long the woman had been dead. The man sniffed in the air as if he smelled something and then muttered about them having to wait for a report. Aukland cleared his throat and said it probably happened early in the morning. He moved his head to one side, signaling towards the living room. "Come on," he said, "let's go talk."

They left the kitchen with DiGrazia joining them. Aukland asked if Shannon had been sick. "You look almost as if you've been suffering from exposure," the coroner noted.

"Not that I know of. But then again, what the hell do I know?"

Aukland gave him an odd kind of look and then shook his head. He told him he'd heard Shannon had been put on departmental leave. "Right now I wouldn't mind volunteering for that," Aukland added. "They're really pissing me off in there. You realize how big a favor they're doing letting us watch? Tight-assed little pricks."

"Why are they involved?"

"Because they're experts from their elite Sex Crime unit.

And we have a serial killer," Aukland said with an unhappy smile.

"There was one several days ago in Boston," DiGrazia said.

"And the Roberson murder," Aukland added.

Shannon turned to DiGrazia. "I thought you had the kid all wrapped up?"

"I was wrong. He didn't do it."

Shannon was going to say something else but he let it drop. DiGrazia's expression demanded that he let it drop. He asked Aukland what they had on Rose Hartwell's murder.

"It's hard to tell standing on the sidelines, but it doesn't look like there's any physical evidence. No skin, no blood, no semen. There's a slight discoloration along the wrists that shows her hands were tied. Probably with some sort of fabric, maybe a towel. Whoever did this has a pretty good knowledge of forensics. How closely did you look at that knife?"

"What do you mean?"

"You probably couldn't tell from the angle you were standing at. The knife went right through the back of her neck and stuck a half inch into the table. It severed her windpipe. My guess is she died of asphyxiation. And, Bill, it probably wasn't fast."

"Any other wounds?"

"No, just the one. It was more than enough, though."

"And there was one like this last week in Boston?"

"A carbon copy. And you have Phyllis Roberson. For the most part the profiles match."

Shannon looked out the window, squinting. "How'd you find out it wasn't Roberson's kid?"

Aukland shrugged. "The blood we found on the pillow didn't match either Roberson or her son. Also the timing didn't fit. With the amount of time it took her to bleed to death, the son couldn't have done it. He was in school at the time the internal bleeding had started."

DiGrazia's thick ears had turned bright pink. "With what we had at the scene anyone would've picked that kid," he said.

Shannon asked, "What about the scratch marks on his arms?"

"It probably happened the way he said it did," Aukland said. "Her internal bleeding was slow so it took a while for her lungs to fill up. In the meantime, her son came home, found her like that, tried to pull the knife out of her throat, and well, you know what happened next." Aukland showed some yellowed teeth as he smiled. "I almost think our killer planned it that way; leaving her dying with that knife bobbing out of her throat so her son would do what he did. The blood, though, doesn't make any sense. He was so careful not to leave any other physical evidence. Do you know how difficult it is to kill someone like that without leaving any physical evidence? You think he would've realized he left a few drops of blood."

"I guess he got careless."

"The sonofabitch plants newspaper stories about Janice Rowley's murder in the kid's room to frame him, is so damn meticulous with the murder, and he leaves blood behind in plain sight?" DiGrazia asked.

"He probably got so excited with the murder he didn't realize it."

Aukland thought about it and shrugged. "Maybe," he conceded. "I'm going back in there and keep my eye on things."

DiGrazia grabbed Shannon by the arm. He told Aukland they'd join him later. Then to Shannon, "Let's go to your place."

Once inside his apartment Shannon tried to call his wife at work. DiGrazia cracked his knuckles impatiently as Shannon left a voice mail message.

"What do you think, we got a serial killer?" he asked as soon as the phone was put down.

"You don't think so?"

"That's right. I don't."

"A copycat murder?"

"Nope," DiGrazia said, shaking his head. "No details were released on any of the murders." He took a cigarette out, slipped it into his mouth, and then raised an eyebrow at Shannon and offered him one. Shannon declined.

DiGrazia lit his cigarette and inhaled deeply and then stood and watched as the smoke curled around him. "I think we got someone who wants it to look like a serial killer," he said, the smoke drifting past him, his face all of a sudden anxious, his eyes like hard red marbles. He sat down on the sofa and leaned forward, licking his lips.

"Phyllis Roberson was having problems with her ex," DiGrazia explained. "She was suing him for back child support. A lot of money, Bill. And her ex didn't want to pay. You know, spite. Real bad blood between the two of them."

"Roberson's ex and Brad Hartwell got together and planned this?"

"No, but they're both criminal lawyers. They both work in the same courts."

"So?"

"So maybe they know the same people." DiGrazia took another drag on his cigarette and then stubbed it out, all the while his eyes focused on Shannon's. "Maybe by pure luck they hired the same guy. And maybe this genius had the idea to make it look like a serial killer to cover up the motive. Maybe he got the idea reading about the details of Janice Rowley's murder. Shit, Bill, we have two women with marital problems murdered. You know the statistics as well as I do. Seventy-five percent of the time it's the husband."

"What about the other woman—the one killed last week?"

DiGrazia shrugged. "I think she was thrown in to confuse the issue. I'll show you her file when you come down to the station."

"Were any of them forced entry?"

"No, they were all let in. So what's your gut feeling, a serial killer or something else?"

"My gut feeling is you're suffering from sleep deprivation."

"Come on—"

"It's too complicated for a hit man. And I can't see a hit man throwing in a third body just to be cute."

"You're not using your imagination, pal. Try thinking outside the box a little."

"Okay, how about this—whoever's doing this is enjoying it. It's taking a long time for these women to bleed out."

"Shit, Bill, that's just a smoke screen. There's been nothing sexual with any of these victims. And you got strong financial motives for both Roberson and Hartwell to be killed. I'm telling you, this serial killer business is just to throw us off the trail."

"What does the FBI think?"

DiGrazia made a face like he had swallowed sour milk. "Fuck 'em," he said, scowling. "I haven't mentioned squat to them. They can keep searching for their serial killer for all I care. You want to come down to the station later today? I'll bring in both hubbies for interrogation."

"We better make it tomorrow. I need to clean myself up and take care of things with Susie."

DiGrazia's face fell slack, not bothering to hide his disappointment. "Okay, we'll do it tomorrow," he said. "I should go home and get some sleep anyway." He leaned back against the sofa. "It's good to have you back, Bill."

"Thanks."

"You really don't know where you were?"

"Other than where I woke up, no idea."

DiGrazia leaned further back into the sofa, his eyes narrowing as he appraised his partner. "I could look into it," he said. "But a crack house in Roxbury doesn't sound good. It'd probably be better if I didn't."

"Probably," Shannon agreed.

Susie called later. Shannon told her he wasn't sure if she'd be there this time.

"I wasn't," she corrected him. "I've been at work."

"You know what I mean."

"I know what you mean." There was a hesitation where Shannon could only hear a soft hum over the line. Then Susie asked if it was over.

"Our marriage?"

"No. Not our marriage. Your—the sickness."

"I certainly hope so." He started to laugh. "At least for this year."

"At least for this year," she agreed, and then she started to cry. When she was able to, she told him she'd be home as soon as she could.

Susan Shannon reached Pig Dornich at his office. "My husband just came home," she told him.

"No kidding." He sounded disappointed, almost hurt. "Just like that?"

"Just like that."

"Do you know where he's been?"

"He didn't say."

"Would you mind if I speak to him?"

"Why would you want to do that?"

He hesitated. "About that other matter—" he started.

"I don't want you speaking to him. I don't want him knowing I hired you. And about that other matter, maybe we better—"

"I'll tell you what," Dornich interrupted, cutting her off before she could finish firing him. "I feel bad about not finding him. Pretty lousy, actually. Let me spend a few days, free of charge, looking into things. Maybe I'll get lucky."

"I can't afford—"

"Free of charge," Dornich repeated himself. "One thing," he asked, "do you know if your husband's been in the area?"

"I don't know. All I know is I don't want you talking to him."

Dornich started to promise he wouldn't but the line went dead on him before he could finish. All in all he really did feel lousy. He had been knocking himself out looking for Shannon; the last three days he'd been at it almost nonstop while charging his client for only a small fraction of his time. The case had become a sore spot for him and it had been picked at enough to leave it bleeding and festering. He knew it was a race, that his man was going to be coming home any moment, and he wanted to find him while he was still out there. He wanted to know what the sonofabitch had been up to.

After his talk with Joe DiGrazia, he hit the mean streets around Boston, showing Shannon's picture, trying to find out if his man had a weak spot for hookers. None of the girls knew the guy. Dornich spent a few more fruitless hours driving around the strip clubs neighboring the city. Again no luck. Later that night he joined Joe DiGrazia as they barhopped 'til closing time, showing Shannon's picture around. After last call they spent the rest of the night cruising alleys and side streets. They came across a few minor crimes; drug deals, prostitution, and the like, but nothing else. No Shannon. Not even as much as a clue.

The next day was purely routine; checking out Logan airport and the bus terminals. After that he drove down to Providence and then back up to Nashua. The problem was, if Shannon had left the city he could've done it any number of ways; hitchhiking, stealing a car, even with a bicycle. So Shannon could've been anywhere.

By the end of the week Dornich was spending half his time driving around the Boston area and the other half checking the wire services and contacting out of state law enforcement offices. At no time did he even get a whiff of Shannon. It hadn't been a complete waste of time, though. He found out his client had been wrong about Shannon's parents. The mother was dead, but the father wasn't. He had an address and a phone number. The older Shannon was living in Mountain View, California. He wouldn't talk much over the phone, just that he hadn't seen his son in over fifteen years and he'd just as soon go another fifteen.

Pig Dornich picked up the photostatic copies that the *Sacramento Journal* had sent him from their archives. He read the articles slowly, carefully, letting his eyes linger on each paragraph. When he was done he read them again. Then he leaned back in his chair and closed his eyes and wondered what went on in that house between a thirteen-year-old Bill Shannon and Herbert Winters.

Chapter 17

Shannon's eyes opened before the alarm went off. Susie's small body was against his. He could feel her chest rising and lowering as she breathed. He could feel a moist heat coming from her body.

They didn't talk much yesterday when she got home. There wasn't much to say. He couldn't tell her where he'd been and she was too worn out to blame him. The silence, though, was different than usual. There was nothing heavy or oppressive about it. It was almost comforting. Almost as if the last few years had been stripped clean. As if they still had a shot.

The alarm went off. Shannon watched as Susie started to stir. Watched as consciousness seeped into her. She pushed herself out of bed and turned off the alarm, and then turned and stood looking at him, her eyes struggling against the morning light.

"How are you feeling?" she asked.

Shannon stretched lazily. "Better than I would've thought."

"I didn't know how you were going to look when you showed up yesterday. Whether you'd be all beat up or worse. At least you came home in one piece this time."

"Seems like I did."

"Yes, it does." She sat on the edge of the bed and put a hand behind Shannon's neck. "Maybe a few pounds lighter, but at least you weren't coughing up blood or anything."

"And no rat bites this year."

Susie withdrew her hand from his neck. "That's not funny," she complained.

"No, I guess it's not. I'm sorry. I just wish I knew what I'd been doing out there."

Susie tried to smile at him but didn't have much luck with it. After a while she got up and told him she was going to take a shower.

As Shannon lay on his back he found himself feeling strangely at peace. He thought about the two women, Rose Hartwell and the one in Boston, both lying dead with knives sticking out of their mouths. He tried to imagine what the woman in Boston looked like and came up with some vague impression. None of this affected his sense of well-being. The water for the shower turned on and Shannon listened to its soft drone. He let it numb his mind as the images crystallized and then faded away.

Later, as Shannon was shaving, he heard a muffled cry. He felt his heart drop to his feet as he ran from the bathroom. Susie was standing by the front door holding a newspaper. She turned to face him, her eyes pained, confused. "Rose—" she started, "oh my God . . ."

Shit, Shannon thought as he moved to her and held her.

There were a few curious stares as Shannon entered the squad room. Most of his fellow officers asked how he was doing. A couple, like Ed Poulett, just smirked. Joe DiGrazia looked relieved to see his partner. He got up from his desk and greeted him.

"I talked with your neighbor, Brad Hartwell, last night." DiGrazia kept his voice low as he leaned his thick knuckles against Shannon's desk and edged forward. "The guy didn't seem too shook up about his wife's murder."

"As I was telling you before, they were having problems."

"Yeah, well, let me tell you about your neighbor. He's got a big mouth. He likes to talk. If he is involved, buddy boy, he'll be bragging about it and we'll nail him." DiGrazia hesitated. "How'd things go with Susie?" he asked, his voice barely above a whisper.

"Pretty good—"

The phone rang. Captain Martin Brady wanted Shannon in his office.

Brady looked uncomfortable as he sat behind his desk, his face frozen in a queer kind of smile. Sitting to the right of him was a man with a long, dour face. From the way he was grimacing it was a good bet he was suffering from some sort of intestinal problem. Shannon recognized him from Hartwell's apartment. Brady nodded at Shannon and asked him to close the door.

"Enjoy your time off?" Brady asked.

Shannon told him it flew by.

"Well, good, good." Brady pushed forward quickly. "I'd like you to meet Special Agent Douglas Swallow."

"Glad to meet you," Shannon acknowledged. Special Agent Swallow made no movement at the introduction. Shannon didn't bother to extend his hand.

"Doug is out of the FBI's Sex Crime unit," Brady explained. "He's helping out with the investigation of a couple of murders we've had. You know about that, though, don't you?"

"Joe filled me in."

"You investigated one of them?"

"As it turns out, I guess I did. At least somewhat."

"Where have you been?" Agent Swallow broke in. His voice had a sharp crack to it.

"What?"

"You don't understand English?"

"What's going on here?" Shannon demanded of Brady.

Brady placed both his hands on his desk, palms up. "Doug

has a few questions to ask you."

"And why's that?"

"Because of the way you reacted at Roberson's murder site," Swallow said. "Because your neighbor was murdered yesterday by potentially the same individual. And because no one knows where you've been the past week."

Shannon took an almost imperceptible step forward. "I've been on disability leave," he stated softly.

"They're all good points, Bill," Brady argued. "Now, we're not accusing you of anything, but they're good points and we'd like to understand things better."

"Should I be getting a lawyer?"

"Not unless you've done something where you need a lawyer. Have you, Bill?"

Shannon shook his head. "I don't need a lawyer."

"Of course you don't. We never thought you did. We just have some questions, that's all. There's nothing for you to get upset about. And nothing leaves this office."

"Where have you been the past week?" Swallow demanded.

"I don't know."

A loud noise escaped from the FBI agent. Brady's round, pudgy face seemed to deflate at the same moment as if a pin had punctured it. "That's not helping any, Bill," he started.

"I really don't know," Shannon explained. "Six days ago I blacked out. I came out of it yesterday."

Agent Swallow looked incredulous. "You're trying to tell us that you don't—"

"That I don't know where I've been," Shannon said, nodding. "I came out of it in a basement of an abandoned building in Roxbury yesterday afternoon. That's the first thing I remember since I blacked out."

Brady and Swallow exchanged glances.

"This isn't good, Bill," Brady said.

"I'm sorry."

"You're trying to tell us you don't remember what you've been doing?" Swallow demanded.

"That's what I've been trying to tell you."

"This so-called blackout . . ."

"A week ago Wednesday, I was sitting at the bar at the Black Rose trying to see how much bourbon I could pour into me. Next thing I remembered was yesterday."

Swallow got out of his chair and started pacing. "This is bullshit," he said.

"I've been sick," Shannon tried to explain. "It's what happened."

"You willing to take a polygraph?"

Shannon shrugged. "If I have to."

Swallow got within a half foot of Shannon, his face pinched, the skin around his mouth drawn tight. "If you have to, huh?" He shook his head. "Were you with anyone?"

"I don't know."

"I want an address for your abandoned building."

Shannon gave it to him. Swallow slowly backed away and sat back down in his chair. Brady exhaled a lung full of air through his mouth, the noise escaping from him in a slow hiss. "This really doesn't leave us much choice, Bill."

"What do you mean?"

"Your behavior has been, at the very least, erratic. And this doesn't sound good at all."

"I've been sick."

"I understand that, but still . . ." Brady shook his head slowly, almost painfully.

"We need physical evidence from you," said Swallow.

All Shannon could do was stare at him.

"We need a blood sample to match against—"

"Fuck you."

"I thought you were willing to cooperate?" Brady asked.

"What the fuck are you talking about?"

"And what the fuck are you trying to pull?" Swallow demanded, his face reddening, his lips receding into a razor-thin smile. "You give us this bullshit story about blacking out for a week."

"I told you I blacked out for five days—"

"Bill," Brady said, "both your blood type and the type found at the Roberson murder site is O positive."

"You think I had anything to do with that murder? Come on, Martin, O positive is the most common blood type out there."

Brady let out a long sigh. "Unless you cooperate, I'm going to have to suspend you. At least until we can prove you didn't have any involvement with these murders. If you give us a sample we can have it cleared up in—how long would it take, Doug?"

"With some luck, an hour. It depends whether we can rule him out with a quickie DNA test. If there are enough matches we'll have to send the samples to Washington for a more complex analysis. If that happened it could take a couple of weeks to get the results back."

"It's all up to you, Bill. You can make it hard for everyone, especially yourself, or you can make it easy. Which way is it going to be?"

Shannon felt a hotness flushing his face. He looked at both men; Brady with his soft acquiescent smile and Swallow with his dour hostility. Fine way to treat a fellow police officer, he thought bitterly.

"Fine," he said. "If Special Agent Swallow wants my blood, he can have it."

"I'm glad you're being reasonable," Brady said. "Hopefully, we'll get this cleared up today. Doug, if you don't mind I'd like to talk to Bill privately for a minute."

"I'll be right outside," Swallow said. He moved quickly as he left the office.

Brady shifted uncomfortably in his chair as he considered Shannon. "This business about blacking out . . ."

"I've been sick—"

"Yes, I've heard that before. You already told me you were drinking heavily. Are drugs involved?"

"No."

"Just alcohol then?"

"I'm not an alcoholic." Shannon hesitated. "This problem I have, it's some sort of illness. I've been seeing a therapist about it."

"This has happened before?"

Shannon nodded.

"And DiGrazia knows about it, doesn't he?" Brady asked angrily. "Goddammit! And all these years Joe's been lying to me about it."

"I'm trying to work this out—"

"So when you have these blackouts you don't know what you do, is that what you're trying to tell me?"

"Martin," Shannon started helplessly, "I'm trying to get help with this."

"For all you know you could be killing these women."

"No. Not a chance. I wasn't gone when Roberson was murdered."

"What do you mean you weren't gone?"

"I hadn't blacked out yet."

"When do you have these blackouts?"

"After I've been sick—"

"Always the same time every year, is that it?" As Brady looked at Shannon his face softened. "What's behind them, Bill?"

Shannon turned away. "I really don't know. That's what I've been seeing a therapist to find out."

Brady started to say something and then closed his mouth. He sat back in his chair, his eyes glassy, his lips pressed tightly together. It became very quiet in the office. A painfully uncomfortable quiet. Finally, Brady told Shannon how much he didn't like the situation.

"It's something I can manage—" Shannon started.

"Obviously, it's not. Not when you can't function for weeks at a time."

"It's over, Martin. At least for this year."

"Uh-uh."

"What do you mean?"

"I'm putting you in for a psychiatric evaluation. Pending the results, you'll be assigned desk duty. You want to file a union protest?"

Shannon stared straight at Brady. His hands were shaking. He told the captain that he didn't want to file a union protest.

"You sure? We can call your union rep right now."

"I'm sure."

" 'Cause I don't want to impinge on your rights—"

"I said I'm sure."

"Okay, I need your service revolver."

Shannon removed it from his shoulder holster and handed it to him.

"You have any others at home?"

"Me? With any unlicensed weapons? You should know I wouldn't break any departmental regulations."

Shannon turned to leave but Brady stopped him.

"Bill, remember, if I wanted you off the force you'd be off the force right now."

"Is that all?"

"One more thing." Brady paused for a moment. "This has been bothering me for several months. How did you know where to find Janice Rowley?"

"I really don't know. I just woke up knowing I had to get in my car and start driving. I didn't know I was going to find her until I did. Why, are you going to blame her death on me, also?"

Brady ignored the question. "Cooperate with Swallow. Let's get this cleared up and over with."

Shannon sat in a small windowless room, waiting for his test results. The room was no larger than a prison cell, about six feet by nine feet. The door was closed. Shannon had heard Agent Swallow lock it from the outside. Aside from the chair he was sitting on, there was no other furniture in it.

An hour passed before the door opened and Agent Swallow gestured for him to get up. He looked more constipated than anything else. He waited until Shannon had joined him in the hall before telling him the test results were negative.

"Tough luck, huh?" Shannon remarked as he turned to leave. He was halfway down the hallway before he heard Swallow barking at his back.

"I don't want you anywhere near this investigation," Swallow yelled, his voice straining to a croak. "You understand me?"

Shannon kept walking. There was't much else he could do.

Chapter 18

That night Shannon dreamt about Herbert Winters again. Like before, Shannon was pulled from a mindless, blissful drifting to have Winters hovering over him, grinning like there was no tomorrow. And like before, Winters seemed like a caricature of the man who had tortured him twenty years earlier; now balding, fortyish, his features bloated, his body looking as if a few extra layers of stucco had been slapped on.

But he still had that malformed chin. He still had those pale, rattlesnake eyes . . .

For a long while Herbert Winters seemed content just to grin at Shannon, his eyes dead within his fleshy face. There was an odor that came off him. A sour rancidness. It assaulted Shannon's senses. Winters noticed the effect and grinned even wider.

"The smell of death," he said with a sly wink.

Shannon tried to pretend he wasn't there. Tried to keep from breathing in that smell. It was like garbage and rotting flesh and sickness all mixed together. It hung in the air and made his skin feel dirty.

"You know all about that smell, don't you?" Winters asked. "You inhaled a big whiff of it from your mom that day. And an even bigger whiff of it from me, didn't you, boy?"

Shannon didn't answer. He squeezed his eyes shut and tried to keep from smelling that smell. Breathing in through his mouth didn't help any.

"You just can't get enough of it, can you, Billy Boy?" Winters asked, laughing lightly, the fat on his body rolling gently. "Is that why you like working homicide so much? To be around that smell?"

Shannon didn't want to answer him but he couldn't help himself. He heard his voice telling Winters it was so he could put shit like him away.

"I don't think that's it," Winters said after thinking about it. He shook his head, his lips forming a small pout. "No, I just don't think so. I think you need that smell. But by the time you get to the body it's faded. It's all but gone. And the little that lingers is no longer enough for you, is it?"

Shannon clamped down hard on his teeth. He tried like hell not to breathe.

"That's why you had to kill those women. So you could get that smell fresh. So you could inhale it deeply into your lungs. So you could let death fill you up."

"I didn't kill anyone."

"Keep telling yourself that, boy." Winters started making a laughing noise deep in his sinuses. "You forget I'm part of you. I know what you've been up to, Billy Boy.

"And don't take too much comfort in those test results!" Winters snapped at once, his dead-fish skin beginning to redden. "All those test results showed was that you didn't kill Roberson. It proved nothing about those other two women."

"Roberson and those other two were—"

"Were what?" Winters rudely interrupted. "Killed by the same person?" He burst into laughter, his thick body now convulsing wildly. It sounded like he was choking on food. "Says who?" he sputtered out when he could, his eyes now alive, now glistening with amusement.

"They weren't killed by the same person," he explained after a while. "Remember one thing, Billy Boy. You and me are part of the same ball of wax. When you went bye-bye last week, you let me out of the bottle. And, Billy, you may not remember all the gory details, but I do. I have to tell you we had a hell of a time—"

The smell had become unbearable. It had become like a thick, oozing liquid. Shannon had an image of it filling up his lungs. He felt like he was drowning in it, and like a drowning man he started to panic. In a mad rush he felt himself moving away from the smell . . . Winters's image dimmed. His voice started to fade . . . The smell . . .

Shannon woke up. His heart pounding, his skin clammy wet, the sheets around him damp. For a brief moment he thought he detected that smell. He jerked himself upright, inhaling deeply as he concentrated. He forced a stillness within him as he desperately tried to find if that smell was anywhere around. But it was as elusive as his peace of mind, and similarly, just as distant.

Shannon exhaled and looked over at Susie. He touched her gently along the cheek to make sure she was still alive and then let his fingers gingerly trace the outline of her small body. She murmured softly in her sleep.

The last thing he wanted to do was wake her. If she found out about his dream she'd leave him for good. He had no doubt about that. Because he wasn't supposed to have another breakdown, at least not 'til next year.

Lying among dirty sheets ten miles away in an eight-dollar-a-day rooming house was the flesh and blood embodiment of Shannon's nightmare. On cue, his eyes opened and his lips formed into a crooked smile, framing an almost nonexistent malformed chin.

He was pleased with how things turned out. More than pleased, really. He had guessed right about the blackouts, and more importantly, how that little piece of shit didn't have a clue what he did during them. It was the reason why he could never visit the little pissant during those times. You can't visit someone who's not there.

He started laughing. A thin, wheezing sound. It oozed out of him like a noxious gas filling the room. "Just wait, Billy Boy," he breathed softly in a wispy, singsong voice, "you might think your nightmare just ended but it hasn't even begun. And when it happens it's going to be a real eye-popper. You can bet on it."

It took a long while before he stopped laughing. Before he closed his eyes again.

Of course, the man wasn't Herbert Winters. Winters was long dead, his corpse cremated twenty years earlier. But while the man may not have been Herbert Winters, he knew what had happened in that house that day. He knew because Herbert Winters wasn't alone.

Chapter 19

Charlie Winters knew early on he had a special bond with his cousin, Herbert. They were born within a month of each other and physically they looked more like brothers than cousins; both around the same size and skin coloring, both damned with the same pale, almost albino eyes, both inheriting the same deformed chin from their fathers. Charlie knew they had far more than their physical similarities in common. Even as young as age six, Charlie knew they shared a uniquely perverse outlook on life. At that age it wouldn't have been something he'd have been able to put in words, but it was still something he knew. That deep in the core of their hearts they were the same.

Over the years they became inseparable as they fleshed out the basic truths that were driving them. Of course, their lessons were learned in secret, first with small animals and then later progressing to neighborhood dogs and cats. They were quiet about it and careful, and it wasn't until the Chilton girl disappeared that they found out they hadn't been nearly quiet and careful enough. It was then that they realized there had been a growing groundswell of suspicion towards them and the Chilton girl brought it all out into the open—the dirty, hateful glances, the inquiries, and outright accusations. They were all baseless, of course. There wasn't a shred of evidence linking them to the girl's disappearance or her mutilated body when it was finally discovered, so they feigned innocence and the townsfolk ended up having to accept it; even the County Sheriff who would've beaten the truth out of them if their parents hadn't been able to afford the best lawyers in North Carolina.

It was an eye-opening experience for them, though, and the lesson they learned from it was invaluable. No matter how careful they thought they were, it wasn't careful enough. And just as important, they'd better not stay in any one spot for too long. After all, a skunk can only hide its stripe for so long. Eventually, you end up smelling it out.

In any case, a drifter from Texas murdered a young girl outside of Durham six months later and over time it became accepted that this same drifter must've also done in poor Marjorie Chilton. Not right away, because it's hard to dispute the obvious, especially when it's staring you straight in the face every day with pale albino eyes, but over time. Eventually, their own parents stopped giving them those funny looks when their backs were sort of turned. Eventually.

So Charlie and Herbert bided their time. It killed them inside, but they knew they had no choice. That as much as they had thought otherwise, they had fooled no one. So they waited and made plans and studied, all the while fighting against the desires that were burning fervently within them.

When they were eighteen they left Mornsville together. They bought a Chevy Nova (they learned their lesson about being careful, and just as important, being inconspicuous). And they went off into the world to fulfill their dreams and aspirations.

They stuck mostly to large cities where people of their kind could blend in without being noticed. Herbert had a knack for finding elderly shut-ins or recluses where they could steal license plates without it being noticed. Whenever they traveled to a new area, that would be the first thing they'd do.

They were on the road for two years crisscrossing the country before they ended up in Sacramento. It was in a local supermarket that Herbert caught a glimpse of Mrs. Shannon. That was all that was needed. Just a glimpse of her. Just something as random as that. They followed her back to her house and gained entrance as she struggled with her groceries and the door, and then kept her alive for an hour as they did things to her.

Near the end Charlie went upstairs and took a nap. They had spent most of the night driving from Los Angeles and he was tired and wasn't much into it. This one was basically Herbert's. As he napped, he heard the woman's muffled screams and a peaceful contentment warmed him over.

When he woke he was surprised to see that over three hours had passed. Herbie should've been finished long before then. He should've woken him and they should've been traveling fast out of Sacramento. Annoyed, he crept downstairs to the kitchen and found Herbie sitting down, the side of his face swollen and smeared with blood, his shirt collar soaked in it. There was a body in a crumpled heap on the floor next to him. The woman was in the same spot as when Charlie had left earlier, lying flat on her back on the kitchen table. Now, though, she was staring blankly up at the ceiling with an eight-inch carving knife sticking out of her open mouth. The padded handcuffs they had used on her had been taken off and were on the floor. As Charlie moved closer he noticed the body on the floor was that of a small teenage boy.

Herbie gave his cousin a hard smirk. "Like my handiwork?" he asked. "I thought I'd give her something nice and hard and long to suck on."

"What happened to you?"

Herbie ran a hand across his cheek and stared enigmatically at his bloodied hand. "This little piece of shit snuck up on me." He pushed the boy's body with his boot and then paused and offered his cousin a crooked smile. "Even gods bleed, Cuz. Believe it or not." He turned his gaze from his hand back to the body on the floor and gave the kid a kick in the ribs. The boy moaned with the blow.

"He's still alive?" Charlie asked incredulously.

"Yeah, he's going to be alive a bit longer." Herbie gave the boy another kick in the ribs and the boy let out another unconscious moan. "As soon as he wakes up from his nap we're going to spend some more quality time together. I'm not anywhere close to being done with him."

Long shadows were forming across the dead woman's torso. Charlie glanced anxiously at a clock on the wall and saw it was four o'clock. "Look, Cuz," he said, "it's getting late. We have to get out of here."

Herbie was shaking his head adamantly, his eyes hardening into sharp, pale crystals. "Sorry, this little piece of shit is going to get to know hell real well before I send him to it."

"Cuz, this is stupid. We're putting ourselves at risk—"

"You want to leave now; okay, fine, let's take him with us."

All Charlie could do was stare at his cousin with his mouth hung loosely open. "Take him with us?" he sputtered when he was able to. "That's brilliant, Cuz. Let's invite a national manhunt to come looking for us. Man, let's just get rid of him and get the hell out of here."

"I need more time. Another hour."

Charlie licked his lips. His mouth felt bone dry. This was crazy. Among other things, their car was parked three blocks away in a supermarket lot. It had borrowed plates and the longer it stayed there the better the chance it would draw suspicion to them. He tried to talk some sense into his cousin.

"We could make this look like some sort of satanic deal," he said, talking in a quick, panicky rush. "We could cut their hearts out and write some shit on the wall. Cuz, we got to get moving."

"I need another hour."

"But—"

"Stop it, Cuz," Herbie ordered softly.

The way he said it stopped Charlie cold. He knew the look on his cousin's face and he knew what would happen next if he didn't stop it.

Herbie rubbed a thumb across the gash on his cheek and grimaced. "You can stay and join me if you want," he offered, "but not if you're going to keep acting like this. I don't need you making me nervous."

"Why don't you wake him and get it over with?"

"I said I don't need you making me nervous!"

Charlie swallowed down what he was going to say and forced his mouth shut. The exasperation was too much. He picked up the padded handcuffs from the floor and shoved them into his pocket. He felt too jittery to stick around. He also knew the more jittery he acted, the more Herbie would stretch things out. "Fine, give me the keys. I'll meet you by the car in an hour."

"What do you need the keys for?"

"What do I need the keys for? You got to be kidding. The car's been sitting in that lot for over three hours. I need to move it before it draws any attention."

"It can sit another hour."

"But—"

"I said it can sit another hour." A petulant smile had twisted Herbie's lips. "It's your choice whether I'm here another hour or another twenty-four. It's all your choice."

Charlie took a step forward with the intention of snuffing the kid himself, but the look Herbie gave him stopped him. Anyway, he knew it wouldn't help. It would only make Herbie more determined that they sit there twiddling their thumbs for the next twenty-four hours. That much was obvious. Reluctantly, he headed back upstairs.

"Fine," he said, "let me know when you're done."

★ ★ ★ ★ ★

Charlie spent the next half hour pacing around the upstairs of the house working himself into a tizzy. The last two years they had been so careful the way they varied the details of each murder, and in fact, making a study of it. They had spent hours reading everything from forensic material to books on police procedural and criminal behavior to make sure there were no patterns to their murders, that there would be nothing the police could tie together, and more importantly, nothing that could bring the FBI in.

And now this. Usually Herbie didn't throw these type of tantrums—at least not to this extent. All because that piece of shit kid had to cut him. In a way he could understand it, but still Herbie was putting them at risk. It just wasn't worth it. The more Charlie thought about it, the more infuriated he got. When he heard the screams it was too much for him. Goddamn him, he thought, he couldn't even gag him first?

He reacted to the screams without really thinking about it—flying down the stairs, his eyes bloodied with rage, his hands squeezing into fists. When he reached the kitchen he froze, not quite comprehending what he was seeing. It wasn't what he expected. Everything was flipped around from the way it was supposed to be. The kid was on top of Herbie, slashing away at him with a carving knife as if his cousin were a side of beef. And Herbie's head wasn't laying quite right, sort of at a ninety-degree angle to his body. Charlie realized his cousin's head had, for the most part, been cut off from his body.

He heard a noise from behind. Someone was trying to kick down the door. Without thinking, he turned and scampered back upstairs and ended up squeezing into the back of the master bedroom closet, pulling some blankets over him.

Somehow, the police didn't search the house. If they had, they would have found Charlie Winters cowering in the closet.

But they didn't. They took it for granted that Herbie had acted alone and they didn't bother searching upstairs, at least not carefully. Later, when the police were gone, Charlie slipped into the night.

He felt like a dead man. Numb and dazed, his world crashing all around him. The unfairness of it all was staggering. Him and Herbie were meant to be together. Now they weren't and they never would be again. Charlie Winters couldn't accept it.

For months afterwards he drifted, not quite sure what to do. There was no pleasure in anything he did. Nothing but a numbness he couldn't shake. Herbie and him needed each other. They fed off each other. Without his cousin nothing made any sense. The world seemed pointless.

Nine months after his cousin's death he was stopped by the police for a burned out taillight. He had been traveling through Seattle, driving straight through from Portland. In the back of his trunk was a thirteen-year-old boy he had picked up along the way. Normally, before he had stopped thinking clearly, the boy would've been either dead or properly anesthetized. But he had stopped thinking after Herbie's death. As the officer wrote him up for the taillight, a thumping noise came from inside the trunk. The officer was quicker with the gun and Charlie Winters was arrested, convicted, and sentenced to eighteen years for kidnapping.

His fellow inmates labeled Winters a child molester, reasoning he had kidnapped the boy for purposes other than money. His first week in prison a group of "gorillas" held him down and took turns turning him out. Later, each one of them were found with their throats cut and their testicles hanging from their mouths. The message got out that Charlie Winters was someone to be left alone. It became gospel.

Even still, the next couple of years were a time of utter bleakness for him. Despondent, he lay on his cot and waited as the days blended into nights. Off and on he would think about his cousin and the unfairness of it all. It would stick deep enough in his craw that he'd start to choke on it. That little shit of a kid. He would've given anything for an hour alone with that little shit. But there was nothing he could give. Nothing to change that he was trapped within a six-by-nine-foot cage. Nothing to do but wallow in his misery.

His salvation came one day when a guard gave him a book on metaphysics.

He saw the light then.

It wasn't the light the guard intended him to see, but for Charlie Winters it was as bright as the burning sun.

The ideas from the book—as they were twisted within his mind—summed up everything he and Herbert had known were true but had never quite put into words. Especially about man being god-like. Of course, the concept of every man being god-like was laughable to Winters, but that him and Herbert were was inescapable. As was their reason for being. To punish and inflict pain. For all time. To keep coming back to earth over and over again to spread their suffering. One day him and Herbert would be reunited. The book (again, as it was twisted within his mind) all but said so. In the meantime, he would have to carry on for both of them and the book showed him how he could do it while in prison. Because you can only lock the body behind bars. If you can learn to leave the body . . .

And all he had was time to learn . . .

It took a year of practice before he succeeded, but Charlie Winters never had any doubts or wavered in his faith. The book had made it all crystal clear to him. When it finally did happen it only lasted for a few seconds before he was sucked back in. It was so fast, he almost didn't realize it. Most people would've talked themselves out of it, blaming it on a hallucination, but Charlie knew it was real, he knew it wasn't any dream. And he laughed good and hard over it because he had found his way out.

With practice he got to where he could leave his body just about any night. It was like learning to play the piano, things at first that were impossible and clumsy, over time became second nature. Movement became easy. Thought became reality. Think about a place and you were there. Think about a person and you were inches away. Eventually, he got to where he could stay out for hours before being sucked back in.

He spent his time out watching Shannon. There was some satisfaction in observing the relationship between Shannon and his father, knowing that him and Herbert were at the root of it. But it wasn't enough. Not nearly enough.

He needed to hurt him.

He needed to keep on hurting him. Again and again. For as long as there was breath in that piece of shit.

All he could do, though, was watch so that was all he did. Patiently. Night after night. Waiting for when things would change. Because, in his heart, he knew they would. That it was only a matter of time.

And he was right.

One of his times out he learned how to slip between the physical and dream worlds. It happened accidentally, without him even trying. Once he knew how, it became as easy as breathing. As easy as pulling wings from a fly. Instead of just watching Shannon, he began to visit him in his dreams. Methodically working on him, breaking him down piece by piece. Following his plan to the letter. Because death by itself wouldn't be enough.

Winters patiently stuck to his plan. Not doing too much at any one time, but little by little nibbling away at Shannon. All the while waiting for his sentence to run out. He refused the early paroles that were offered and bided his time, waiting for when they would have to release him unconditionally. By this time the Correction Office knew what he was and they knew what he would do once he was out, but when his time ran down they had no choice. They had to set him loose.

That was a month before Janice Rowley's murder.

Thinking about Shannon had brought the bile up into his throat. He spat on the floor and then lay gingerly back among the dirty sheets. The blood seeped from his face as he concentrated on the inside of his eyelids.

Charlie Winters's breathing became more shallow. His facial muscles relaxed and a lightness softened his features. He had a busy night in front of him. So many people to visit . . .

Chapter 20

When the alarm went off Shannon jumped out of bed and asked Susie if it was okay if he took the first shower.

"I want to get to work early. See if I can make up for the time I lost," he said, forcing a half smile.

As he stood under the water Susie opened the shower door. Her face was set in a troubled frown.

"Are you okay?" she asked.

"Still feel a little beat, but sure. Why?"

"Both your pillowcase and the sheets on your side of the bed are soaked through."

"Maybe I got some virus," Shannon said. "But I feel better right now."

Shannon turned back to the shower. He could feel Susie standing by the open shower door watching him. In his mind's eye he could see her frown deepening, becoming more worried, more pained. It seemed a long time before she moved away.

Of course, Shannon wasn't feeling any better.

That he was still having nightmares worried him. And this specific nightmare . . . Was there any truth to it? Were Phyllis Roberson and the other two women killed by different people? As he tried to sort it out in his mind, an uneasiness spread through him. The more he thought about it, the more twisted his insides became. Like a sheet caught in a hurricane.

As it turned out he didn't leave any earlier for work. He hung around waiting for Susie. After dropping her off at the Fresh

Pond train station, he doubled back to the apartment and called Elaine Horwitz's office. The receptionist was able to squeeze him in for ten-thirty.

Elaine Horwitz had a pasty, almost sickly look about her. She sat at her desk, fidgeting, unable to look directly at Shannon. Her attitude was detached and vaguely hostile. Shannon apologized for abandoning her at the restaurant. Horwitz seemed taken aback by the apology.

"I had no right going with you," she mumbled, some red blotching her pale skin.

"You were just trying to help me through a rough time," Shannon said.

Horwitz's blush deepened. She fidgeted with her glasses and tried to look at Shannon. Her mouth fluttered briefly, unable to keep its composure. "How are you doing, Bill?"

"Not so good." He told her about his blackout, his trouble at work, and finally about his dream.

She sat quietly, taking it all in. "This person you dreamed about—you're sure it's the same man who murdered your mother?"

"Yes."

"I suppose you must've seen pictures of him at some point," Horwitz thought out loud, "or maybe it's simply the image you've imagined him to be. It sounds like an anxiety dream, similar to when a college student dreams about having to take an exam for a class he's never attended." She ran a finger along her lip, pausing. Then she smiled slightly. "That's all there is to it, Bill," she added. "You're anxious about the psychological evaluation you've been ordered to undergo. There's nothing sinister underlying it."

Her appearance shifted subtly, becoming more confident, more self-assured. "Tell me about your blackout," she asked, meeting Shannon's eyes.

He shook his head. "I can't remember any of it. All I know is I was gone for five days and when I came out of it I was lying in a basement in Roxbury."

"When exactly did you black out?"

"It was the day after we went out to dinner."

Elaine Horwitz nodded knowingly. "That's why you didn't make it to our session."

Shannon didn't bother to correct her. Their appointment had been for three o'clock. He remembered later that day, sometime past six o'clock, he had been sitting at the Black Rose pouring bourbon into himself. It was after that he disappeared.

"I'd like to have you hypnotized," Horwitz said.

Shannon found himself nodding. It was something he wanted, too. Elaine Horwitz would find out the truth about how he had been tortured, but that didn't matter. He could live with it. What he couldn't live with was not knowing what he had done while he was gone. He needed to know if there was anything behind that dream. He asked her when they could do it.

Mark Bennett sat in front of Shannon, his tight, curly hair damp, his lips forming a bland, pleasant smile. He led Shannon through a series of exercises, eventually sending Shannon down an imaginary spiral staircase. When Shannon reached the bottom, Bennett had him place a hand in front of his face and open his eyes.

"Concentrate on a spot where your fingers and hand join." He paused, giving Shannon some time to follow his instructions. "Have you found that spot?"

Shannon murmured affirmatively.

"Strings are now attached to your fingers," Bennett told him. "They're pulling them apart. You can't fight it."

Shannon's fingers splayed outward, his hand tensing as he

struggled to keep them together.

"You can drop your hand and relax. The strings are gone."

Bennett turned sideways to Horwitz. "Okay," he murmured under his breath, "let's see what we can dig up."

He addressed Shannon in a soft monotone, asking him if he could remember the last place he was on February seventh. Shannon told him it was a bar in Cambridge, the Black Rose.

Bennett placed Shannon back at the bar. He had Shannon describe the inside of it in detail.

"Is anyone sitting next to you?"

"There's a heavy blond on my left. The seat on my right's empty."

"How many drinks have you had?"

"Nine." Shannon counted them slowly. His speech became slurred. His facial muscles tightened, forming the sullen look of a man who's been drinking hard.

"What time is it?"

"I don't know."

"Are you wearing a watch?"

"No."

"Is there a clock on the wall?"

"No, but the blond next to me's got a watch."

"Can you see it?"

"Yeah, let me look . . . it's six-thirty."

Horwitz made a noise. She indicated to Bennett to ignore her. "Sorry," she murmured, "just realized I have to bill one of my patients for a cancellation."

Bennett turned back to Shannon and asked him to move forward by ten minutes. "Do you know where you are?" he asked.

"Yes," Shannon answered, his speech no longer slurred, "I'm in a basement."

"Where?"

"In Roxbury."

"That doesn't make sense . . ." Bennett started, confused. Horwitz figured it out. She told him Shannon was leaping forward to when he came out of his blackout. Bennett moved Shannon backwards, minute by minute, until he was out of the basement and back at the bar. He tried it again, and Shannon again skipped from the bar to Roxbury. The time that existed between those two moments passed by without any awareness, as if it never existed to Shannon. Bennett narrowed down the moment when Shannon blacked out to six-thirty-six. He tried some more to crack into Shannon's blackout and then gave up. "I've never seen anything like this," he told Horwitz.

"Okay," he sighed as he rubbed a hand across his face. "Let's go back to when you were thirteen. You've just come home after playing street hockey with your friends. This is the day your mother has been murdered. You're at the front door. What do you see?"

Shannon sat silently, his brow furrowed, thin lines of concentration spreading out from the corners of his eyes. "The front door's not locked," he said in a thin, nervous voice. "And all the lights are out. It's not right. Mom never leaves the door unlocked when she's not home."

"What happens next?"

"I open the door and walk in. I'm in the family room."

"What do you see?"

"It's a mess. There are grocery bags on the floor. Food all over the place. A carton of milk has spilt out. The carpet's wet . . . Something bad's happening . . . I can hear it."

"What do you hear?"

Shannon didn't answer.

"What do you hear?"

"I don't know."

"Try to explain it."

"It's just a noise."

"Where are you now?"

"In the kitchen."

"What do you see?"

Shannon shook his head, his lips pressing hard together.

"Tell me what you see."

Shannon's lips became thin, bloodless lines as they pushed harder together.

"What are you doing in there?"

No answer. "You're doing something," Bennett accused suddenly, the words rushing out of him. "Your dad knew about it, too, didn't he? Didn't he? Answer me!"

Elaine Horwitz blinked stupidly at him. Bennett seemed taken aback by his own question.

"What are you doing?" Horwitz demanded.

"I don't know." Bennett leaned forward, his elbows resting on his knees, his hands cradling his head. He dropped one of his soft, white hands over his eyes and squeezed the flesh around his temples. "I really don't know why I asked that." And he didn't; the thoughts had just bubbled out of him. He had a strange sensation that they had been whispered to him and that other things had been whispered to him. He felt a sudden chill.

Shannon still had his eyes closed. His breathing had become more shallow, to the point of being nonexistent.

"Get him out of it," Elaine Horwitz ordered.

"I'm really sorry, Elaine, I have no idea what made me say those things—"

"Please, just bring him out of it!"

Bennett looked helplessly at Horwitz. He wanted to explain what happened but there was no explanation, at least none that made any sense. Reluctantly, he turned to Shannon to talk him out of his hypnotic trance. Nothing happened. He tried it again without any response.

"What's wrong?" Horwitz asked.

"Sometimes it takes a few times," Bennett lied. He had never had that happen to him before. He had never even heard of that happening before. The golden rule of hypnosis is they always come out when you tell them to—no matter how deep they're in it they come out. No matter what, they come out. He went over it a half dozen more times without any reaction. A panic overtook him. Without realizing it, he grabbed Shannon by the shoulders and started shaking him.

"Stop it!"

"Give me a moment, Elaine—"

"Let go of him now!"

He turned briefly but before he could respond Shannon caught him in the mouth with a left jab, and then a hard right into the middle of his forehead. The hypnotherapist staggered back a few feet and then Shannon was on top of him, sending him crashing to the floor. Shannon's hands found his neck. As his air was cut off, Bennett's face turned a mottled red, his tongue thickening as it pushed its way out of his mouth. As Shannon increased the pressure, Bennett's tongue pushed further out.

Elaine Horwitz watched in horror. She stood paralyzed until it fully hit her what was happening and then she moved quickly, grabbing Shannon around his chest, trying to pull him off. The dullness disappeared from his eyes. He looked puzzled and then disappointed as he stared into Bennett's face. Recognition seeped in and he released his grip.

"I'm sorry," he said as he got off the hypnotherapist.

Bennett started to cough and then rolled onto his knees, vomiting. The bruises along the side of his throat stood out like a knife wound. Shannon stared blankly at them and then sat back down in his chair.

"I'm sorry," he repeated.

After a while the vomiting stopped. Bennett tried to stand but his knees buckled under him and he fell back onto the floor. As he lay in kind of a sprawl, he put a hand to his mouth where he'd been hit and pushed at his teeth with his thumb.

"They're loose," he said.

Horwitz tried not look at him. "Should I call an ambulance?" she asked.

He pulled his hand away from his mouth. "Oh, God," he groaned as he looked at it. "I'm bleeding."

Horwitz called for an ambulance. When the attendants came, they noticed the bruises along Bennett's throat and looked suspiciously at Shannon. One of them asked what happened.

"There was an accident," Horwitz explained weakly.

They didn't seem to like that explanation until Shannon showed them his police badge. Then they put Bennett on a stretcher. After they left, Elaine Horwitz found she couldn't stop shaking. In a voice that didn't sound quite right to her, she told Shannon not to blame himself for what happened.

"You were someplace pretty awful, weren't you?" she asked.

Shannon didn't say anything.

"You were back with your mother. But you weren't alone, were you, Bill? He was there with you."

Shannon murmured that he didn't know what she was talking about.

The adrenaline of the last twenty minutes caught up to her. "I'm not stupid," she said, her voice cracking. "I saw the way you attacked Mark. I saw the look on your face. You haven't been telling me the truth about how your mother died."

She paused, waiting for him to say something. When he didn't, she told him she couldn't see him anymore. "I can't treat you if you're going to lie to me," she said stiffly.

He looked up at her briefly, then without saying a word, got up and walked out of her office. As the door closed behind him,

Elaine Horwitz felt a chill run through her. She grabbed herself and leaned forward, trying to keep from shaking. She couldn't stop it, though. It went through her like an electric current. It made her teeth chatter. And then she got hysterical.

Chapter 21

The bartender gave Shannon a tired, well-practiced smile. "What can I get you, buddy?"

Shannon asked for a bourbon. He was sitting at the bar at the Black Rose, sitting at the same stool he had sat on before blacking out a week earlier. The bartender poured him a shot and slid it in front of him. He asked if Shannon wanted to start a tab.

Shannon nodded. He didn't recognize the guy but that didn't mean anything. He held out his hand and introduced himself. The bartender, a bit dubiously, accepted it and gave back his name as Tom Morton.

"Tom, let me ask you something. Do you remember seeing me here a week ago?"

"I don't get you, buddy."

Shannon showed an embarrassed grin. "About a week ago I got really shit-faced and am trying to piece some stuff together. I know I was drinking here around six-thirty. I'm trying to figure out what I did afterwards."

The bartender's broad face darkened. "Yeah," he said, nodding, "I remember you."

"Was I with anyone?"

The bartender removed the shot glass from in front of Shannon. "I think you better leave."

"Why's that?"

"Come on, buddy, get out of here, okay?" The bartender

started to reach for something under the bar. Shannon took his badge out and laid it out in front of him. As the bartender looked at it he moved away from what he'd been reaching for.

"You're a cop?" he asked, his voice sounding queer.

"That's right. What's going on?"

The bartender didn't say anything.

"I asked you what's going on?"

"Yesterday a couple of FBI agents were in here showing your picture around," he said, a pained expression creasing his face. "That's how come I remember you."

"That's it?"

There was a hesitation while he looked as if he had a bad attack of gas, and then he told Shannon they wanted to know if he had left with anyone. "They were also showing another picture around."

Shannon stared at him until he let it out that it was a picture of the woman who had been stabbed to death on Beacon Hill the previous week.

"They wanted to know if you met her here," he added.

"Did I?"

The bartender gave Shannon an odd look. "I don't even remember you here," he said. "They came back later and asked around to some of our regulars. Betty was the only one who remembered you. She said you were drinking alone."

The bartender put the shot glass back in front of Shannon. "On the house," he said before walking away.

Shannon looked long and hard at it. His mouth all of a sudden felt dry. He found himself wanting the drink, wanting it badly. His hand shook as he picked it up. He held the glass for a moment, his arm stiff, the joints in his fingers throbbing. Some of the alcohol spilled on his sleeve. With some pain, he forced the glass back onto the bar.

He got up and left, the bourbon softly whispering to him . . .

Of course, Elaine had been right earlier, he had gone someplace pretty awful. He had gone right where the hypnotherapist had led him. Right back to Herbert Winters.

As he left the Black Rose, Shannon found himself wondering about the dreams he'd been having, about why he felt so helpless in them. Why he felt so weak and ineffectual in them. Earlier, when he was under hypnosis and thought he was lashing out at Herbert Winters—when he thought he was squeezing the life out of him—it felt better than anything he could remember. When he realized it wasn't Winters but the hypnotherapist, for a brief moment anyway, he didn't want to let go. He didn't want to give up that feeling. He would've given anything to have been able to hold on to it.

But there was nothing to hold on to.

Shannon drove aimlessly as he tried to sort the events out in his mind. He had almost killed that man because of where he'd been brought to. What he didn't know was if he had ever been brought there before—if that was where he went during his blackouts—because if he did, God knows what he would be capable of.

He tried to swallow. His mouth felt as if he had gargled with a handful of sand. As he drove past a liquor store, he involuntarily slowed down. The world seemed to slow down with him. A bottle of bourbon would make everything so much easier. Especially after a few shots. Especially then.

He didn't stop for the booze. As much as he wanted to, he didn't stop. Instead, he headed towards the Central Square precinct. He wasn't even sure why until he got there.

Chapter 22

As Shannon made his way through the precinct, he passed DiGrazia at his desk and gave him a nod. The look DiGrazia returned stopped him dead in his tracks. He walked over to his partner and asked what was eating him.

DiGrazia had turned back to his paperwork. He ignored Shannon.

"It sure looks like something's eating you. Come on, what's your problem?"

"Whatever it is, it's not as big as the one you've got," DiGrazia murmured without looking up.

"What are you talking about?"

DiGrazia just smirked. His eyes, though, remained dead.

Shannon pulled up a chair. "Look," he said, "if you're pissed at me for not helping interrogate Roberson or Hartwell's ex's, I'm sorry, I couldn't. I've been put on desk duty. Brady wants me to keep away from the investigation for the time being."

"Why would I want you to help me interrogate them?"

"What you were telling me before—"

"Forget that," DiGrazia said. "I wasn't thinking straight. Probably suffering from sleep deprivation. The FBI's right. These ain't no paid hits. What we got is a true psychopath. But where the FBI is fucked is the way they're going at it. You know why?"

Shannon shook his head.

"I'll tell you, pal. I don't think Roberson and the other two were killed by the same guy."

"Why's that?"

DiGrazia showed a thin smile, his teeth barely breaking through it. He stared at Shannon for a long moment before asking if something was wrong. "You sound kind of sick," he added.

"Nothing's wrong. Why weren't they killed by the same guy?"

"Are you sure nothing's wrong?" DiGrazia asked, ignoring Shannon's question. "Your voice doesn't sound quite right. Like maybe you need a drink of water or something."

"Cut the crap, okay? You got something to say, spit it out."

DiGrazia shook his head, making a tsking-type noise. "Getting kind of touchy, are we? Now what was I talking about—oh yeah, why Roberson wasn't killed by the same guy as the other two. It's really pretty simple. She was stabbed in the throat. The other two were stabbed in the mouth. We got different individuals doing these murders. The FBI shouldn't've made the assumption they did. They should be doing what I'm doing right now. Want to guess what that is?"

Shannon found himself shaking his head.

"I'm doing a computer search for other murders where women have been stabbed in the mouth. I figure twenty years is enough to go back—"

DiGrazia stopped himself and gave Shannon a long, thoughtful look. "You don't look so good all of a sudden," he said. "What's wrong, sick or something? Jesus, you look like you're falling apart right in front of me." There was no warmth or empathy in his eyes, nothing but a cold detachment.

"Man, you're white as a sheet," DiGrazia continued after a long moment, his bare-fanged smile tightening. "You look like you've just seen a ghost. Is that what's troubling you, pal, ghosts around?"

Shannon didn't say anything. He just turned and walked away.

DiGrazia watched as his partner made his way down the hallway. Shannon's reaction was interesting. More than interesting. Even if he hadn't had that dream he'd think so. And maybe even if he hadn't gotten those twenty-year-old newspaper clippings sent to him—maybe even then . . .

That morning he had found an eight-and-a-half-by-eleven-inch envelope against his apartment door. Stuffed inside were photostatic copies of newspaper clippings. The articles were twenty years old and detailed the murder of Shannon's mother. He had read them halfway through before putting gloves on. Now the envelope and its contents were inside a plastic evidence bag locked away in his bottom desk drawer.

He hadn't yet decided what to do with them. He would like to get them dusted for fingerprints because if there were any, and they matched Shannon's, that would be that. Because if Shannon had left it for him, it would've been a cry for help; a plea to stop him before he killed again. Word had come down that physical evidence had cleared Shannon of the Roberson murder, but as he had reminded Shannon, Roberson hadn't been stabbed in the mouth. The other two had. Just like Shannon's mother.

And that dream he had . . .

DiGrazia almost never remembered his dreams, but this one he couldn't get out of his mind. It was so damn real, so damn much like being pulled through a nightmare. Every god-awful detail of it.

In it DiGrazia had become aware of a presence nearby, a presence that seemed to have floated out of nowhere. As it moved towards him he could smell it as if it were real, he could just about taste it in his throat. It was worse than raw sewage.

Worse than anything he had ever imagined. And it was so strong, so overpowering . . .

It was next to DiGrazia then. Without looking at it, DiGrazia knew that it was something obscene, something malignant. The smell, though, kept DiGrazia from facing it. Even if he could have, there wouldn't have been much for him to see because it kept too close to him, most of the time right up against him as it whispered into his ear.

DiGrazia at times caught brief glimpses of it. He remembered seeing its mouth, a tiny slit that was more of a knife wound than anything else. The image of it stood out in his mind. Along with those hands; bloated, dead-white hands.

It told DiGrazia that he was who Shannon became when he blacked out. That he was the one in control when the two women were murdered. It—he—talked for a long time, his breath hot and fetid against DiGrazia's ear. His voice becoming excited as he talked about the murders, about the horror each woman went through. The hotness of his breath was unbearable. He told DiGrazia that he appeared briefly in November. He asked DiGrazia to seriously consider how Shannon was able to find Janice Rowley's body and whether Roper was a little too neatly packaged as her murderer. He promised there would be more murders. That he was just getting his second wind.

DiGrazia woke up with his heart pounding. He felt dirtier than he had ever felt in his life. It was as if that smell had somehow permeated through his dream and had gotten into his skin and his hair. For a brief heartbeat he could smell it and it sent his stomach reeling and him stumbling for the bathroom. After he was done he took a long shower, scrubbing himself raw. Later, he found a bottle of whiskey and tried to make sense of his dream.

He had just about decided it was nothing but his nerves, and maybe some resentment towards his partner. After all, he got his ass chewed off by Brady for keeping Shannon's blackouts a secret. But when he found that envelope outside his door and read through the clippings, he began to look at the dream differently. And he couldn't keep from thinking about the obvious. He couldn't keep from replaying that dream. That god-awful dream . . .

DiGrazia made a decision about the evidence bag locked away in his desk. Later, he would check its contents for prints. If there were any and they matched Shannon's, he'd nail his partner to a cross. He'd fucking skin him alive.

Shannon stood quietly in front of Dr. Ronald Chaucy's office. His talk with DiGrazia had unnerved him and he wasn't quite sure what to do next. He started to move away and then found himself opening Chaucy's office door and walking in. Dr. Chaucy, a plump man of about fifty, had his eyes closed and his hands folded across his belly. The doctor had been working as a psychiatrist for the Cambridge Police Department for fifteen years, mostly doing prisoner evaluations, occasionally evaluating the competency of an officer. He opened an eye as the door closed behind Shannon and reluctantly pushed himself upright.

"Hello, Bill," he murmured as he cleared his throat. His eyes bulged slightly from his round face. Thick layers of skin sagged under his jaw. "Martin told me you'd be coming around."

"Sorry for interrupting your nap."

"I was meditating." Chaucy shrugged his rounded, stooped shoulders. "Why don't you take a seat?" Chaucy said as he turned towards his desk and picked a few papers from it. As he read through them, a frown pulled down his lips. He reached back to his desk and picked up a notepad and a pen.

"Martin filled me in somewhat," he said. "Why don't you tell me what's going on with you, Bill?"

Shannon sat across from the psychiatrist. "I'll tell you, Ron, I really don't know."

"Tell me about your blackouts—are drugs or alcohol involved?"

"I was drinking heavily before it happened." Shannon hesitated. "But I don't think the booze had anything to do with it."

"Uh huh." Chaucy scribbled something into his notepad. "Why's that?"

"I just don't think so."

"How often do you have these blackouts?"

"Once a year."

Dr. Chaucy blinked several times. "What do you mean, once a year?"

"I black out every year around this time. I usually come out of it a week later."

"Every year . . ." Some more scribbling. "Going back how far?"

"I don't know, probably about ten years now."

"You don't remember when it first happened?"

"It's been going on for ten years now." Shannon tried to smile. "I kind've gotten used to it by now."

"How frequently do you have these blackouts?"

"As I said, once a year."

Chaucy pushed a hand across his face. When it passed over his mouth a deep scowl was left behind. "You have no memory at all during these episodes?"

"None at all."

"And the duration's usually a week?"

"Usually. Sometimes it's a day or two longer, sometimes a day or two less. This last time it was less."

Chaucy's scowl deepened. His eyes glazed over as he stared at Shannon. "What's behind these blackouts, Bill?"

"I don't know." Shannon forced a sick smile. A heavy weariness passed through him like a chill. All he wanted to do at that moment was find a place to lie down. "My mom was murdered February tenth. I was thirteen at the time and I discovered her body when I came home from school. My therapist thinks I black out to get through that day. I don't know what I think anymore."

"How was your mother murdered?"

"She died of asphyxiation."

Chaucy was nodding slowly. A transformation had occurred. It was subtle, but obvious. Shannon realized the psychiatrist was now viewing him as some sort of specimen instead of as a colleague.

"What do you think you do during your blackouts?"

"I don't know."

"You must have some idea."

"I really don't know." Shannon shrugged weakly. "What usually happens when a person blacks out?"

"What do you think happens?"

"I don't know. Does another personality take over?"

"You think you have multiple personalities?"

"That's not what I said. I was just asking what usually happens when people black out."

Chaucy rested his notepad on his lap and brought his hands up to his chin, pushing his fingers together and forming an apex. His jowls drooped softly over the tips of his fingers. "Why do you think another personality is taking over when you black out?"

"I don't—"

"Yes, you do, Bill," Chaucy stated softly, expressionless, his eyes staring at Shannon as if he were a lab animal. "Do voices tell you about these other personalities?"

"Ron, I don't hear any voices—"

"Or do you see them in your dreams?"

Shannon felt his heart drop to his feet. He tried to say something but couldn't.

"What do they tell you, Bill? What do they tell you about Phyllis Roberson or Linda Cassen or Rose Hartwell?"

"I don't know what you're talking about." Shannon pushed himself out of his chair. When Chaucy listed those dead women, Elaine Horwitz's name popped into Shannon's mind. A sense of urgency got him to his feet. "I have to go," he said as he stumbled forward. "We can finish this later."

Dr. Ron Chaucy looked alarmed. "Bill, please, sit down." He started to get up but Shannon was already out the door.

Chapter 23

Charlie Winters had a nice, warm feeling inside as he lay curled up in the back of Elaine Horwitz's metallic blue Saab. It had gotten overcast and a thin drizzle of freezing rain had started to fall. Winters knew she wouldn't bother looking in the backseat. She'd notice him eventually, but not until it was too late. At least for her, anyway.

He inched his way up and peered out the side window before sinking back down. The layout was picture perfect. The car was parked behind the brownstone Horwitz had her office in. The lot was small—only four cars parked in it—and secluded from view. No witnesses, no one to hear her scream.

He lay back down and closed his eyes and listened to the soft patter of freezing rain against the roof of the car. It soothed him. As he relaxed, he visualized what was going to happen. He let it unwind frame by frame, like a movie playing out in slow motion. The clicking of high heels as Elaine Horwitz rushes from her building to get out of the raw weather. Door swinging open. Her sitting in the front seat, too preoccupied to bother looking around. A sock shoved in her mouth and Winters's hand hard against her throat applying just enough pressure to squeeze the consciousness out of her. Then dumping her limp body into the trunk and hog-tying it with the quickness of a rodeo veteran. All told, no more than thirty seconds elapsing. Winters had done it enough times in the past to know how long it would take.

His hand inched into his jacket pocket and fingered an envelope containing strands of Shannon's hair. Earlier in the day, he had visited Shannon's apartment. The hair was taken from Shannon's hairbrush. Later, much later, a few strands would be placed on Horwitz's body. One or two gripped within her dead hand.

Slowly, he played out in his mind what was going to happen to the psychologist and it brought a genuine smile to his lips. As he lay in the back of the Saab he started to feel nostalgic. It was like when Herbie was alive and they would hide together in their victims' cars. Most of them never bothered looking in back before getting in. The few that did, well, it didn't help them any because there was never anyone around to hear their screams. And they never got a chance to scream for long.

Winters felt a heaviness pull at his eyelids. His body sunk deeply into the plush leather. It was four-thirty. Enough time for a little cat nap.

The sound of footsteps woke him. He stretched lazily and sniffed in the air, trying to smell his victim. The footsteps stopped, then someone talking. Two people talking. As he recognized the voices, he froze. From the position he was lying in he could see Shannon and Elaine Horwitz in the rearview mirror. They were less than twenty feet away.

Winters pushed the rear passenger door open and crawled out. A Honda was next to Horwitz's Saab. He tried but couldn't squeeze his thick body under it. To the right was a Dumpster. Keeping on his hands and knees he made his way over to it.

He pushed himself as close to the Dumpster as he could. From the Saab, with the lights on, he'd be seen. In his mind's eye he imagined the headlights turning on and Shannon locking eyes on him from the passenger seat. Acting solely on instinct, he boosted himself up until he was hanging halfway over the open Dumpster and then fell in.

Shannon took an involuntary step towards the noise. "What was that?"

Horwitz appeared emotionally wrecked, her face drawn, her lips as bloodless as the thin layers of snow coating the ground. "What was what?"

"That noise. Something's in there."

"I don't know. Either a raccoon or a cat. What difference does it make?" A sudden calm relaxed her features. The corner of her mouth pulled up slightly. "Bill," she said, "this is pointless. I shouldn't see you anymore as your therapist. I'm not up to it."

"I still don't understand why."

"For one, treating multiple personality disorders is beyond my training. You need clinical help—a psychiatrist specializing in this area."

"But you've been telling me you don't think that's my problem."

"It doesn't matter, you seem to think it is."

"I don't know." Shannon was shaking his head. "What else could be happening to me when I black out?"

"Most people who suffer from extended memory lapses or blackouts do not have multiple personalities. Sometimes it's physical, most often it's caused by the subconscious needing to suppress certain memories. Multiple personalities are very rare."

Elaine Horwitz stopped and gave Shannon an odd look, almost as if she were seeing him for the first time. "You've had these suspicions for a long time, haven't you?"

"I don't know. I don't think so. It's . . . it's just those dreams I've been having." Shannon looked helplessly at her.

Dammit, Horwitz thought, not the wounded-deer look.

"All I know," Shannon continued, "is that right now I'm

hanging on by a thread and seeing you is one of the few things keeping me going."

"Regardless of Freud, dreams don't necessarily mean anything." Elaine Horwitz let out a long sigh. "If I were to continue seeing you, I'd need you to be completely honest with me. You can't keep holding things back from me."

Shannon nodded weakly.

Horwitz felt her resolve melt away as she looked at him. For some reason she didn't fully understand she felt her eyes starting to tear.

"I'm getting all wet out here," she said, struggling to keep from crying and laughing at the same time. She grabbed his hand and gave it a squeeze. "Why don't we go to Harvard Street, get some coffee and continue this?"

Shannon followed Horwitz to her car. As he opened the passenger door he only half noticed the envelope lying in the rain. Inside, Elaine Horwitz turned to him.

"Do you smell something?" she asked, wrinkling her nose.

Shannon smelled it, also. A faint odor of something rotting. It was vaguely familiar.

"Maybe an animal got under the engine and died," Shannon suggested.

They opened the hood but didn't find anything.

As the Saab pulled away, Charlie Winters emerged from the Dumpster. Pieces of ice and garbage fell off him as he dropped to the ground. He stood for a long moment in the twilight, his face chalk white, his skin wet and shimmering with rage.

At first there was nothing but violence swirling within him, but as he stood immobile, his gloved hands clenching and unclenching, he started to feel the withdrawal symptoms; a suffocating tightness filling up his chest and then his body shaking uncontrollably. The anticipation had been building up for days, and like an addict getting a taste of the junk only to then have the needle ripped from his fingers, he now needed his fix more than ever.

The shaking was hitting him hard, leaving him barely able to hobble out of the lot. Being careful earlier, he had parked his car eight blocks away. Those eight blocks were now an eternity. He cursed Shannon and then the rest of mankind. As he made his way through the neighborhood, walking in short, shuffling steps, the people he passed gave him a wide berth, the more perceptive ones crossing the street at the sight of him. He'd look back over his shoulder at each one of them, a dryness in his mouth, his head pounding, trying to decide if they'd do. Trying to decide how safe they would be. How easy they would be.

As he hobbled along he spotted her—a college girl, no more than eighteen, struggling with both groceries and the front vestibule door of a small brick apartment building. He swallowed hard as he watched her, his throat constricting. Blindly, automatically, he started to move. A patrol car pulled up next to him. The officer in it shined a flashlight in his face.

"Sir, I would like to talk with you."

Winters turned towards the patrol car, his eyes squinting against the light. Behind him he could hear the vestibule door closing shut. The echo of it vibrated in his head.

"Did you hear me?" the officer repeated.

"I heard you," Winters whispered in a soft, wispy, singsong voice.

"Do you live in Brookline?"

The officer holding the flashlight was middle-aged with a square, red face and a marine style crewcut. He involuntarily grimaced as he smelled Winters.

"Do I have to live in Brookline?" Winters asked, a soft lisp worming its way into his voice.

"What are you doing here?"

"I'm walking to my car. Is there a law against that?"

The officer kept the flashlight aimed at Winters's face. "Would you like to tell me how you got so dirty?"

"Poor personal hygiene. Again, is that breaking any law?"

The flashlight moved up and down over Winters before settling back on his face. Winters was asked for identification.

"And why do you need that?"

A shadow dropped over the officer's eyes. "I'll only ask you once," he said. The muscles along his jaw tightened as he reached out to open the door.

Winters handed him the Washington State driver's license he got after he was released from prison. The officer took it from him and told him to wait. He then rolled up the window of the patrol car and got on the police radio.

Winters stood in the freezing rain and waited, the water running streaks of dirt and grime down his face. After about five minutes, he knocked on the window of the patrol car. The officer inside gave him a dull stare, his hand resting on his service revolver.

"Excuse me, Officer," Winters said, his soft, singsong voice straining to be pleasant. "It's cold and I'm getting wet. And I think I'm beginning to feel ill. I would like my license back."

"You just stay put," the officer ordered.

"I would at least like to see your identification," Winters said, his thin, twisted lips pulled up cheerfully. "I'd like to know who I'm going to sue for this harassment."

The officer looked long and hard at Winters and then, with his eyes dulling a bit, flashed him his identification. Winters made a mental note of his name.

"Do you mind if I sit in the patrol car?" Winters asked.

"You just stand out there and wait."

Ten more minutes passed before the officer rolled down the

window and asked for a local address. Charlie Winters gave him the rooming house in Somerville he was staying at. It was another ten minutes before the officer opened the door of the cruiser and stepped out. He walked over to Winters until he was no more than a foot away. If he could've stomached it he would've gotten closer. Using his right hand he started to slide his handcuffs from his belt.

Winters spoke quickly, softly, "I'm sure at this point you know about my prison record. I'm sure you also know I've paid my debt to society, and that there are no outstanding warrants out for me. What you don't know is that I spent my twenty years in prison studying law books so I'd be able to sue anyone who chooses not to observe my constitutional rights."

The officer hesitated. After a long ten-count the handcuffs slipped back onto his belt. "What are you doing in this neighborhood?" he demanded.

Winters fingered his malformed chin. "I told you before, I'm walking to my car."

"Yeah, I think you're doing a little shopping."

Winters didn't say anything.

"Looking for another boy to put in your trunk?"

Again, Winters didn't respond. The officer spat on the sidewalk, nearly hitting Winters's boots. "I don't want you ever in Brookline again," he said.

"I thought this was a free country."

"That's a mistake pedophiles like you make."

"I'm not a pedophile," Winters said with both sincerity and hurt.

The officer held out Charlie Winters's license, waited until Winters started to reach for it, and then dropped it. Winters reached down and picked it up off the ground.

"You've kept me out here over a half hour," Winters said. "I'm wet and I feel ill. Could you give me a ride to my car?"

The officer didn't bother answering him. He got back into his patrol car and then followed alongside Winters as he hobbled the remaining three blocks to his beat-up Subaru.

The officer pulled the cruiser up to a forty-five-degree angle to the Subaru, blocking it from being able to pull away. He got out and shined his flashlight through its interior.

"Would you mind opening the trunk?" he asked.

"Do you have a warrant?"

The officer shook his head. "If you'd like to wait, I could try and get one tomorrow morning. We could make a night out of it."

The trunk was opened. As the officer bent over it and poked around, it was all Charlie Winters could do to keep from slamming the trunk on the cop's neck. It just wouldn't work. He'd have the cop but they'd have him. Maybe not right away, but eventually. So all he could do was stand there and take it. Blood boiled in his eyes as he plastered a thin smile across his face.

When the officer was done he returned to his patrol car and pulled it up and waited for Winters. He followed Winters out of Brookline and halfway through Boston before veering off. All the while Charlie Winters made plans for him. He recited the cop's name to himself. Ed Podansky. Eddie Podansky. Eddie baby.

A family man, right, Eddie baby? Yeah, I'm sure you are. Wife and kiddies, right? More the merrier, Eddie, more the merrier. 'Cause we'll all have a big surprise for you later tonight; me and your fat little wife and your fat little kids. Chips off the old block, are they? Well, their little faces will be burning in the window for you tonight. Guaranteed. The rest of them might be someplace else, but their faces, Eddie, their piece-of-shit, fat, little faces . . .

As he pulled up to a pay phone he was feeling better. Information didn't have an Ed Podansky listed in Brookline but did have one in Brighton. He got the number and tried calling it.

An answering machine clicked on and then the cop's tired voice saying he couldn't come to the phone right now but please leave a message.

He couldn't come to the phone . . . The answering machine message shouldn't have been like that. It should've been something about how him and his fat-assed wife couldn't talk now because they were too busy beating their children or banging away at each other. It should've been something like that. Since it wasn't, the cop had to've been divorced with his wife and kiddies living elsewhere. He knew they existed. Charlie Winters could feel their existence. Eventually he'd find them in his dreams, but not for tonight. For tonight it would have to be someone else.

He spotted her then. The someone else. A hooker, young, strung out on heroin, on the street trying to hustle some money. She looked tired and worn out and cold. All she was wearing was a short, black leather jacket and matching mini-skirt and boots. As cars rolled by, she halfheartedly tried to slow them down by flashing them some skin. There weren't any takers. Winters sighed to himself as he put the phone back down. Hookers were cheap and easy and not all that satisfying. How can you really enjoy yourself when they're faking the emotion and not giving a shit about what's happening? Oh well, Winters thought sadly to himself as he headed across the street. Oh well, a body's a body.

Chapter 24

Did he know about them?

Shannon could honestly answer that he didn't. Whether he had suspicions about them was another matter. Any lawyer cross-examining him on the stand would have a hard time proving otherwise.

But he sort of knew about them, didn't he? About the things Susie would tell when he'd be fading in and out around his yearly breakdowns. The way she'd claim he'd act. But, then again, Susie had stopped telling him about those things years ago, and it was easier to simply ignore, to pretend they never happened . . .

His suspicions went further back than Susie, though. They went back to when he was a teenager living in California. Back to maybe a year after his mom's death. By then, he and his dad had stopped acknowledging each other's existence. They lived in the same house, cooked food in the same kitchen, sometimes sat in the same rooms, but they never talked or even looked at each other. More specifically, they'd look through each other. Days, sometimes weeks, of that would go by; all the while a low burning rage would be filling up Shannon's lungs, both stifling and suffocating him. When the pressure would get too great, when he could no longer breathe because of it, he'd have to get someplace alone. Then it would all come out of him; the rage and the anger and the tears. It would pour out of him like the insides from a gutted animal.

But did they really exist? Were they voices whispering to him or was it just noise echoing through his mind? Because there was nothing concrete, nothing substantial. Only a vague sensation of whispers dying deep in his head.

But he'd have a sense of what the whispers were telling him (if they were, indeed, whispers and not simply his own mind racing towards a breakdown), or more specifically, what the whispers were saying, because they never seemed directed towards him. About what a patsy he was being or if they were in his shoes they'd kick the shit out of the old man instead of the wall of his room or how unfair it all was. Especially, how unfair it all was.

Back then he ignored them. But he did have suspicions about them.

He had gotten back late that night. Susie eyed him somewhat suspiciously as he walked into their apartment but accepted his explanation that he'd had a late session with his therapist. For the most part it was true. He and Elaine had spent hours talking, first at a coffee shop and then at a restaurant.

Elaine had insisted on knowing the truth and Shannon had broken down and told her all of it, the words just sort of bubbling out of him. He told her what he found when he got home the day his mother was murdered. He told her the things Herbert Winters had done to him and what his father later accused him of. When he was done he couldn't look at her. Instead of feeling any sense of relief, all he felt was disgust.

"Bill, there's nothing for you to be ashamed of."

"Yeah, right."

"Bill, please, look at me."

He forced his eyes up to where he was looking at her. "You know," he said, "when I picture my mom in my mind I can only see her dead. I'd give anything if I could close my eyes and see her alive."

"Do you have any pictures of her?"

"Not a single one." He shook his head. "The only image I've got of her is what's in my head."

"I'm so sorry—"

"There's nothing for you to be sorry about."

"I can still feel for you, Bill. Knowing what you went through, I'm amazed at how well adjusted you've turned out."

Shannon couldn't help laughing. "Yeah, I could be a poster boy for mental health, couldn't I? Me and all the little people living inside me. We could make it a group shot."

"First of all, I doubt you're suffering from multiple personality disorder. As I've been telling you all night, your dreams are not any indication of it and I haven't seen any symptoms. Second, most of the year you are healthy."

"Yeah, but not all of the year."

"No, not all of the year. But considering what you suffered through, first with your mother's murder and then all those years of emotional abuse from your father, most of the year's pretty good. We just have to figure out how keep you from breaking down during that one small opening every year."

Elaine Horwitz took a sip of wine, a warm smile spreading over her lips. The smile made its way up to her eyes, leaving them sparkling.

"You know," she said, "for the first time since I've been treating you I really feel positive. Like we've turned a corner."

Shannon didn't feel quite so optimistic, but he kept quiet about it. If nothing else, it was nice to see Elaine smiling. They finished their dinner. Elaine, over coffee, told him she'd find a psychiatrist who specialized in multiple personality disorder to evaluate him but she didn't believe anything would come of it.

★ ★ ★ ★ ★

That was all hours ago. It was now almost four in the morning. Too quiet to sleep. Too damn quiet to do much of anything. He could feel Susie's small, warm body against him. He could feel her chest barely rising with each breath. So quiet. Eventually, he closed his eyes and stopped thinking. Eventually.

Winters was waiting for him. As Shannon drifted into unconsciousness he saw Winters off in the distance, his malformed face cold and expressionless. Like polluted ice. From far away he could smell the foulness from him. As Shannon watched, Winters's bloated body flew towards him.

"I've got a lot to tell you, Billy Boy," Winters breathed in his singsong voice as he moved closer, now only a foot from Shannon's face. "You've been a busy little shit tonight. We've both been busy tonight."

Shannon froze. For a moment he thought about lashing out at Winters. As he imagined himself grabbing Winters by the throat, as he imagine himself throttling that smirking thing, he felt his strength drain out of him. His arms fell dead at his side.

"I don't know what you're talking about," he forced himself to say.

"Sure you do. You let me out tonight and I had fun, Billy. We both had a hell of a time."

"I still don't know what you're talking about."

"No, you don't, do you?" Winters asked, bemused. "You don't even know anymore when you let me out, huh? But you do know I'm in you. You know I've been fermenting inside you for years, Billy Boy, getting nice and ripe. You can smell the ripeness, can't you? Breathe deeply, Billy Boy."

Winters took a long, deep breath and winked. "I got news for you, Billy, there are others, but I'm the dominant one inside you now. I'm the one who comes out whenever I want, 'cause in reality I'm the true essence of you."

Winters watched as the numbness spread across Shannon's face. "What's the matter, boy?" he asked, "the truth a little too painful?"

"That's nothing but crap—"

Winters shook his head sadly, his small knife-wound of a mouth smiling sympathetically. "You know it's the truth, boy. You know you let me out after you left that redheaded sweet thing of yours. What's too painful to remember, we simply choose to forget, is that it? Well, let me refresh your memory, boy. Let me tell you what we did tonight.

"We found us a whore, Billy," Winters continued after waiting patiently for Shannon to respond, "just a young thing, no more than eighteen. A cold, unhappy, frightened little girl. And she was exactly what we were looking for, Billy. Exactly what we were looking for. And in a way we were exactly what she was looking for.

"A knife just wouldn't do for tonight. Not the way we were feeling. For tonight we needed something special. You remember all the things we used? You remember what we pushed into her until she hemorrhaged and died? Think hard and try to remember. Try and remember how long it took."

Shannon looked like he was deep in thought. Winters's grin turned darkly obscene. "Think harder, Billy Boy. Give it everything you got."

"That smell," Shannon murmured.

Winters laughed. "Just like fresh gardenias, huh?"

"Earlier today. That smell . . ."

"What the hell are you talking about?"

"It was in Elaine's car. We both smelled it when we got in. I thought an animal had died under her hood."

Winters blinked twice.

"It was much fainter than this. But it's the same smell."

The little color in Winters's face drained out of it. His slit mouth froze into a forced grin. "You're confused, Billy."

"No, that smell—"

"Yeah, you are, you little shit. You're losing your mind, Billy Boy. You don't know whether you're coming or going anymore."

"I know about that smell."

"You know why you know it, huh?" There was a long pause. "You want to know why you know it?"

Winters stopped, a caginess momentarily pushing his lips into a small circle. When he continued his soft doughy features were relaxed, his grin again playful.

"You know it because it's from inside you, Billy. Deep inside you. It comes out when you let me out and sometimes even a few hours before me. And you did let me out tonight. Liza Keenan would attest to it if she could. If rigor mortis hadn't frozen that cute little mouth of hers, she'd tell us all about it, if she still had a tongue that is. Remember that name, Billy Boy. Liza Keenan. Try and remember all the fun we had with that whore."

Winters's image started to drift away. Shannon stood and watched as it floated off into the distance and then disappeared completely. Then there was nothing but blackness. A moment later there wasn't even that.

When Shannon woke later, he thought about his dream. He played it back in his mind slowly, analyzing each detail of it. What Winters had told him about the smell was bullshit. It had been in Elaine's car before either of them had gotten into it. The rest of the dream was bullshit, also. He could account for every minute from when he left Elaine to when he showed up at home. The dream was nothing but crap.

Still, he wondered about that smell. About what it was doing in Elaine Horwitz's car.

★ ★ ★ ★ ★

Joe DiGrazia showed up later that morning. As Susan opened the door for him, he looked through her, his face showing as much compassion as a granite block.

"I need to talk to your husband," he told her.

"Hi, Joe. Bill's in the bed—"

DiGrazia brushed past her. Susan, surprised, followed him to the bedroom. Shannon propped himself up as his partner walked in.

"I'd like to talk to your husband alone," DiGrazia grunted over his shoulder.

"Is this about Rose?" Susan asked.

"Rose Hartwell?"

"Yes."

DiGrazia slowly turned to face her, his granite face clouding ominously. "Why'd you ask that?"

Susan tried to smile but it got stuck halfway. "I-I don't know. I guess because Bill hasn't said anything to me about it."

"That's kind of odd, isn't it? Your neighbor gets murdered and your husband, who's a cop, doesn't tell you anything about it. Why do you think that is?"

"Joe, leave her alone."

"No, I want to hear what Susie has to say."

"I said leave her alone," Shannon ordered. He turned to his wife and suggested maybe it would be better if he and Joe talked in private. Susan looked apprehensively at him, doubt wrecking her mouth. She nodded and left the room.

"What's going on with you, Joe?" Shannon asked after the door closed behind his wife.

"Come on, buddy boy, you should know better than that."

"What are you here for?"

"What do you think I'm here for?"

Shannon sighed wearily. "I'm not in the mood for this. Cut

the crap, okay?"

"No, come on. You're a bright guy. Tell me what I'm here for."

"I have no idea."

"You've been with me on enough murder investigations. Come on, make a guess."

Shannon didn't say anything.

"You disappoint me, partner," DiGrazia said, shaking his head as he showed his disappointment. "I want to search your apartment. If I have to, I'll get a warrant."

"Why?"

"I have my reasons. Do I have to get a search warrant?"

"Joe, I didn't kill those women."

DiGrazia shrugged nonchalantly. "I believe you, but we don't know what happens when you black out. We don't know who takes over then."

Shannon felt himself trying to swallow. "What are you talking about?"

"Maybe you got another personality inside you. Maybe he's the one who killed those women."

"W-why do you think that?"

DiGrazia shrugged again and let a smirk form over his lips. "Let's call it a hunch, partner."

Shannon felt very cold around his temples. He only half heard himself ask DiGrazia what he was looking for. DiGrazia started to say something but stopped himself. His smirk disappeared. Doubt softened the hard ridges around his eyes. He pulled an envelope from his inside coat pocket and handed it to Shannon. Inside were the photostatic articles that had been left outside of DiGrazia's apartment. As Shannon read through them he felt his heart turn to cold sludge and then sink to his feet. Before DiGrazia had showed up he had half convinced himself that Herbert Winters was somehow still alive, that he didn't really leave Winters with his head hanging by a thread, and that Winters was now out there committing these murders. It was the only thing that made sense. At least it explained that smell in Elaine's car and the dreams he'd been having. The articles ended that possibility. It stuck a goddamn stake right through it.

"How'd you get these?" Shannon asked.

"They were left outside my apartment."

"Any idea who left them?"

"I got a pretty good idea."

"Joe, they didn't come from me," Shannon said. One of the articles showed a wedding shot of his mother, Lily. She couldn't have been more than twenty in it. It was the first time since her murder he could imagine her without a knife sticking out of her mouth, without her dead eyes staring up at him. Without rigor mortis hardening her skin. He had forgotten how beautiful she was, how alive she once was. He had forgotten how much he missed her.

"I was hospitalized for six months after the murder," Shannon said, his eyes transfixed on his mother's picture. "I never saw any of these." He felt a grittiness on the paper. "You dusted for prints?"

"Yeah. There was nothing. I'd like to search your apartment."

"I told you I never saw any of these."

"Yeah, I know you did." DiGrazia started to rub his knuckles impatiently. "Maybe you didn't. Maybe you got other personalities that collected them for you. I've got to know if the originals are here."

Shannon felt himself choking up as he looked at his mother's picture. "Go ahead," he said. "Search all you want."

DiGrazia started on the bureau, methodically searching through each drawer and then pulling them out and checking the inside of the wooden frame. Shannon watched for a while and then laid back down on the bed and closed his eyes. He tried to imagine his mother the way she had been in her wedding picture, but each time her image would shift into a grotesque death mask. After a while Shannon stopped fighting it.

DiGrazia had moved over to the closet. Off and on Shannon would hear the fat man grunt as he pulled boxes out and searched through them. Shannon wondered about who left the articles for DiGrazia. It was a good question. Someone in the area knew about him and that someone wanted to make sure DiGrazia knew about him, also. A thought struck him. Maybe Elaine had checked up on him and knew all about him before the other night. Maybe she had gotten the articles and left them for DiGrazia. But why? Did she believe he was capable of killing those women? As he tried to sort it out in his mind, DiGrazia interrupted him.

"Okay, Bill," he said, "I'm done in here. Would you help me flip over your mattress?"

Shannon stared blankly up at him.

"I'd like to look under your mattress," DiGrazia repeated.

Shannon got off the bed and helped DiGrazia flip the mattress over. There was nothing under it.

"I'm going to search the rest of the apartment," DiGrazia said. He turned towards the door and stopped to wipe some sweat from his forehead. "I'll make something up for Susie," he grunted as he left the room.

Shannon sat back down on the bed. Elaine had seemed genuinely surprised the other night when he had told her what really happened with Herbert Winters. Or did she? He tried to re-create their conversation in his mind. He tried to picture the way she looked at him when he told her about Winters. Because if she had left those articles for DiGrazia, if she really thought he might've murdered those women . . .

DiGrazia was standing in the doorway. Shannon almost didn't recognize him the way his partner was looking at him. "I'd like to show you something," DiGrazia said.

"What?"

"Come on. It will take a minute."

Shannon followed DiGrazia out of the room. "What did you tell Susie?"

"Nothing." His voice was cold and brutal, barely above a whisper. "She was already gone."

In the living room, the sofa had been pushed away from the wall and a wooden panel that provided access to the bathroom's shutoff valves had been removed. DiGrazia got on his knees and shined a flashlight into the opening. He waved for Shannon to take a look.

"You see that?" he asked.

Pushed under some pipes was a plastic bag that Winters had left behind when he had visited the apartment. DiGrazia reached in and pulled it out. Inside were twenty-year-old newspaper articles.

DiGrazia, stone-faced, studied Shannon. "It would be a good idea if we went down to the station," he said. "Do you want to try to call Susie first?"

Shannon declined without giving the matter any thought.

Chapter 25

When they arrived at the station Shannon was shuffled into an interrogation room. A half hour later he was joined by DiGrazia, Agent Swallow, and a third man he didn't recognize. The third man wore a cheap suit and had a badly pockmarked complexion. His skin reminded Shannon of chipped glass.

Swallow took over the interrogation while DiGrazia and the other man watched. The questioning focused on Shannon's movements the previous night. There was nothing about his mother's murder or the newspaper articles or any of the other women's murders. Instead, Swallow kept going over a timetable of Shannon's movements, from when he was with Elaine to when he later arrived home to his wife. At first, it surprised Shannon. After a while he caught on.

"Tell me about who you found last night," Shannon said.

DiGrazia and the guy with the cheap suit kept their poker faces intact. Swallow's color dropped a shade.

"Why don't you tell us about her?" Swallow said after a long ten-count.

Shannon shook his head. "I don't know anything about it. It just became obvious that's what this is about. What did you find?"

"You want to make a guess?"

"Another woman forced to swallow a knife?"

Swallow flashed a look at cheap suit. He, in turn, stared straight ahead at Shannon, his eyes glazing over.

"Very funny," Swallow said.

"I don't think she would've been able to swallow much of anything," DiGrazia added.

"It would be tough," cheap suit said vacantly.

"Especially with her tongue ripped out of her mouth," Swallow noted. He opened a briefcase and took some photos from it that he dropped in front of Shannon. They were crime scene photos of what had probably been a young woman, although it was tough to tell through all the gore. As hardened as Shannon had become to this type of stuff, the pictures turned his stomach. He looked each one over before handing them back to Swallow.

"You think I could've done this?" he asked.

Swallow showed a smug I-got-you-by-the-balls smile. "Now why would I think that?"

"Fuck you." Shannon felt a hotness burn his neck. "I didn't black out yesterday and I didn't commit any of these murders." He turned towards cheap suit and demanded to know who the hell he was.

The man's mouth tightened a bit. "Detective Ed Foley," he said. "I'm working this murder out of the East Boston precinct. Did you know this girl?"

"No, I never saw her before."

"You sure?" Swallow asked. "Take a closer look."

Agent Swallow handed him back one of the photos. Shannon forced himself to take a long, hard look at it before shaking his head and telling him he didn't know her.

Agent Swallow frowned. "Even if she were my own daughter, I don't think I'd recognize her from this. I mean, Jesus, look at it. It looks like her head's been pushed through a lawn mower. Maybe you know her, though. Ed, what's her name?"

The East Boston detective curled his lips before announcing that the woman's name was Liza Keenan.

Shannon had tried to brace himself. He knew it was coming, so he had tried to brace himself. He could feel a vein start to pulse along his temple. He shook his head slowly. "Never heard of her," he said. From the corner of his eye he could sense DiGrazia's face darkening.

Agent Swallow looked almost amused. "You want to think about it a little harder? Maybe you ran into her one night?"

"I'm getting sick of this," Shannon said. "What do you think you got?"

"Absolutely nothing." Swallow's smile had crept back in place. "I'm just hoping you can help us better understand whether your blackouts or your mother's murder have anything to do with this mess. You want to guess what killed her?"

There was some noise from out in the hallway and then someone pounding on the door. Agent Swallow turned towards the commotion, a look of annoyance rubbing out his smugness. A key turned in the lock and a red-faced man of about forty bulled his way in.

"I'd like to know what the hell's going on!" he demanded, his voice blasting out like a bullhorn.

"I'd like to know the same thing," Agent Swallow shot back. Thin veins started to push out of his forehead. "You better have a good reason for being here."

"I've got a hell of a good reason," the red-faced man stated angrily. "It's called the Constitution. Let me introduce myself. Russ Korkin, Mr. Shannon's attorney. Maybe you can explain to me why you're questioning him without me present?"

"He's helping us with an investigation—"

Korkin snorted loudly. "Yes, of course," he said. "Are you charging my client?"

Swallow opened and then closed his mouth. "I haven't decided. I was hoping he could help us clear up a few issues—"

"He's not going to help you do anything. My client is through talking. Again, are you charging him or is he free to leave?"

Agent Swallow stared at Shannon before looking back at the red-faced attorney. "I haven't decided yet," he said as if he were spitting out phlegm.

"While you try to make up your mind, why don't you and these other two gentlemen get out," Korkin said, pointing a thumb at DiGrazia and the East Boston detective. "I'd like to talk to my client alone."

"Bill, is this the way you want it?" DiGrazia asked.

"This is exactly the way he wants it," Korkin answered for Shannon. He then sat down and crossed his legs and waited for the three detectives to clear out. As he waited, he clasped his hands behind his head and whistled the theme song for *Cops.* When the door closed behind them, Korkin sat upright and held a hand out to Shannon.

"Your union hired me as soon as word got out about this. It's a good thing you've got friends here. Now, before you say a single word, I want to know if this interrogation room is private or if it can be observed from outside."

"It's private."

"Thank god for that." The attorney looked as if he were going to slap Shannon across the side of his head. "You ought to know better than to agree to questioning without an attorney."

"I've got nothing to hide—"

Korkin glared angrily. "You ought to know better."

"I said I've got nothing to hide. I haven't done anything—"

"That's good," Korkin said, cutting him off. "That's all I want to hear about the matter, understand? Nothing else. What did you give them?"

"They were trying to get a timetable for last night."

"And?"

Shannon gave the attorney the same rundown he had given Swallow. Korkin smiled as he took it in. When Shannon was done the attorney shook his head and let out a sigh.

"You shouldn't have said a word without an attorney present," he said. "You really should've known better."

Shannon didn't say anything.

"Eh!" Korkin waved the issue away. "It doesn't matter. You know what they got on you?"

Shannon shook his head.

"An anonymous phone call!" Korkin exclaimed with amazement. "That's all. About an hour ago some punk called up and gave them your license plate. What the hell does that mean?"

"Not much," Shannon said.

"That's right," Korkin agreed. "I mean, shit, you're a cop here in Cambridge, I'm sure you've made life difficult for some of the punks doing business here. So one of them decides to make life difficult for you. Why in the world would anyone take an anonymous call like that seriously?"

"I don't know."

"Probably because your neighbor was murdered recently," Korkin noted. "And probably by the same person who butchered Liza Keenan. But that's probably what gave the punk the idea in the first place to make the call."

"Probably."

Korkin laughed at that. As he laughed his face grew redder. "I'll tell you," he said, "if they do try to charge you, we'll hit them with a twenty-million-dollar defamation suit. Let's keep our fingers crossed. With a little luck we could both be retired in the Bahamas."

The attorney stood up and winked at Shannon. "I'll go check and see what's happening," he said as he left the room.

When he came back his red face had somewhat deflated. "Bad news," he said. "They're not charging you with anything. You're free to go. The Bahamas will have to wait."

Chapter 26

Phil Dornich couldn't keep from thinking about Liza Keenan. A lot of ink had been given to her murder—more than you'd expect for a junked up prostitute in East Boston. The pure brutality of the crime was partly responsible. Even though the papers didn't give many details, they sure as hell hinted at them. It bothered Dornich when he read the articles. There was something oddly familiar about the murder, something he couldn't quite put his finger on. He tried calling acquaintances of his from the East Boston precinct, but they were being vague about it; either they didn't know anything or they weren't talking. It took over a dozen phone calls before he was told about her tongue being pulled out and then another half hour of calls before finding out about the internal damage that had been done to her.

He tried to imagine how difficult it would be to pull a person's tongue from their body. After a while he realized he couldn't even imagine it.

Dornich was rereading the articles when Susan Shannon called. She wanted to know if he had found anything yet. He hesitated before telling her that he had. "I think it would be better if you came to my office," he told her.

Susan tried to get him to tell her over the phone what he had found, but Dornich refused. She finally agreed to meet him at his office during her lunch break.

Dornich closed his eyes and tried to pull out whatever it was that was lurking in the back of his mind. Eventually, he gave up and made a long distance call to California.

Susan Shannon showed up at his office around twelve-thirty. She looked a bit ragged, her eyes reddish, thin lines creeping underneath them.

"I only have about fifteen minutes," she told Dornich after he offered her a seat.

"We shouldn't need much more than that," Dornich said, smiling sympathetically, showing his few rotting teeth. "I'd like to ask you to read something."

Dornich handed her the articles he had gotten from the *Sacramento Journal.* As Susan read them, the skin around her mouth tightened. It gave the fat detective a good idea what she'd look like at fifty. By the time she finished with the articles her hands were shaking. She looked up at him, her eyes nothing more than small black beads. Dornich could see fear in them.

He asked her if she knew about any of it.

"N-no." Her voice cracked. She swallowed and tried again. "All I knew was that Bill's parents had both died. About the way she was murdered . . . our neighbor, Rose Hartwell, was murdered the same way . . ."

"I know."

"What—what do you think it means?"

Dornich tried to make his shrug look natural. He had been thinking about that question off and on since he found those articles. The obvious explanation was that Shannon was involved—that when he blacked out, he repeated his mother's murder. That was the obvious explanation, but it didn't ring true to him. He didn't feel it in his gut and usually his massive gut was right on target. Except recently. Every gut feeling he'd had about Shannon had been wrong, so why not this one . . . ?

"I don't know. It's possible he's involved. It's also possible someone's trying to frame him. Or it could all be a coincidence."

"Do you think he's involved?"

"I don't think so."

His answer didn't seem to comfort her any. All her color seemed to bleed out of her. "The articles say Bill was hospitalized. They didn't say what happened to him," she said.

"Fingers on his right hand were badly broken. Repeatedly. I was able to speak to the doctor who treated him. He still remembers it. He thinks that the damage occurred over several hours. That the murderer, Herbert Winters, used those fingers to torture him."

Susan put a hand over her eyes. "I can't believe this."

"There's something else," Dornich said. "His dad's still alive."

Susan took the hand away from her eyes. She stared blankly at Dornich.

"He's living in California," Dornich explained. "I've got his phone number. He's willing to talk to you if you want."

"I'd like to talk to him."

Dornich hesitated. He took out a handkerchief and wiped some wetness from his neck. "I have to warn you. It's going to be unpleasant. There's some mental illness there."

"Like father like son," Susan muttered under her breath.

Dornich started to say something and then thought better of it. He didn't want to discourage her from talking to Shannon's father. He wanted to see her reaction to what the old man had to say. He reached over and redialed the number to California. "I'm going to put this on the speaker phone."

After a few rings a voice picked up. It wanted to know who was calling. The voice was both strained and hostile.

"Hello, Mr. Shannon," Dornich answered. "This is Phil Dornich calling back from Boston. I've got your daughter-in-law with me."

The line seemed to go dead. Then, in a tight brutal voice, "Okay, I'll speak to her."

Susan had to clear her throat before she could talk. "Hello, Mr. Shannon," she said. "I'm your daughter-in-law, Susan."

There was a soft hiss over the line, something that could've been static but more likely was the old man breathing hard. Then, "You want to know about your husband?"

"Why, uh, yes—"

"I'll tell you about him. First, though, let me tell you about his mother—my wife. About what was done to her." He started to tell her about the murder, the brutal facts that the police had determined. At some point he shifted away from reality to a series of grotesque obscenities that he had convinced himself of over the years. They were hateful and irrational things. Monstrous things. His rantings spewed out over the speaker phone like blood from a burst artery. It was sickening to listen to. After only a few minutes of it Susan had to disconnect the line. By that time her face had turned a queasy white.

"You realize none of that makes any sense," said Dornich.

Susan just shook her head.

"Winters had spent several hours breaking and rebreaking your husband's fingers. Whatever your husband might've done, he had no choice."

"How could he say those things?" Susan asked, her eyes wide open as she stared into the fat detective's face.

Dornich shrugged, lowering his eyes.

"No wonder Bill told me his father was dead," Susan said. She started laughing; a weak, tired laugh. "At least I know why he goes crazy every year." The thought seemed to sober her up. She stood up quickly and then put a hand out and steadied herself to keep from falling back into her seat. "I have to get back to the office."

Dornich watched quietly as she left, amazed at how small and frail she looked. How much older . . .

Chapter 27

Even the best laid plans, huh, Billy Boy?

But I'm not complaining. Because those plans weren't worth shit. You see, Billy, even us gods can screw up occasionally. Especially when we're reacting to the moment, when the adrenaline's pumping so hot through our veins we don't know what's up or down. That's when we're vulnerable. You can just ask poor Herbie.

But, Billy Boy, there's a providence watching out for me. You're out on the street where I need you. It just wouldn't do to have you locked up now. Not while there's so much more that needs to be done. So much more doubt to sow. So much more blood to spill. And bodies to send to the morgue. God knows what I was thinking when I made that phone call . . .

As his consciousness seeped back into his body, Charlie Winters became aware of a sour taste in his mouth. He had been out for hours watching Shannon's interrogation. Now that he was back in his physical body he could feel an ache spreading across his chest. He coughed and spat on the floor. With some disgust he realized the sour taste had been blood.

He probably had pneumonia. That goddamn cop from the night before. Making him stand out in the freezing rain. Winters forced himself to concentrate until he remembered the cop's name. Podansky. Eddie Podansky. When the time was right he'd be dealt with. After Shannon.

Winters tried to sit up but found himself dizzy. He lay back down among the dirty sheets and soiled clothing. Right now it was time to get some rest. Time to make his plans. And not rush things now that everything was so close to working out.

Chapter 28

After Shannon was released he headed across the Boston University bridge and then to Brighton. Without really thinking about it he found a small biker bar and had three quick shots of scotch. As he held his fourth shot he looked at it, mildly surprised, realizing he had no taste for it.

That part of his life was back to normal. He didn't have any desire for alcohol. He didn't really have any need for it. The three shots he poured down were wasted on him.

But the rest of it. The murders. The articles hidden in his walls . . . Liza Keenan . . .

He lifted the shot glass to the window and studied it, studied the way the light filtered through its yellow murkiness. As he stared through the liquid a resolve tightened the muscles along his jaw. A coolness cleared his mind. He put the shot glass back on the bar and got up.

He first called Susan. She confirmed that he had gotten home around eleven-thirty. Her voice sounded brittle, distant. She asked if he had been drinking. When he told her he hadn't she hung up on him. He had a sickening feeling in his stomach that she had been told about Liza Keenan. For a moment he lost his resolve but then called Elaine Horwitz. She was positive he left her at eleven-ten. That left only twenty minutes for him to have driven to East Boston, pick out Liza Keenan, butcher her, and drive back to Cambridge. It would've taken more than twenty minutes to have just driven to East Boston, which meant that he had nothing to do with the murder.

At first he felt an overwhelming sense of relief. Then, just as quickly, a hot flush of anger. When Shannon next called Joe DiGrazia, his hands were shaking.

The old man looked first at Liza Keenan's photograph and then back at Shannon. "Cops were showing me her picture," he said suspiciously. "And yours, too. Why should I be talking to you?"

Shannon showed him his police badge.

"This says you're a Cambridge cop. This is Boston. I don't have to talk to you. Not unless I have a reason."

He had been pushing a grocery cart filled with cans and newspapers when Shannon had stopped him. He brushed past Shannon and started to push his cart away.

"Is ten dollars enough of a reason?"

"Maybe." He stopped and waited for Shannon to hand him the money. When he had it shoved into his pants pocket he gave Shannon an accusatory scowl. "Why those cops showing your picture around?"

"I don't know. Have you ever seen me around here before?"

"No, I've never seen you. That what you want me to say?"

"I want you to say the truth."

"Okay, I've never seen you before."

"But you were here last night?"

"Yeah, I was here last night. Where else am I going to be?"

"You didn't tell the police that."

The old man showed a sly, toothless smile. "They didn't give me any reason to," he said.

"And you saw what happened to that girl."

"No, I didn't!" the old man protested. His face went slack. "At least," he added, "not until after it had happened." Then, very quietly, "I saw him when he was leaving."

Shannon felt his heart skip a beat. "You saw him?"

"Not enough to get a good look," the old man said apologetically. "I was sleeping in that alley behind some crates. I saw him when he walked by. Then I saw what he had done to that girl. And then I found myself another place to sleep."

"All right," Shannon exhaled, "let's go talk to some people—"

"No, you don't! I ain't going nowhere. They'll steal my cart if I go. Anyway, I don't want to go nowhere." The old man started to push off.

Shannon dragged his cart away from him. "You'll lose your cart either way."

The old man struggled briefly and then turned, resigned, to face Shannon.

"It wouldn't help if I went with you," he said. "My eyes aren't that good anymore and it was dark and add to that, I was just waking up. I didn't get a good enough look at him. At least not so I could describe him." The old man shuddered involuntarily, his gnarled face relaxing. "I don't think I wanted to get a good look at him.

"There was something about him that made me look away," he continued, smiling sadly. "I guess I'm just too old to want to face death. At least before it's time."

"Is there anything about him you remember?"

"I'm sorry. There really isn't. Except he seemed evil. That's all I can picture in my mind. Just pure evil. It made my skin crawl when he walked by. And then I saw what he did to that poor girl."

Shannon tried to question him, but the old man wouldn't budge. If he had to guess on it, he'd say Liza Keenan's murderer was big, but he couldn't say for sure. He couldn't narrow down the man's age or what he was wearing. Only that he was white and that he was evil and that he smelled bad. Smelled bad enough that even he could notice.

Shannon sighed. "I need your name."

That got the old man cackling. "What you need my name for?" he asked, showing a wide, toothless grin. "Nobody's used it for over twenty years."

"I still need your name."

"Wouldn't do you or anyone else any good. I don't leave this block much, if you need to find me. Although, I don't know what for. Since I already forgot everything I told you."

Shannon met with Joe DiGrazia and filled him in on what he found. DiGrazia looked skeptical.

"You just left him?" DiGrazia asked.

"It wouldn't have done any good bringing him in. He would've denied witnessing anything. Besides, he really didn't. At least not so he could've given us a reliable description."

"It was still sloppy police work."

"Yeah, well, at this moment I'm not really a cop. And if we want to look at sloppy police work, let's look at me being brought in for Liza Keenan's murder. A couple of phone calls would've cleared me."

DiGrazia looked thoughtful. "I'm not convinced you shouldn't have been brought in," he said at last. "I believe Susie about when you arrived home. I'm not sure if your therapist is being completely honest. I got a feeling she's covering for you."

"That's ridiculous." Shannon couldn't tell whether or not DiGrazia was only trying to get a rise out of him. "There was no evidence I was involved with Keenan's murder. If I was, from the photos I was shown, there should've been some blood evidence. A few minutes of real police work would've cleared me."

DiGrazia shrugged. "It was still worth bringing you in. Something funny is going on with you. You might not have had anything to do with last night's murder, but it still doesn't clear you of the other two. Or explain why you had those articles of your mother's murder hidden in your apartment. The ones you claimed you didn't know you had. And it doesn't explain what you were doing when you blacked out."

Shannon shrugged. "Let's look at what happened. There've been four murders, all presumed to have been committed by the same individual. I've already been cleared of two of the murders, but you and the FBI still keep trying to get me for the other two."

"And we shouldn't be?"

"No." Shannon shook his head. "I think you need to go back to your original theory. That they all were committed by one person. If you do, and you accept the evidence that clears me of Roberson's and Keenan's murders, then you have to ask yourself why it seems like I'm being implicated."

DiGrazia narrowed his eyes, lines along his jaw muscles hardening. "Yeah, why is that?"

"Because," and Shannon couldn't keep from showing a sick smile, "someone out there is trying like hell to implicate me."

"And who's that?"

"I don't know. But he knows what happened to my mother. He planted those articles in my apartment. He had to have, 'cause I never saw them before."

"You're trying to tell me he broke into your apartment—"

"That's right. And he's committing these murders. Joe, he's trying to frame me. I think what he really wants is to convince me I'm doing them."

DiGrazia was drumming his fingers against the table. Frowning, he reached into his coat pocket and fumbled for a cigarette. "If that's true, he has to know about your blackouts," he said after he lit it up.

Shannon nodded. "I've been thinking about that. He must've been watching me, waiting for when I'd black out this year.

Which means he's been keeping tabs on me over the years."

DiGrazia stared long and hard at Shannon. "Dammit," he swore. He flicked his cigarette on the floor and crushed it out with his heel. "Give me a description of your witness. I'm going to bring the sonofabitch in like you should've."

At four in the afternoon Shannon received a call from DiGrazia.

"You sick bastard." DiGrazia's voice was strained to the point where Shannon wasn't sure what was said. At least at first.

"What was that?"

"You heard me." Then, his voice choking, "I found your witness. Goddamn it, I almost believed that crap you fed me. I actually almost believed it."

"What are you so excited about? I told you he wouldn't cooperate—"

"Yeah, you're right about that. At least, not after the way you left him in that alley."

"Joe, talk English to me—"

"Shut up. I don't want you trying to talk to me again. We'll talk later, but not now. Not until we got you dead to rights. Oh, Bill, one more thing, I wouldn't wait up for Susie if I were you. We had a nice long chat before I called you. In English."

CHAPTER 29

It had been raining sheets of water all night. Three in the morning Pig Dornich received the call. A couple of uniforms found the abandoned station wagon in an alleyway in Dorchester. The car was stolen. She was in the trunk. Four of her front teeth had been pulled out of her mouth. Her tongue looked a half foot longer than it should've been, as if someone had pulled on it. As if someone had tried to yank it out of her . . .

That was twenty-one years ago. They never got anywhere with the murder. The victim was a prostitute and those types of deaths happen. Maybe not as brutal and vicious as this one, but they do happen. Dornich really hadn't thought about it in years. At least, not consciously. But once he remembered it . . . what was done to her tongue . . .

But that was all twenty-one years ago.

His office desk was now covered with a collection of faxes, newspaper clippings, and old police reports. They traced a trail of unsolved murders leading from Boston, down the Eastern seaboard, snaking through Florida and Alabama, into Texas, and Arizona. The murders appeared random. There appeared to be no rhyme or reason to any of them. Nothing outwardly that could link them together, yet they were all eerily similar. Almost as if the nature of their randomness was forced. As if they were purposely made to look unconnected.

Dornich felt a dryness in his mouth as he scanned the reports.

In front of him were forty-three unsolved murders. He knew by the time he brought the trail to Sacramento there would be at least a half dozen more. Forty-three unsolved murders . . .

By eight o'clock he was finished. Fourteen more murders had been added to the list—the last one occurring in Los Angeles, four days before Shannon's mother had been butchered. The total count had reached fifty-eight unsolved murders. Dornich had no doubt about who committed them. He couldn't help feeling overwhelmed as he looked the list over. There were so many names on it.

He felt exhausted, but also somewhat exhilarated. Not bad police work for a pig. Not fucking bad at all. Before calling it a night he made a couple of more phone calls; first to North Carolina, then to book a morning flight to Raleigh.

Chapter 30

Susie never arrived home, not even to pack her bags. After watching the six o'clock news, Shannon understood why. He could pretty much guess what DiGrazia told her. He could pretty much understand why she'd believe him.

The lead story was about the murder. The old man's body was found in the same East Boston alleyway that Shannon had stopped him in. It had been a brutal murder, in some ways even more so than any of the women's, and it had been leaked to the media that it was done by the same killer. That tie-in made it a big story. Shannon learned from the news the old man's name was Walter Hough. It didn't seem to matter much anymore.

No one contacted Shannon. Not Agent Swallow, or anyone from the East Boston precinct, or any of the cops he knew in Cambridge. He figured this time they were waiting until they had enough evidence to make it stick.

The night faded by as he half paid attention to the TV. At some point static replaced the talking heads. When he finally closed his eyes, he drifted off quickly. He knew Herbert Winters would be waiting for him. Strangely, he didn't mind. In a way he was looking forward to it.

The smell was there immediately. Then he saw Winters, his face whiter and fleshier than before. Whiter and rounder than a harvest moon. A nasty grin, made even nastier by the lack of a real chin, was streaked across it.

"You shouldn't have killed that old man," Winters admonished lightly.

"I didn't."

"Of course you did." Winters paused to stroke what should've been a chin, his grin shrinking to something more smug. "You let me take over. Don't you remember what happened next? I coaxed him back into the alley. And I didn't let his collection of bottles go to waste. You remember what we did with them? You remember how much fun we had with those bottles, Billy Boy?"

"You're lying."

"Why would I lie to you with us being one and the same?"

"You're not part of me. You've never been part of me. I know that."

"You do, huh?"

"I do. You blew it with that girl."

Winters let loose with a low hiss of a laugh. The sound of air escaping from a punctured tire. "I wouldn't believe what that old man told you, boy. He wasn't going to tell you the truth. He was scared to death of you. 'Cause he recognized you from the other night. So he fed you whatever bullshit he thought he had to—"

"He was telling me the truth. You blew it with that girl. I know where I was when you murdered her. I've got two people who know where I was."

"You don't know what you're talking about—"

"Two people know where I was."

"They're mistaken, boy, because you were there. Goddamn it, you little piece of . . ." Winters's voice trailed off. His mouth closed as he considered what Shannon told him.

"What happened?" Shannon asked. "You couldn't help yourself, was that it? The urge to kill a little too strong?"

Winters didn't say anything.

"Who the hell are you?"

"That's the real point," Winters remarked slowly as life

filtered back into his dead rattlesnake eyes. "It doesn't matter anymore what you think. As long as the police believe you're doing these killings, that's all that matters."

"Who are you!"

"You don't have any idea, do you? Except that I'm not Herbie, because we both know he's long dead. Just like your mommy, right, Billy Boy?"

A white, blinding rage surged through Shannon. He felt himself taking off with it, his hands groping for Winters's throat, wrapping themselves around it, squeezing it. At first there was nothing but shock and surprise in the dead man's pale eyes, and then unbridled fury. As Shannon squeezed harder against his throat, Winters fought back, pushing himself closer to Shannon, his foul rankness assaulting Shannon, weakening him.

"You're the one they'll be coming after," Winters whispered as he clawed at Shannon, his breath hot against his face. His head seemed amorphous as it ebbed in and out. "Especially after tonight."

In the same motion Winters jerked free of Shannon's grip and grabbed Shannon's two fingers, the ones that had been broken as a thirteen-year-old. "You were right about that girl," Winters said with a sly wink. "I just couldn't help myself. But I sure did have fun. And guess who I'm with right now? Even as we speak." He started to bend back Shannon's fingers. "I'm going to make mincemeat out of her," he breathed into Shannon's ear. Then with a hard push he shoved Shannon's fingers back until they touched his wrist. And Shannon screamed.

Shannon woke up screaming. He doubled over in pain and grabbed his two fingers. He rocked back and forth in bed massaging his fingers, trying to quiet the pain that was radiating from them. After a few minutes it became bearable.

His fingers had turned a dark purple. They had swollen to

over twice their normal size. Shannon walked to the kitchen and wrapped ice in a paper towel and squeezed hard on it, trying to numb out the pain. As he stood in the kitchen, he smelled it. It came from his hair and it brought a rush of vileness up from his stomach. He fell to the floor, vomiting. It lasted a long time, long after there was anything left inside. When he could stop, he went to the bathroom and stuck his head under the shower and scrubbed his scalp until he was sure he had gotten rid of any trace of that smell.

When he was done he dried off and made his way back to the kitchen. He slowly, meticulously cleaned the floor and then put some water on for coffee. His fingers hurt like hell. He must've slept on them funny, somehow spraining them, maybe even breaking them. Probably why he had that dream . . . but that smell—somehow he imagined it—because how could it have gotten in his hair? Unless . . .

Unless, and the thought sickened Shannon, unless it was more than a dream. And what did Winters tell him—that he was with her?

With brilliant clarity Shannon realized it was true. Winters was with her.

He called DiGrazia. The answering machine clicked on. Shannon hung up and tried again. DiGrazia answered after the third ring.

"Where is Susie staying—"

"You son of a bitch," DiGrazia groaned. "It's three in the morning."

"Where is she?"

"Goodnight, buddy boy."

"Joe, listen to me—"

"I told you before I didn't want you calling me again—"

"He's with her right now. The murderer."

At first there was only static. Then DiGrazia asked how Shannon knew that.

"He told me."

"What do you mean he told you?"

"I know this sounds crazy but I had a dream where he told me he's with her. And Joe, I know it's true."

There was a long pause. Then, "Who are you talking about?"

"I don't know. In my dreams he's the guy who murdered my mother. Whoever he is, I know he's with Susie."

"Did you smell anything?" DiGrazia asked, his voice barely audible.

"Yeah, I smelled something. You've dreamed about him, too, haven't you?"

There was another long pause before DiGrazia told him he didn't know what the hell Shannon was talking about.

"You're lying, Joe. You know about the smell. You've dreamed about him. Trust me on this, he's with Susie right now. She's going to die if you don't help me."

"I'm not telling you where she is."

"Joe, you've got to believe me on this—"

"I'll tell you what I got to believe. That you're completely wacko. That you're playing the same game with me you did when you called me about that old man in East Boston. Susie probably contacted you already. She let you know where she's staying, didn't she?"

"Dammit, Joe—"

"I'm getting off the phone now. I have to go check on your wife. You better pray she's okay."

"Call me when you see her—"

The line went dead on him.

The killer was with her. He knew it. DiGrazia better fucking hurry.

Shannon couldn't stand still. There was a frantic energy buzzing through him and neither pacing the apartment nor kicking the walls helped calm it down any. A drink would take some of the edge off but there was nothing in the apartment and all the bars were already closed for the night. He checked the kitchen for cigarettes, didn't find any, grabbed his coat and headed outside. There was an all-night gas station off Memorial Drive where he could buy a pack.

As he drove he played back his dream. He had no doubt about it being real. The killer had talked to him. Somehow the killer had invaded his dream, had somehow forced himself into Shannon's subconscious. It was more than just that. The killer's presence had been real. That smell . . . the damage he did to Shannon's fingers . . . as crazy as it sounded, Shannon knew it was true. Absentmindedly he found himself imagining what Elaine would say if he told her about it.

He was with her . . .

Shannon pulled the car over. His knuckles bone white as he squeezed the steering wheel. A dull ache pulsated from his injured fingers. His therapist. Elaine Horwitz.

He was with her. He was going to make mincemeat out of her.

Shannon knew it was true. But he had made a mistake about who the killer was referring to. Now he knew.

The road was empty except for a gray Chrysler sedan that had pulled up behind him. Shannon got out and told the two FBI agents in it where he was going.

CHAPTER 31

Elaine Horwitz sat propped up on her office sofa, her hands tied behind her back, her feet tied tightly together. She was naked. Her panties had been stuffed into her mouth. Charlie Winters sat in an easy chair next to her. His complexion had an unhealthy pasty look, making it seem as if his skin had been dipped in wax. Droplets of moisture beaded up along his upper lip. As if he were coming out of a trance his eyes opened.

"Time to make the doughnuts," Winters said with a twisted grin.

He stood up and grabbed the therapist by her hair, pulling her head up until her eyes were directed towards his.

"I'm going to free your mouth," he breathed softly. "You know what will happen if you make any noise?"

Horwitz didn't respond.

"Even as much as a whimper," Winters added. "Especially a whimper."

He pulled the panties out of her mouth, letting his fingers linger along the inside of her lips. Even through his gloves, he could feel the coldness of her flesh. It excited him. He let the panties drop to the floor.

"You know who I am?" Winters asked in his soft, singsong voice.

"Yes."

"You want to guess how many women I've killed?"

Horwitz shook her head. She tried to keep the terror out of

her eyes. She knew that was what he needed. She knew that was all he needed.

"To tell you the truth I couldn't tell you," Winters answered anyway. "There's been so many. Not that they've all been women. I've had my share of men and boys and little girls. Even babies. I've never been too picky. But for some reason I always seem to gravitate towards women. I sometimes wonder if that's healthy. In a way it seems to be, but you're the trained psychologist and I'm only a layman. Tell me what you think."

"You pick women because you're trying to deny strong homosexual feelings."

Winters made a soft tsking noise as he shook his head. "Oh, please. I was hoping this could be good for both of us, but not if you're going to give me these fucking textbook answers. There's far more to it than that. Far more to it, Doctor. What next, that I was an excessive bed wetter? I tortured animals as a child?"

"You didn't torture animals?"

Winters's eyes dulled. "I wouldn't call it torturing," he said. "I'd call it more experimentation. Developing my craft."

His eyes closed momentarily. Then, striking with an open palm he caught Horwitz hard along the jaw. The blow knocked her off the sofa.

"It's good you didn't scream just then," Winters said, his small mouth squeezed tight. "At least you're perceptive. But you've got to take this seriously. This is an opportunity of a lifetime. How many chances do you get to deal with someone like me? Especially with so much riding on it. Or as far as I'm concerned, so little."

"You don't want to be cured."

"Don't we all want to be cured?"

"No. You enjoy killing too much."

Winters squatted until he was right over Horwitz's body. He

grabbed her along the area of the jaw where he had struck her. "Are those tears, Doctor?"

Horwitz bit hard on her tongue to keep from sobbing. Winters dug his fingers deeper into her jaw.

"I do believe those are tears." He ran his thumb under her eye and felt the wetness. "Yes, I do believe you're crying."

"It's nothing more than a physical reaction to pain."

"I think it's more."

"No," Horwitz said, her eyes expressionless as she met Winters's gaze. "It's nothing more than a physical response."

Winters shrugged. He moved over to an easy chair and sat down, crossing his legs. "Fine. We'll wait. Meanwhile, I want to hear your theories on why I turned out the way I did. Why was it, Doctor? Because of an overbearing mother who deep down resented having a boy? Or maybe because of an abusive father who belittled me every chance he had? Or was it the other way around?"

"I doubt it was because of any environmental causes. Your physical deformities probably played a role in how you turned out, but I'd bet it was as simple as you being born broken."

Winters's small, pale eyes turned cold. "What do you mean physical deformities?"

"Look in a mirror."

"Kind of glib considering your situation, Doctor."

"Does it make any difference?"

"Probably not," Winters said. "But—" he moved off his chair and got very close to Horwitz, his breath hot, his mouth brushing against her ear. "Billy Boy has probably figured it out. He could be on his way right now to save you. If you were a little better at what you did, maybe you could've distracted me. Maybe you'd even be alive when he got here."

"Who's Billy Boy?"

"Come on, Doctor. The man you dream about every night."

"I-I don't know who you're talking about."

"You're lying to me, Doc."

"How—how do you know he's coming here?"

"Because I told him," Winters smirked. His tongue flicked in and out of Horwitz's ear as he talked. "Billy and I go back a long way. Let me show you what I borrowed from his apartment."

Winters grabbed a paper bag and took an eight-inch carving knife out of it. He held it out in front of Horwitz.

"A beauty, isn't it?" Winters asked as he ran his thumb along its blade. "You know, usually I leave the women fully clothed, but with you I wanted to let Billy Boy see what he's going to be missing. I hope you won't be too bashful."

Winters got down on a knee and ran a finger along Horwitz's throat. "If you want to scream go right ahead," he said. "Just keep that beautiful, big mouth of yours wide open."

"Wait—" Horwitz said, keeping her voice low, "you actually can be cured. Would you like to know how?"

"Not particularly. After all, I was born broken."

"You can still be cured," Horwitz insisted.

"To tell you the truth," Winters said, "I think you were right before. About my not really wanting it. Anyway, it's too late now. They could be here any minute."

"But—"

"Ssh," Winters said. He placed a hand on top of Horwitz's throat and started to apply pressure to it. "By the way," he whispered softly, "this is the way we did it to Billy Boy's mom."

A raw panic took hold. As much as Elaine Horwitz tried to fight it, it seemed to grow within her, replacing the very breath that was being pushed out. She knew it was showing in her eyes. She wanted to scream.

A smile broke out over Winters's face. An almost pleasant smile. "That's a good girl," he said warmly. "That's right, darling, scream. Stretch those red lips of yours wide and scream your head off. Wider please. A bit wider. This knife has to go somewhere."

As much as she tried, Elaine Horwitz couldn't fight it.

A Brookline police cruiser was parked in front of Elaine Horwitz's office building. Its lights were off and the cop sitting in it looked bored. Shannon pulled into the parking lot behind the building and ran back to the cruiser. The two FBI agents pulled up behind it.

"Why aren't you in there?" Shannon asked the cop, incredulously.

"You're the guy who called?"

"I asked you why you're sitting here on your ass—"

"Hey, look, it's three-thirty in the morning. The building's empty. There's no sign of any forced entry—"

"Her car's still in the parking lot!"

The cop looked stunned. "Maybe somebody gave her a ride home," he offered defensively.

One of the FBI agents was getting out of the sedan. "Okay, what's this about?"

Shannon ignored him. The entranceway to Horwitz's building was protected by a glass security door. Shannon tried it, found it locked, and kicked it in. Obscenities were shouted out from behind him. Someone tried to grab him by the arm, but he pulled free and ran to Elaine Horwitz's office. The door to it was also locked. A familiar rancid smell filtered through it. He kicked the door and felt it splinter. He kicked it again and fell with it as it crashed open.

"You goddamn psycho," one of the FBI agents was yelling at him, "you better fucking stop right now."

He had a service revolver trained towards the middle of Shannon's body. Shannon ignored it. From where he was lying he could see Elaine Horwitz's desk. There was a body lying on top of it.

"Oh shit," the FBI agent murmured as he fumbled for the lights, the color dropping out of his face. He lowered his revolver.

The body on the desk was Elaine's. She was naked, on her back, her legs limply hanging over the edge, her hands tied behind her. As Shannon got closer he saw the knife angling out of her mouth.

"Don't touch anything!" the FBI agent ordered hoarsely. Elaine Horwitz's normally pale skin had turned an awful gray. Shannon put a hand to her neck. The skin still felt warm. Then her body twitched and a gurgling noise came out of her.

Shannon yelled out for him to get an ambulance. Then to no one in particular, "She's still alive, you sonofabitch."

Chapter 32

The Brookline detective taking Shannon's statement looked uneasy. "Who told you he was going to kill her?"

"I don't know."

"But you said he told you?"

"No, I didn't. I said I dreamed he told me."

"And you don't know who this guy is?"

"No, I don't."

"Nobody told you anything ahead of time?"

"What do you mean?"

"Maybe you heard something? Maybe you had second thoughts what to do about it?"

Shannon just shook his head.

"How about a phone call? Sometimes I get calls in the middle of the night and I don't even realize I'm answering it. Could it have been something like that?"

"No. There were no phone calls."

The detective looked uncomfortable. He drummed his fingers across his desk. He didn't like this dream stuff. Even though Shannon worked in Cambridge, even though he was suspended, he was still a fellow officer. Otherwise the questioning would have gone differently.

"So you'd say you had a, uh, premonition about the attack?" the detective asked hopefully.

Shannon decided to make things easier for his fellow officer. He told him that was what happened. A premonition. When he was first brought to the station he had agreed to a Breathalyzer test and then to giving blood and urine samples, so the detective didn't bother asking about drug or alcohol usage. The tests would answer that better than Shannon could. After signing his statement, the detective asked Shannon if he could wait around. Someone from the FBI wanted to talk to him. Shannon pointed out that there were two FBI agents there now, but the detective just shrugged and turned to some paperwork.

While he waited, he called the hospital Elaine had been taken to but they couldn't tell him much. Only that the damage to her had been severe and that she'd probably be in surgery most of the morning. If she survived that long.

Agent Douglas Swallow arrived after eight o'clock. He seemed uninterested as he read over Shannon's statement.

"Do you have anything to add?" he asked.

Shannon shook his head.

"Well, then, thank you for your time." And Agent Swallow turned away from him.

The FBI agent's attitude bothered Shannon. There was something behind it, some card Swallow thought he had. Shannon tried to think it through, but he was too tired. Instead, he drove to Beth Israel Hospital. The front desk couldn't give him any status about Elaine, only that she was still in surgery.

Shannon sat and waited. A heavy weariness had soaked into his joints. It tugged at him. It tried to force his eyes closed. He struggled against it. He fought like hell to stay awake. At that moment he didn't feel up to facing Winters.

Chapter 33

Pig Dornich had tried calling Shannon from the Raleigh-Durham airport and again after he landed in Boston. He knew about Charlie Winters, about his release from prison four months before the murders started up again, and wanted to talk to Shannon before going to the police. But, and the magnitude of it left him overwhelmed, this was at least sixty murders over a twenty-year period. He tried his best to get ahold of him, but, well, Shannon would just have to hear it secondhand.

While he drove from Logan airport to his office in Malden he thought about the two cousins crisscrossing the country and about all the corpses they left behind. Twenty years ago they ended up in Sacramento. He pretty much guessed what happened with Shannon's mother, that Charlie took a nap while Herbert did the murder. When he had gotten Charlie Winters's arrest report faxed to him he knew why Winters had a thirteen-year-old boy in his trunk when the police had stopped him. He also knew why the recent murders were being done. In a way it was remarkable that things had worked out the way they had, almost as if the sonofabitch knew about Shannon's blackouts. It was as if he knew when they happened, that he knew Shannon could be convinced he was doing the murders himself.

As Dornich pulled into the garage he heard over the radio about Elaine Horwitz. He recognized the name and remembered her as Shannon's therapist. The report had her in critical condition. A grim determination tightened the flesh around his mouth. You're losing your touch you goddamn psycho, he swore silently.

The adrenaline that had been pumping through him fizzled out. He felt tired all of a sudden. Weary to the bone. Looking in the rearview mirror he saw the eyes of an old man. If he had been a little smarter, a little quicker, a little more on the ball, that woman wouldn't have been carved up. Charlie Winters would've been locked up already with the key thrown the hell away.

Dornich stopped outside his door. He smelled a rotting, rancid odor coming from his office. He wondered whether he had left any food out. As he opened the door the smell assaulted him. He realized rotting food couldn't have caused that odor. Maybe if a raw sewage pipe had opened up into his office . . .

Someone tapped him on the shoulder. As he turned he felt something sharp ripping into his gut. His knees buckled and he fell to the floor. His hands felt a sticky wetness as they searched out the knife that had been buried in his stomach. Charlie Winters stood over him, grinning widely.

"The goddamn psycho hasn't completely lost his touch, eh?" Winters asked.

Dornich didn't answer him. His fingers lightly traced his wound. The knife had gone in below his belly and had been pushed up almost a foot, just about slicing him open.

"It's almost as if I've been in your mind listening to your every thought, huh?" Winters asked, waiting patiently for an answer. When he didn't get one he went on, "I wanted her alive when Billy Boy showed up. But, in any case, I don't think she'll be around much longer. Not the way I left her. Which was in a hell of a lot better shape than you're in."

Winters turned away from Dornich and started to collect the papers from his desk. "It's a bitch, isn't it?" Winters asked as he dumped the faxes and reports detailing his and Herbie's murders into a trash can. "You should've gone straight to the police, but I guess you wanted to waddle in with your evidence. What was it, you needed to show them how damn smart you are?" He lit the corner of one of the papers and watched as the fire spread and flared out of the trash can. A thick, black smoke poured into the room. After a while Winters flipped the can over.

"Ashes to ashes," Winters noted.

Dornich moaned softly as the knife shifted inside him. Winters turned towards him, showing a slight melancholy smile. "I almost hate to tell you this," he said, "but you didn't even get a quarter of them. Herbie and I left a hell of a lot more corpses behind than what you found."

Dornich tried to push himself up to his elbows, but fell back to the floor. Winters made a soft tsking noise. "Jesus," he said, "look at you lying like that. Bleeding like a goddamn stuck pig."

He stepped forward and aimed a kick at Dornich's midsection. Dornich, though, caught his foot and pulled it towards him, sending Winters off balance and falling backwards. As he hit the floor, Dornich rolled on top of him, his heavy mass crushing Winters's chest, his clenched fists hammering at his face. And then his hands were searching out Winters's throat, his thick fingers closing around it, squeezing it.

Dornich came close to squeezing the life out of Charlie Winters and Winters knew it. His eyes bulged as they reflected the horror of that possibility. His tongue thickened as it pushed out of his slit-like mouth. He tried to scream. A strangled, gasping noise came out. Like a cat hacking on a hairball. The sound brought a slight smile to Dornich's mouth.

Ultimately, though, it was a race, one which Pig Dornich just didn't have enough time to win. The little life he had left dripped out with his blood and he collapsed lifeless on top of his killer.

Winters had to struggle to pry Dornich's dead fingers from his throat and then to push his corpse off of him. As he lay on the floor gasping for air a horrible fury raged in his eyes. When he could move he turned to the dead man. By the time he left, Pig Dornich's office looked worse than any slaughterhouse.

Chapter 34

Shannon felt someone nudging him. He opened an eye and saw DiGrazia sitting next to him, pushing him with an elbow.

"You were drifting off, buddy," DiGrazia said.

"Thanks. How'd you know I'd be here?"

"A lucky guess. I wanted to let you know Susie's okay. How's your therapist doing?"

"She's still alive. That's all they're telling me."

DiGrazia lowered his voice. "How'd you know about it, Bill?"

"You've seen my statement?"

"Don't give me that. How'd you know about it?"

"Just what was in my statement. I dreamed about him. He told me he was with her and he was going to kill her. When I called you I thought he was referring to Susie. Later, I realized it was Elaine. You've dreamt about him, too, haven't you, Joe?"

DiGrazia stared at the wall across from him. Grudgingly, he nodded. "Once."

"What did he look like?"

"I couldn't tell you. I really didn't see him, he was too close to me. He kind of stood off to the side of me whispering things."

"But you smelled him?"

"Yeah, Jesus, I smelled him. When I woke up I just about crawled on my knees to the almighty porcelain goddess. And I gave one hell of a devout prayer."

"He's real, Joe. Elaine's office had that same smell. A few days ago that smell was in her car. The sonofabitch was probably hiding in it waiting for her. When he saw me he must've jumped out. He must've been what we heard moving around in the Dumpster. Sonofabitch. What kinds of things did he whisper to you?"

"About how you were killing these women."

Shannon nodded slowly, the muscles tightening along his jaw. "Yeah, what do you think?"

"I'll tell you what our friends at the FBI think. That you set this up. An accomplice of yours attacked Elaine Horwitz to throw us off."

"They really think that?"

"Your friend Swallow does."

"And I just happen along and save her life?"

"We don't know that yet. Anyway, it wouldn't matter. If she lives and she doesn't know the guy's a friend of yours, how does it hurt you?"

A muscle along Shannon's jaw began to twitch. "What do you think?"

"I think it's what it looks like. Someone's pulling a pretty masterful frame job on you."

"You tell Susie this?"

"No. I want her afraid of you. This way she stays hidden and safe. I don't want this psycho picking her next. I'm sure you don't, either. And anyway," DiGrazia paused and showed a thin smile, "I could be wrong."

"I have to talk to her."

"Sorry, pal. By the way, she's staying out of work until I tell her it's safe, so don't waste your time bothering anyone at her office. If your therapist recovers we'll get a description of the guy and that will be that. You got any ideas who's doing this?"

Shannon shook his head. He knew DiGrazia was right. If Susie were home she'd be in danger. If he knew where she was the killer would probably end up knowing, too.

"No," he said, "I keep thinking it's Herbert Winters, that maybe I left him alive, but I checked with the California state police and he's long dead. I can't think of anyone I've ever put away who'd be up to this. How about you?"

DiGrazia sat silently for a moment, a darkness clouding his face. "All this is beyond me, pal. Especially this dream shit."

They sat silently for a few minutes. Finally, DiGrazia suggested that Shannon go home and get some rest, that he would call him when there was news about Elaine Horwitz.

"You might as well," DiGrazia added, "you're not going to be allowed to see her."

There were a pair of messages on his machine from a Phil Dornich. Both messages had Dornich stating he was a private detective hired by Shannon's wife and that he had important information for him. Shannon replayed them and then searched through the yellow pages. He found Dornich's ad, the one Susan had circled. When he tried calling the number, he got an answering service. Dornich had been out the past few days but was expected back any minute. Shannon left his name and number and hung up.

It was almost one o'clock. Shannon didn't feel like resting. He didn't feel like facing Winters, at least not yet. He got in his car and headed towards the Dornich Detective Agency.

The door to Dornich's office was unlocked. When Shannon opened it and looked in, a wave of nausea rolled through him. With over a decade on a city police force he had seen his share of killings and mutilations, but he had never seen anything close to this. Gore and blood were splattered everywhere and what was laying on the floor was a perverse mockery of a human body. Shannon turned away for a moment, steadied himself, and then reentered the office.

The familiar rancid smell had mixed with smoke and the combination stung Shannon's eyes. He noticed the trash can laying on its side and the charred ashes that had spilled out of it. He had to step carefully to avoid the pieces of flesh and gore that littered the floor. The corpse had literally been torn to pieces. It looked like both a knife and hands had been used. Maybe even teeth.

Shannon made his way to the trash can, sifted through the ashes, but didn't find anything useful. He returned to the body and knelt over it. The corpse's suit jacket had been ripped to shreds and was soaked through with blood. He found a blood-smeared and ripped plane ticket receipt in the jacket's inside pocket. Shannon held it up to the light but couldn't make out the printed destination. He checked the dead man's pants pockets and came up with a set of car keys. As he stood up he noticed for the first time that all the fingertips had been bitten off the dead man's hands.

After leaving Dornich's office, Shannon found a men's room down the hallway. Another corpse lay on the floor. The body was that of a man in his seventies. His head had been crushed and he had been stripped to his underwear. One of the sinks was filthy, streaked with a mixture of blood and dirt. A pile of soiled paper towels littered the floor next to it. Shannon moved to the sink at the end and washed his hands and then tried to remove the blood droplets from his shoes and clothing. He got most of the blood off his shoes but only smudged it into his pant legs and coat.

The FBI had followed him to Dornich's office building. He peered out the front door and saw their car still parked outside, the agents in it both looking bored.

The back exit of the building led to an adjoining parking lot. After a few tries, Shannon found the car that matched Dornich's keys. In the trunk was a suitcase with an airline baggage tag still attached. The tag read NC.

North Carolina . . . Mornsville, North Carolina.

Shannon had parked his car in front of Dornich's office building. He left it there with the FBI agents. Instead, he cut through a back alley, and then another office building and another alley before hailing a cab.

He was able to get a three-ten flight to Raleigh-Durham. While airborne he dozed off several times. There were no intrusions by Winters. No death. No pain. Just blissful nothingness.

The plane landed a few minutes after five. It was past dinnertime before he drove into Mornsville.

Chapter 35

Malcolm Winters had the same chin, or lack of chin, as his son, Herbert. The rest of him, though, was different. Frail, hunched over, his eyes pained, his face sagging. His wife, Ethel, was a brittle thing of a woman. All wrinkles and bone. Step on her and she'd crack like a stick. The room they were in had a scrubbed, powdery smell. No hint of that familiar, rotting odor. Everything clean and in its place. Medical journals lined several book shelves.

"He left home when he was eighteen," Mr. Winters explained.

Sitting was too much for Mrs. Winters. She popped off the floral-patterned sofa, her hands nervously pulling at each other. "Are you sure I couldn't get you anything?" she chirped out in an unnaturally brittle voice.

Shannon declined. Mr. Winters took hold of his wife's arm. Reluctantly, she let herself be guided back to the sofa.

"There was no way to know that he would do what he did," Mr. Winters said. "We gave him a good home. We never hit him. We did everything you're supposed to do.

"There was never any hint at all," he said after a long pause, "except for that poor Chilton girl."

Ethel Winters put a hand to her face as if she were about to weep. "There were all those animals," she said.

"There were no animals!"

"Of course there were. Those stray dogs and cats—"

"How were we supposed to know he had anything to do with them?"

"You knew. We both knew. Just like we knew about little Marjorie Chilton."

"That's ridiculous!" Mr. Winters snapped back at his wife, his sagging face growing beet red. He turned back towards Shannon. "At the time, neither us had any suspicions about that girl. There was no reason for us to have had any. There were no reasons for anyone to have had any."

Ethel Winters stared at her husband in stony silence before looking away, her lips pressing hard and virtually disappearing within her lined, wrinkled face.

"Of course, anyone can look back with hindsight . . . but how can anyone expect a thirteen-year-old boy capable of doing something like that? How could you think that of your own child?" Mr. Winters asked.

"He was only six when he started with the animals," Ethel Winters said.

Mr. Winters ignored her. "If I had any idea that he had done those things to that little girl I would've had him committed. I wouldn't have let him walk free. You have got to understand he was a quiet, introverted boy and people were suspicious of him because of that, and well, his appearance. He was unnaturally pale, almost an albino. And along with inheriting my chin . . ."

His voice trailed off as he lost himself in thought. Then, almost pleading, "I'm a doctor. If there were any indications of deviant behavior, of psychosis, don't you think I would've picked up on it?"

"You ignored it," his wife said.

"I didn't ignore anything!"

"I can tell you firsthand he was as psychotic as they come," Shannon said.

"I know you can," Mr. Winters agreed, trying to smile. "I feel sick inside about what happened to you and your mother. I wish there was something I could've done to have stopped it. I've been wishing that for twenty years."

"I appreciate your concern," Shannon said dryly. "Do you have any other children?"

Mr. Winters shook his head, surprised.

"How about any friends who might've been with your son?"

Mr. and Mrs. Winters looked at each other. "We told the other detective all about that," Mr. Winters said.

"About what?"

"About my brother Earl's boy, Charlie. The two of them were together all the time as children. They left Mornsville together. Didn't that detective tell you any of this?"

Shannon shook his head.

"God help us," Ethel Winters murmured, "the two of them even looked alike. Ugly little bastards."

Charlie Winters's parents were both dead. Neither Mr. or Mrs. Winters had heard from their nephew since he left Mornsville with their son. "I told the police that he might've been involved with what happened to you and your mother, but I never heard anything more from them," Mr. Winters said.

Before Shannon left, Mrs. Winters moved close to him, her bony hands touching his arm. "The FBI had told us they were investigating Herbert for other murders. They never found any, but I know there were others. God help me, I'm afraid to think how many there were."

Shannon was able to get on a ten o'clock flight back to Boston. He dozed off quickly, almost as soon as he closed his eyes. Charlie Winters was waiting for him. Winters's rotting, sickish odor was waiting for him.

"I know who you are, Charlie," Shannon said.

"You're a day late and a dollar short, bright boy."

"What's that supposed to mean?"

Winters smiled. A thin, diseased smile. "Everybody knows about me. They've been showing my picture on the news all night. As it turns out, you were the last to know."

"You're lying—"

"I wish I were, bright boy. Sad to say I'm not. And even sadder, our special little relationship is coming to an end. After tonight."

"Elaine must have recovered—"

"No, sorry chump, she's dead as a doornail."

"Then how'd they find out about you?"

Winters's pale, rattlesnake eyes dulled a bit as he stared at Shannon.

"Damn you! Answer me!"

"You see, I don't have to," Winters said after a while, "but I'll trade you. You tell me why you didn't call any of your cop friends after speaking to my aunt and uncle, and I'll tell you how I got careless."

"I was waiting until I got back to Boston."

"You're lying. Even in your dreams you're a little pissant liar. I think you were planning on keeping it a secret. I think you were going to try to track me down so you could enact your little lying pissant revenge on me. And to hell with all the innocents who would die in the meantime. And, Billy Boy, there would be plenty. Is that it?"

"Fuck you."

"If you want to trade you have to trade fair. Is that it, Billy Boy?"

"Okay. That's it. I was going to find you and then cut your fucking ugly head off just like I did your cousin. And then I'd have a pair of the god ugliest bookends on earth."

"That wasn't so hard, was it?" Winters said. "Except, I'm not keeping my end of the bargain. You see, I just keep taking from you. Taking and taking without giving anything back. I took your mommy and, for the most part, your daddy from you. I took your childhood, your career, and even your sanity. And I took that pretty bitch redhead you dream about. Oh yeah, earlier tonight, I took your dago cop partner."

Winters nodded slowly, his face expressionless, his skin a grim, icy white. "That's right," he explained, "I got him tonight. I snuck up behind him. I think he smelled me at the last second but before he could completely turn around I had an ice pick in his kidney. And then we had some fun. A couple of hours of hard rock and roll.

"So come on," Winters asked, "what's left for me to take?"

"You sick piece of shit."

"That's not it," Winters said, shaking his head with exaggerated pity. "That doesn't even make sense. Why would I want to take a sick piece of shit away from you? Come on, think harder. It's really pretty easy. Even for such a bright boy."

"What do you want?"

"I want you to guess what I can still take away from you. I'll give you a hint. It's an old joke. Take my *blank,* please."

Shannon didn't say anything. Winters was only a few feet from him, his body bobbing up and down as if it were floating on the ocean. He wondered if he could end it right there, if killing Winters's dream self would kill off his physical self. He wanted to try it more than he ever wanted to try anything. Winters seemed to sense what Shannon was thinking. He started to chortle, his slit mouth twisting into a smirk.

"You don't want to try that, now," Winters admonished softly, his singsong voice rising and falling with the bobbing of his body. "If you did, I'd have to break your fingers some more and you'd wake up screaming like a baby. Like last time.

"Anyway," Winters added, "being such a bright bulb, you've

probably guessed what's left for me to take. If you woke up now you won't be able to stop me. I'd just have to go ahead and take it. Tonight. Besides, if you could kill people off in their dream states, don't you think I'd be doing it?"

Shannon took a step back. "Okay," he said, "what do you want from me?"

"In a minute. Just so we're clear, I'm talking about your wife. You know, take my wife, please. I'm with her right now. She's all dressed up like a Christmas turkey. And I've got the carving knife."

"Why do you think I care? She left me."

"You care, Billy Boy. You don't want her to end up like all the others, do you?"

Shannon found himself involuntarily shaking his head. "For the last time, what do you want?"

"The same as you. I want the two of us to get together tonight. Have a little dance. Make a little romance."

Shannon agreed and Winters gave him the address where he had Susan.

"I'll be watching you," Winters warned. "Just like I can meet you in your dreams, I can watch you while you're awake. If you speak to anyone, call anyone, I'll know about it. And I'll do things to her that I've only dreamed about. Imagine that, things that someone like me has only dreamed about. Then I'll disappear. So don't be stupid, bright boy."

Winters body floated off, floated until it became a small, white point. Floated off until there was nothing.

Turbulence jerked Shannon awake in his seat. For a brief heartbeat he could still smell the odor, for a bit longer he could taste it in his throat. He found himself gagging from it. The woman sitting next to him was eyeing him somewhat suspiciously.

"Are you okay?" she asked.

Shannon nodded and, when he could, he muttered something about having a bad dream. He found a pen and wrote down the address Winters had given him. He couldn't afford to forget it. Then he fell back into his seat, feeling his heart skipping on him, racing away like a rabbit's.

He knew Winters was with Susie. There was no doubt in his mind about it. The sonofabitch psycho had told him the truth. And he knew Susie would be kept alive until he got there. About watching him, Shannon knew that was true, also. As impossible as it sounded, he knew it was true. But if Winters were watching him, he wouldn't be able to do things to Susie, he'd have to be concentrating his energies on Shannon. Unless he took occasional breaks, thinking that watching Shannon ninety percent of the time would be enough. Even still, Susie would be kept alive.

As much as he tried telling himself otherwise, he knew Winters had also told him the truth about DiGrazia. It fit together. Joe would've gone to pick up Susie after the case broke against Winters. Somehow Winters followed him and got to him—probably as he was opening the door to wherever he had Susan hidden. Or maybe the psycho found Susie first and waited for Joe. Anyway, Shannon knew it was true and knew Winters would've taken his time killing his partner. And he knew Winters would've forced Susie to watch.

A numbing calm took over. It was almost peaceful. Something like death. The plane wouldn't be landing for a couple of hours, but that was okay. Susie would be kept alive. There was nothing to do but wait. Wait and let himself slip into the blissful numbness. And he welcomed it.

Charlie Winters's eyes opened slowly and, as they did, they focused on Susan Shannon. She was lying spread-eagle on the kitchen table, each of her limbs tied by wire to each of the four table legs. If she struggled the wire would slice her skin. Her own eyes were large and shining brightly with terror. A dish rag had been stuffed in her mouth. All her clothing had been removed.

Seeing her terror excited him. He closed his eyes momentarily and breathed deeply. He could just about smell her terror. A barely palpable pungent smell. Sweeter, though, than the heavy, rotting, death odor that he carried.

He stood up and leaned over her so that his face was inches from hers. Even though she was gagged he could hear the sudden intake of her breath. Pure unadulterated fear exploded in her eyes and it sent a dizzying rush of exhilaration through him that nearly floored him. He had to back up a few steps. He ran his tongue slowly over his lips and swallowed.

"Did I frighten you?" he asked in his soft, singsong voice.

She made a muffled noise that sounded something like "please."

Charlie Winters could barely contain himself. He picked up the carving knife that he had left lying against her neck and ran the blade over the length of her body, pushing the skin down but not cutting it. He did a complete trace of her body, ending back at her throat.

"You don't want any sudden movements," he whispered into her ear, his breath stale and harsh, "because those wires I've tied around your wrists and ankles will cut straight to the bone. Probably even clean through it. Understand, sweetmeat?"

She nodded her head, tears leaking from her eyes.

Winters took hold of the index finger on her right hand and slid the knife under it. The drive to cut it off was pounding in his head. For a long moment he stared, transfixed on her finger. Then he let it go and took a step away. If he started now he wouldn't be able to stop and that wouldn't be any good. He needed her alive for when Shannon showed up.

Those were the plans he had improvised. They weren't his original plans, but his original plans had gotten shot to hell because he had let Eddie Podansky live.

Podansky. He had gotten careless with him. He should've found his family and taken care of them and then taken care of Podansky. But he had let things slide and the Brookline cop was alive to make the connection between him and Elaine Horwitz. After all, Podansky had stopped him only a few blocks from Horwitz's office, and the cop was suspicious as hell to begin with. And it wasn't a difficult leap from Charlie to his cousin Herbert and then to the recent killings.

Since the six o'clock news, his prison picture had been shown repeatedly over the airwaves and there was no disguise for a man who looked like Charlie Winters.

He knew about it over an hour before the news. While out of his body he had eavesdropped on DiGrazia. Then DiGrazia was on the phone with Shannon's wife, telling her about Winters, and arranging with her to pick her up. Hearing Susan's voice over the phone allowed Winters to navigate to her. After that it was simple. He knew where she was and he knew when DiGrazia would be picking her up. All he had to do was hide in the bushes with an ice pick and wait.

Charlie Winters forced himself to look away from his prisoner. It just wouldn't do if he got started now, because if he did there would be nothing left of her by the time Shannon got there. Nothing but pieces, anyway. He let out a lung full of sour, fetid breath as he sighed heavily and then sat back down and closed his eyes. A few moments later he was out of his body and watching Shannon.

Chapter 36

It was past midnight before Shannon was able to pick up a taxi from Logan airport. He gave the cabbie the address that Winters had given him and then sat back and stared absentmindedly out the window. The cabbie, a bulky middle-aged man with a thick Russian accent, tried to make small talk and he didn't let Shannon's lack of responsiveness deter him. After a while he settled in about the recent serial murders.

"At least they know who the person is," the cabbie said, nodding his bald, square head.

Shannon didn't respond. He kept his gaze directed towards the window, watching the freezing rain bead up on the glass.

"My shift don't start 'til eight," the cabbie went on, "so on TV I saw his picture. Very ugly man."

"Is that so?" Shannon muttered.

"Yes. Very. I hope they catch him soon. I have wife and children home alone while this sicko loose. I don't like it."

"I wouldn't worry about it."

"Why shouldn't I?" the cabbie asked, scowling. "He could hurt them just like others. What a world, huh? When they catch him I hope they exterminate him. Like bug."

The cabbie stopped talking. The streets were, for the most part, empty and the taxi was able to speed along, stopping only briefly at red lights and not at all at stop signs. The city had a weird, desolate feel to it. As if it were lifeless. As if the buildings were nothing but tombs for the dying. Shannon watched blindly as the city sights passed by. After a few minutes the cabbie broke the silence, commenting about how the killer didn't deserve to live another second among decent people.

"Not with things he did," the cabbie declared stubbornly.

"I agree with you."

"The judges, they probably let him out on technicality."

"That won't happen."

"Let's hope not. Worse than animal."

The address Winters had given was in Arlington. When they got close to it, the cabbie asked if Shannon knew which house it was. Shannon said he didn't.

"With this rain I can't read numbers," the cabbie complained as he slowed down and stuck his head out the window to try to read the number posted on one of the houses. He slowed down three more times before pulling up to a small cape. As Shannon paid him, the cabbie noticed the red smudges on his overcoat but didn't comment on them.

Shannon walked up to the front door and stopped. He didn't have a gun, he didn't have anything he could use as a weapon except for his car keys and they wouldn't do any good unless he could get in close. He left his keys in his pocket. If Winters was watching him, he didn't want to give him any idea of what he was thinking.

If he were watching him . . .

The thought struck Shannon that if Winters had been watching him he would've stopped by now. He would know that Shannon was right outside the front door and he'd be hiding near it, waiting for him.

Shannon knelt low and moved alongside the house. Blinds had been closed on all the windows and the lights were off. What did Winters tell him, that Susie was dressed up like a Christmas turkey? Which, deciphering his perverse sense of humor, meant he had her in the kitchen, just like him and Herbie had had his mother. Shannon continued on to the back of the house, picked up a small plaster statue of a saint, and tossed it through what he guessed was the kitchen window. As it crashed through, he took a headfirst dive after it. His foot, though, caught in the blinds and, instead of rolling as he fell, he went straight down, hitting the floor with a thud and jamming his shoulder. As he scrambled to his feet he saw Susie tied to the kitchen table. Then something hit him hard on the back of the neck, the blow pushing him back to the floor. Broken glass cut both his hands and face.

"That was stupid," a soft, singsong voice breathed into his ear, "if any of the neighbors heard anything and call the police I'll have to kill both of you."

"Yeah, so what?"

"Kind of cavalier, Billy Boy. Believe it or not, I'm not planning on killing either of you. Not if I can help it. I've got other plans. Wonderfully, nasty plans."

A knee pushed hard into Shannon's back, knocking the wind out of him. His right hand was jerked behind him and his two fingers, the ones that had been broken years earlier, were grabbed.

"Ah, here's what I'm looking for," Winters whispered. Metal clamped down on those fingers and twisted upwards until the bones snapped. Shannon couldn't help screaming. The floor muffled the noise somewhat.

"A nutcracker," Winters confided cheerfully. "I love using them." Then softly, "You need to control yourself better, Billy Boy. As I already told you, if you make noise and neighbors call the police, I will have to kill both of you. Then I'll give myself up and rest comfortably in prison. If we're not interfered with, I'll just continue on as planned. So be a man like your dago partner had been. I did much worse to him and he didn't once scream like a baby. At least not 'til the end."

"You smell like shit," Shannon grunted, his breathing labored. Pain forced hot tears into his eyes. "Ever consider taking a bath?"

"I've been trying to get nice and ripe for you, Billy Boy." Winters held on to Shannon's broken fingers and used them to force him to his feet.

"Up and at 'em," Winters whispered from behind. "I have something to show you."

Winters, using Shannon's broken fingers, forced Shannon into the dining room. Lying in a corner was what looked like a pile of raw meat. Up close it was a human body. Even though most of the skin had been removed, Shannon was able to recognize his partner. He tried to twist around to get at Winters, but Winters applied more pressure to his broken fingers. The pain forced Shannon to his knees.

"I've been as busy as a bee today," Winters whispered casually. "His cousin, or at least most of her body, is upstairs. She came home as I was finishing up with my whittling. Your wife had the best seat in the house for both killings."

Winters moved closer until his breath was hot against Shannon's ear. "Look at him," he ordered. "Want to guess how painful it must be to be skinned alive? I'd have to think it would be a hell of a lot worse than only having your fingers broken. He took it like a man, Billy Boy. No screaming, no crying. You really ought to be ashamed of yourself."

"You're nothing but a fucking psycho."

"It doesn't matter what I am. What matters is I got you on your knees cowering because of a couple of broken fingers. And I got your wife tied up and ready for action. Put your other hand behind your back. Now."

Winters worked on his broken fingers until Shannon complied. Then Winters tied his hands together, binding the rope tightly around both broken fingers. The throbbing from his fingers went all the way up his shoulder. It was like nails had been driven into his bones. Winters grabbed him by his injured fingers and forced him back to his feet and into a chair. He pulled up a chair opposite Shannon.

"For years I planned on skinning you like that," Winters said.

It was the first time Shannon had actually seen him. For the most part, Winters looked as he did in the dreams. He had the same slit mouth, and under it, nothing. It was as if a hatchet had been taken to his face, cutting off anything below his razor-thin lips. His skin color, though, was more waxy than pale. Maybe even a bit jaundiced. And his eyes were more sick than dead.

"I've been waiting a long time for this little face-to-face," Winters said.

"God, are you ugly," Shannon intoned in a low, guttural voice. "You even look worse than you smell."

Winters's eyes dulled a bit. "Another comment like that," he said, "and I go into the other room and cut off one of your wife's appendages. Maybe a finger, maybe something else. Understand, you little fuck?

"Also," Winters added after waiting for a response, "you try anything stupid and the same thing happens. She loses a piece of her. My choice which piece."

"You have no chance in getting away with this—"

"I know that," Winters acknowledged. "I'll be caught and I'll grow old in prison. It's a fate I've accepted. Just as I've accepted instead of killing my victims, I'll only be able to slip into their dreams and torment them. But that's much later. After tonight, anyway."

"Just get this over with," Shannon said. "I'm tired of listening to you and I'm tired of smelling you."

"No. I've waited a long time for this, Billy Boy. A very long time. We're going to have a nice little chat first, and then we'll have all night to do the things we need to do. And please, don't try to pretend you don't care."

"I really don't anymore."

"Of course you do. After all the things I've done to you? And your wife lying in the other room helpless?" Winters nodded slowly, a dull glint in his eyes. "You care, Billy Boy.

"Now," Winters continued, "let me tell you what I originally planned for you. Because what I settled on is so much better. I want you to fully appreciate it.

"It was going to be similar. I was going to show up in your dream and tell you I was with your wife. I was going to give you an address. Same as what I've already done. Except the address was going to be for a young, sweet little coed and FBI Agent Swallow would be fervently waiting there for you. The reason he'd be waiting for you is because I've been visiting him in his dreams, telling him that you'd be killing this sweet, little girl next. Of course, by then, he'd also know the carving knife used on your redheaded bitch therapist came from your apartment.

"The whole case would be circumstantial, but you'd be found guilty of my murders. And you'd spend the rest of your life in prison, or at best, an insane asylum. And I'd be there every night, visiting you in your dreams."

"Too bad the case against you broke," Shannon said.

"Not really. Because what I've improvised is really much sweeter. Have you figured it out yet?"

Shannon didn't answer. As his hands shifted, the rope pulled tighter around his fingers, driving the imaginary nails deeper into his bones. His body stiffened as the pain immobilized him.

A smugness twisted Winters's small, bloodless lips. "I think you got it. Any questions before we get started?"

"Go to hell."

"Come on. You must have some curiosity. Haven't you at least wondered how I slip into your dreams?"

"Okay, I've wondered about that."

"It's because I'm a god. At least, spiritually. My body might bleed and break, just like Herbie's did, but inside I'm a god. And tonight you are going to suffer my wrath like no one ever has."

Shannon couldn't keep from laughing. "A little full of ourselves, are we? You, a god? Jesus. You're nothing but a freak."

The skin around Winters's mouth tightened and a light pink flushed his cheeks. He moved quickly out of his chair, slapping Shannon hard across the face with an open palm. The blow sent Shannon and his chair tumbling to the floor. Winters reached down and grabbed him by both his hair and his broken fingers and jerked him to his feet.

"Enough chitchat," Winters whispered from behind. "We got a busy night ahead of us."

Winters forced Shannon back to the kitchen and to the table Susan was tied to. Using the carving knife and holding Shannon's broken fingers, Winters cut the rope tying Shannon's hands together. He then twisted Shannon's broken fingers until he heard an audible gasp, and then he slapped the knife's handle into Shannon's free hand.

"You know what you're going to do," Winters breathed into Shannon's ear.

Shannon tried swinging the knife around, trying to get at Charlie Winters's thick body, but Winters simply applied more pressure on the broken fingers until Shannon collapsed against the table, the side of his face resting on Susan's stomach. He couldn't help noticing how cold her skin felt. As he was pulled away from her, he saw the fear in her eyes, the wetness around her cheeks. Anger swelled up within him. He tried to swing the knife around and again was forced to collapse against the table.

"Is that the best you can do?" Winters asked. "Gawd, are you a weak, little shit."

"I'm going to kill you," Shannon breathed through the pain.

"Is that so?"

More pressure was applied to his injured fingers. The pain sucked the breath out of him. From behind he could hear a wheezing laugh ooze out of Winters. The pressure continued. The pain seemed to build on itself, becoming something unbearable.

Shannon looked into Susan's eyes. He told her that no matter what was done to him, he would not hurt her. "And I won't let this sack of human garbage hurt you, either."

More wheezing laughter came from behind. The pressure increased.

"I would take the dish rag out of her mouth so the two of you could talk, but I'm afraid she would scream. Even though she'd know I'd have to kill her, she'd still scream. I don't think she could help it. But you can talk, Billy Boy. Why don't you tell her how my cousin had you whimpering like a baby and pissing in your pants?"

Winters raised the pressure a notch.

"Come on, Billy," Winters breathed in his singsong voice. "You can do it."

"I was thirteen at the time," Shannon said, trying to keep his eyes level with Susan's. It was a struggle, though, the pain forced him to look away. "My mother was already dead before I got home. They broke my fingers and tortured me. I don't know how long it went on for. I don't remember too much about it. Even at the time I don't think I was fully conscious of what was happening. I think I was in shock. Now, it's nothing but a blur in my mind."

"I think you're a liar," Winters said. "I think you remember every little detail of what happened."

More pressure. Constant, continuous. The imaginary nails driving deeper into his bones.

"One thing you didn't lie about," Winters said, "is that pain will make a weakling like you do anything. But you can stop it if you want."

He gave the injured fingers a harder twist.

"All you have to do is cut her," Winter said. "One drop of blood, that's all. You cut her and show me a single drop of blood and I stop. After all, how much could a cut like that hurt her? I'm sure she'd want you to. I mean, trading all that pain for only a single drop of blood. You pick the spot, sport."

"You killed Janice Rowley—"

"That's right, bright boy."

"You framed Roper."

"Of course I did. Weak little shit. One little dream visit and he smothers himself. Come on, sport, show me the blood."

The pressure continued. Winters's singsong voice droned through it, mixing with it, intensifying it. Shannon's hand shook as he held the knife against Susan's thigh. A small cut was made, drawing blood.

The pressure stopped. "You broke your promise," Winters said. Then to Susan, "He's really quite a liar. I don't know who he's trying to fool with this gallantry crap. He doesn't love you. The person he pines away for, who he dreams about every night, is his therapist. A real cute piece of meat, although a bit pale for my taste, and probably at this point a bit too stiff."

"I'll tell you what I do dream about," Shannon forced through clenched teeth, "the way it felt cutting off your cousin's head. It's like I'm there again. Seeing him scared shitless, smelling him crap his pants. I shove the knife into his neck. And all I want is to do it again."

"Now you know why I do what I do," Winters said. He twisted Shannon's injured fingers until the pain shot off like a fireball, firing deep into his brain. Then the red glare faded into blackness.

As Shannon regained consciousness, he heard Winters whispering things to him, his words slurred and nonsensical. After a while, he realized Winters wasn't whispering but talking loud enough for Susan to hear. He was detailing what Shannon would have to do to stop the pain.

"You see," Winters was saying, "you cut her after only ten minutes of pain. I can keep it going for hours, probably even for days. By then you'd be begging me to let you do these things to her. And in your heart you'll want to do them. You'll be dying to do them. So why go through all that when you know how it's going to end up? We both know you're nothing but a pissant weakling."

Shannon shifted the knife so he was holding the blade and then flicked it over his shoulder. Winters dodged it and the knife clanked off the wall.

"You're going to have to beg me to let you retrieve it," Winters said.

The pressure was turned on. His fingers had swollen and the pain now was far worse than before. It seemed to fill him up, to push deep into his skull, hard against his eye sockets. Shannon begged to retrieve the knife. Winters ignored him. Shannon kept begging. It seemed an eternity before Winters moved him away from the table to where the knife had landed, all the while increasing the pressure. After Shannon picked it up, Winters moved him back to the table, back to Susan.

More pressure. Just as the room would start to slip sideways on him, just as his consciousness would start to fade into blackness, the pressure would be modulated down. Then it would be increased.

"If you want it stopped," Winters said, "you're going to have to push the knife into her throat. Not enough to kill her, or even do much damage, but enough to leave it bobbing up and down."

Shannon looked at Susan and then at the knife's blade. Through the pain he started laughing.

"I know what you're thinking," Winters whispered softly. "But it won't do any good. If you kill yourself I'll do horrible, horrible things to her. Far worse than what I'm asking of you."

"That's not what I'm thinking, shithead."

His injured fingers were twisted violently. Consciousness flickered away for a heartbeat.

"Enlighten me," Winters demanded.

"It was really pretty funny," Shannon said, still laughing.

"Go on."

"It was about, ha ha, you and your cousin."

"Yes."

"I was thinking how you must've been there while I cut his head off."

Winters pushed his broken fingers back. Consciousness slipped away for a moment. Then Shannon started laughing again, harder than before.

"You were probably standing there watching. Ha ha, too chickenshit to do anything."

"Your front door was being broken down. I thought the police were coming."

"But they weren't. It was just my neighbor. And you were too chickenshit to do anything with a thirteen-year-old boy with broken fingers and a forty-year-old tax accountant."

"Shut up."

Shannon's broken fingers were jammed back. His consciousness faded for a moment. Then he was laughing again.

"What did you do, hide in the closet? Too chickenshit to move?"

"I said shut it!"

"What a fucking god. The god, ha ha, of chickenshit!"

There was a hard, violent twist. Then pain exploded through him. It seemed to blow him towards the ceiling. His body rising as if he were filled with helium. All pain was gone, all feeling was gone, any concern he had had dissipated. He looked down and saw both Winters and himself, or at least his body. It was like those other times with Herbie and his father. He had somehow detached himself from his body and was observing the events from a distance. It all seemed only vaguely interesting to him.

Charlie Winters's face had become pinched. Thin, hostile lines pushed up from his forehead. He was straining as he used both hands to twist Shannon's broken fingers. And Shannon's own body just laughed harder through it all.

Then Winters stopped. He stood for a moment, confused, staring at what was in his hands, not quite comprehending that the two broken fingers had separated from Shannon's body. Had, in fact, been ripped from the body.

It was as if Shannon were watching it all from outside of himself. Watching as his body turned and pushed the knife into Charlie Winters's neck. Watching as the confusion drained out of Winters's face, only to be replaced by wide-eyed disbelief and then fear.

From what seemed like through a haze, Shannon watched as Charlie Winters's head was hacked from his body. Even as his head rolled free his lips kept moving, at least for a few seconds, screaming in panic the word "no" . . .

Shannon knew he was missing his two broken fingers. Even still, he could feel a throbbing ache from where they should've been. He stood up slowly and let go of the knife. Winters's head had rolled a few feet from his body. Shannon tried not to look at it. He tried to stare straight ahead, trying hard not to even catch a glimpse of his mutilated hand.

He heard a muffled noise from behind. Susan's small body was convulsing as she sobbed. Shannon stumbled over to her and removed the dish rag from her mouth.

"It's going to be all right now," he said, trying as hard as he ever had to smile.

"I'm so cold. Please get me something."

"Sure. I'll be right back."

He made his way upstairs. A woman's torn body lay in one of the bedrooms. He removed both the quilt and a sheet from the bed. The sheet was used to cover Winters's head and body. He lay the quilt over Susan.

"Just another minute. I need to find something to cut these wires with."

"Bill, you need to call an ambulance—"

"What else did he do to you?"

"Not for me, for you."

"I'll be okay. Just a minute . . ."

Shannon searched through the house until he found a wire cutter. He didn't seem to have much strength in his left hand and it took a while to snap the wires, but eventually he had them off Susan.

"I know better than to ask if you're okay," he said.

Her face twisted slowly into the saddest clown smile Shannon had ever seen and then she started bawling. As she did, Shannon tried to hold her. He tried like hell not to bleed on her.

"He lied about what he told you," she said when she could. "Your therapist, Elaine Horwitz, survived. I heard it on the news earlier today."

And then she just sobbed harder.

Charlie Winters knew he was dead.

Instead of being drawn to a white light, he had been pulled through some sort of black void. The book he had read in prison had stated that leaving your body and dying were basically the same thing. This was different, though. He felt anchored to where he had been pulled to. Movement didn't seem possible. And his essence, or spirit, or whatever it was that defined him, had changed shape. He had the sensation that he had become gnarled and gnome-like.

They came as a group. The ones he'd recently murdered. Joe DiGrazia, Pig Dornich, Phyllis Roberson, the hooker in East Boston, all of them. There were even some he recognized from his days with Herbie. There were a few he didn't recognize. Somehow he knew they were guides.

They milled around him, looking at him as if he were insignificant, as if he were unimportant to them, and then they turned from him. None of them had spoken, none of them acknowledged him. It was as if he didn't exist. Then they were gone.

The quiet was unlike anything Charlie Winters had ever experienced. A pure, absolute quiet. He almost welcomed it when he heard them.

The noise they made was like razor blades being scratched over glass. Millions of blades over millions of pieces of glass. A pure, raw terror filled him as the blades scraped closer, as the noise screamed through his every fiber. He still couldn't see them, but he could sense they were almost on top of him.

They were on him then. Shredding him, engulfing him, their blades ripping his being to infinite pieces. Just as the quiet before had been absolute, his agony now was also pure and absolute.

When he had first learned how to slip into the dream world and then into other planes of existence, he searched for Herbie. He never found him, though, and he now knew why. Herbie suffered this same fate, or rather Herbie must still be suffering this same fate. Because Charlie Winters knew the shredding would never end. He knew the agony would never end.

It wasn't supposed to be this way. The book had stated there was no hell, that you would keep going back to earth until you improved yourself to where you could enter a higher plane of existence. Which meant him and Herbie would keep going back to earth. That was how it was supposed to be.

Through the pure, absolute agony he felt an overwhelming sense of betrayal. It was all so damn unfair. After all, there wasn't supposed to be any hell.

A voice cut through the swarming mass, it cut through the agony screaming through Charlie Winters's consciousness. It told him: "You can't believe everything you read in books, Charlie."

Chapter 37

It had been ten months since Shannon had seen Susan. After that night with Charlie Winters, Shannon spent the next five days in a hospital as doctors tried to reattach his two fingers. They were unable to, though—the damage to both his bones and muscles had been too severe. When he got out he found that Susan had moved into her own apartment. She told him she needed some time alone. He agreed that it would probably be best.

Six weeks later, she asked for a divorce. They did it quickly. Afterwards, Shannon moved to Colorado. Since then he had spoken to her over the phone only a few times. Two days ago, she had called to tell him she'd be visiting him. Before that he hadn't heard from her in over half a year.

Her plane was twenty minutes late. Shannon found himself oddly at peace. He felt no anxiety, just a warm calm. He watched as Susan got off the plane. She looked thinner and paler than he remembered, but she was still beautiful. A worried frown pinched her face as she searched for him. When she saw him she tried to smile. Shannon walked over and helped her with the overnight bag she was carrying. He told her he was surprised to get her call, especially about her wanting to visit him.

"I thought you could use some company this time of year. How are you, Bill?"

"Pretty good. We'll talk later, though."

He got the rest of her baggage and carried it through the airport to his car. They drove in silence as they circled around Denver to get to Interstate 80. Once on it, they headed east towards Boulder.

"I guess it used to be much easier getting to Boulder from the old Stapleton airport," Shannon remarked.

"That's interesting. When are we going to talk, Bill?"

"Soon. Let's just enjoy the ride right now. It's very pretty out here."

After a while they could see the mountains. The plains were covered with snow and seemed to stretch forever. What Shannon liked most about Colorado was how he could go for miles without seeing anything but wide open space. He enjoyed driving the highways there, especially the trip between Denver and Boulder. It relaxed and soothed him. When he reached Boulder the traffic became more congested. He parked at the end of the Pearl Street mall and took Susan to one of the small bistros lining the street.

"The food's really quite good in this town," he told her. "Very healthy, wholesome stuff. I've become a vegetarian, but this place has good veggie and meat dishes."

"After what we went through a year ago, I don't want to ever look at meat again," Susan said, her color dropping a shade.

Shannon couldn't help noticing how tired her eyes looked. As thin as she had been before, it was obvious that she had lost weight. Her cheekbones were more pronounced, her lips slightly larger against her face. The overall effect made her look both somber and sad.

"You look tired," Shannon said.

Susan started to laugh. "I should. I haven't been sleeping very well."

A waitress came with the menus. Shannon suggested that they split a pizza. Susan said that would be fine, and Shannon ordered one with olives and broccoli along with a bottle of wine.

When the waitress left, Susan asked why he ordered the wine. She looked as if she had been struck.

"I thought you'd be asking why I'd order something with broccoli."

"I'm serious. Why did you order that?"

"It's okay. I don't drink much, only a glass or two of wine with dinner. Every once in a while I have a beer."

"You promised me you'd stop drinking—"

"That was years ago, and besides, I would've thought any promises we had were voided with our marriage." Shannon took a deep breath and let it out slowly through his nose. "I'm sorry," he said. "That wasn't very nice. I know you're concerned about me drinking, especially with February tenth only a couple of days away, but there's really nothing to worry about. I've never been an alcoholic and I now know what caused my problems before. I also know they're never going to happen again."

"I don't understand. I thought we knew already, that it was because of what happened to your mother—"

"No. It was because of him, and he's dead now." Shannon had left his glove on his right hand. His face tensed as he grabbed where his two fingers had once been. "It's been almost a year," he said, grimacing, "and I still get these damn phantom pains."

"Are you okay?"

"Just a minute." After a long ten-count the muscles along his jaw relaxed. He let go of his gloved hand and leaned back in his chair. "Jesus, that was a bad one. It felt like my fingers were still there and were being bent back to my wrist."

There was a wetness around Susan's eyes. "You don't have to wear that glove for me."

"That's okay. I feel more comfortable with it on." Shannon looked away from her. "I never told you this, but somehow he was able to get into my dreams. That's how I knew where to find you that night."

"I know. He told me."

"Yeah, I guess he would. My blackouts probably started when he first learned how to do it. You see, he had a long range plan to destroy my sanity. I think what he really wanted to do was convince me I had multiple personalities and that he was one of them. He had all those years in prison to work on me, to leave whispers and doubts in my mind. Around the anniversary of my mother's death he'd whisper a little louder and dig a little deeper. My body's defense against him was to shut itself down. Alcohol would help at first, but only for a while. When his whispers would cut through the booze, I'd have to shut down completely. If I didn't, I probably would've gone insane. So that's what caused my blackouts."

"You never remembered dreaming about him?"

"No. He didn't want me to. While he was in prison he only wanted to weaken me. After he got out that changed."

"Do you ever dream about him now?"

"Sometimes, but they're only dreams. He doesn't exist anymore." Shannon paused before continuing. "I've been experimenting with some New Age–type stuff since I've been here. Along with meditation, I've been doing a lot of dream work. That's where you try to be aware of every aspect of your dreams. I've been keeping a journal of them. Something else I've been trying to do is learn to leave my body. I guess you'd call it astral projection."

Shannon looked away from Susan and focused his gaze towards the front window. "I know it can be done."

"You've been able to leave your body?"

"It happened at the end with him. It also happened with his

cousin and once with my father. All three times it was as if I was thrown out of my body. If it hadn't happened, at least with him and his cousin, I probably wouldn't have survived, the pain would've been too much for me."

Shannon turned his gaze back to Susan and offered her a weak smile. "I've been trying to learn how to do it, but I haven't had any luck. My teacher tells me it's because I refuse to give up the notion that evil exists. The way he explains it is that if I believe that the universe is a potentially evil place then I won't feel safe about entering it. I don't know, though. It's hard not to believe in evil, especially when you get as close to it as we have."

"How would he explain Winters?"

"That his spirit was broken. Sounds like bullshit to me."

"I have to agree with you. Bill, why do you want to leave your body so badly?"

"I guess it's because of what he was able to do. If he could visit me and other people in their dreams, maybe I could do the same thing, or maybe even visit people in different dimensions. Maybe like my mother, or maybe Joe. I figure it's worth the shot."

"I took a one-day course in it myself."

"Really?"

Susan nodded. "I saw it listed in a brochure and decided to try it. It was on a Saturday in Harvard Square. The instructor went over a bunch of exercises, which were really nothing but giving yourself suggestions before falling asleep. Is that what you try to do?"

"Yeah, basically."

"My first night trying it, I sort of woke up, feeling as if I were spinning out of my body. Then I noticed I was hanging over the bed. I became afraid I was going to fall down and wake up the couple in the apartment below me. Next thing, I was awake and lying in the middle of the bed. I still don't know if I really had an out-of-body experience or if I just dreamed it."

"You had one. Jesus, I'm jealous. Your first time trying."

"It was the only time it happened so far," Susan said. She hesitated. "At first I didn't know why I wanted to try it. It just seemed like something I needed to do. Later, I realized it was because I wanted to find Joe so I could apologize to him. I wanted to tell him how sorry I was about what happened to him."

"Yeah, I guess we both want to do that."

"But I have a good reason." Susan's face darkened. "He made me watch it. Halfway through, he offered to let me take Joe's place. He told me if I asked him to skin me, instead, he would let Joe live. I just couldn't do it . . . I just couldn't . . ."

"He was just playing with you. He wanted you alive for when I showed up. No matter what you said he would've done the same things to Joe."

The waitress brought the wine to the table. Shannon filled two glasses with it.

Susan dabbed her eyes with a napkin, then took a deep breath before looking up. "I've been wanting to ask you something."

"Sure."

"I thought you would've started seeing Elaine Horwitz after our marriage ended. I was surprised you didn't."

"Is that why you wanted the divorce?"

"I thought you wanted to be with her."

Shannon shook his head slowly. "I'm not at a point where I could get involved with anyone. I know most of his victims are dead, and I know we were lucky to survive, but we were still victimized by him, and with me it went on for twenty years. What I need to do now is get healthy. I know I'll never be completely whole; all I have to do is look at my hand to realize that, but I need to heal quite a bit more before I can sort out my feelings."

Susan's eyes seemed to soften as she met Shannon's gaze. Neither of them spoke a word until the waitress came and delivered their pizza to their table. "You don't think you could get involved with anyone now?"

Shannon thought about it for a long moment. "At least no one new," he said.

She kept looking at him as she moved a slice of pizza onto her plate. "Are you working or anything?" she asked.

"You know I'm getting disability and that covers my expenses. I'm spending quite a bit of time with my meditation and the other things I told you about, but I'm also freelancing a couple of days a week for a small detective agency in Denver. I'm only taking assignments where I feel I can do some good. I kind of like it. Eventually, I'll spend more time with it."

Susan continued looking at him. As she took a bite of the pizza, she turned from him and stared straight at it. "This is damn good pizza," she said.

"I told you the food's good here."

"This could be the best pizza I've ever had."

"I was hoping you'd like it."

"I do." She paused. "I'll tell you, I could really see living in a town with pizza this good. You think they need legal secretaries here?"

"I'd have to think so. At least in Denver."

"You know, I think I'm getting sick of Cambridge."

"I don't blame you."

"With the taxes—"

"And the traffic—"

"And it gets so humid during the summer."

"It gets hot here," Shannon said. "But it's a dry heat."

Susan took another bite of the pizza. "I really could see moving here. But I'd need a place to stay while I got settled."

"I'd be glad to put you up," Shannon said.

"It might take a while before I could get my own place."

"However long it took."

Susan reached under the table and took hold of his gloved hand. They sat that way for a long time before either of them touched their pizza.

"Even if it took a lifetime," Shannon said.

ABOUT THE AUTHOR

Dave Zeltserman's dark, short crime fiction has been published in many venues, including *Ellery Queen's Mystery Magazine, Alfred Hitchcock's Mystery Magazine, New Mystery, Hardboiled* and *Hot Blood.* His first novel, *Fast Lane,* received numerous praise, including Ken Bruen calling it one of "the most entertaining debuts since Jim Thompson" and Poisoned Pen Bookstore including it as one of their top hard-boiled books of the year. *Fast Lane* has since been translated to Italian by Meridiano Zero. Dave's third crime novel, *Small Crimes,* will also be out later in 2007. Dave lives in the Boston area with his wife, Judy, and when he's not writing crime fiction, he spends his time working on his black belt in Kung Fu and running his *noir* fiction web-zine, www.hardluckstories.com.